Wild Swimming at Croftwood Lake

Victoria Walker

Copyright © 2025 Victoria Walker

All rights reserved.

ISBN: 978-1-7399441-8-6

No part of this publication may be reproduced, distributed, or transmitted in any form or by any means, including photocopying, recording, or other electronic or mechanical methods, without permission.

The story, all names, characters, and incidents portrayed in this production are fictitious. No identification with actual persons (living or deceased), places, buildings, and products is intended or should be inferred.

For all the Wild Swimmers

x

1

Nora Hartford was making the most of a perfectly still, bright morning. It was her favourite time of day. The sun had broken over the horizon and her mind was empty, focused only on the next stroke as she stretched her hands out into the water ahead of her, and pulled herself forward almost silently. Her breath hit the surface of the water producing clouds, reminding her that despite the sunshine, it was the end of January, and far from balmy weather.

Taking a moment to assess herself, making sure she wasn't getting too cold, she decided that another loop around the small island in the middle of the lake would be fine. She carried on, past the small wooden dock that extended out over the water where she'd left her clothes, and around the side furthest from the woods which led to her cottage.

Suddenly, before she could fathom what was happening, something splashed into the water right in front of her.

'Argh!' she gasped, trying to wipe the water from her eyes while she frantically tried to stay afloat.

Once she had steadied herself, Nora could see that a dog was happily paddling around in front of her, not caring that it had almost launched itself right on top of her.

'Tatty!'

Treading water, she looked beyond the edge of the lake to see a man in the distance striding towards her. He was tall and slim and wearing too much tweed for someone his age. Was he a farmer?

'Tatty! Out!' the man shouted and the dog obediently hauled itself out of the water and shook itself dry before running back to its owner, who was still some way away from the lake.

Nora fully expected him to carry on walking towards her, maybe shout at her for being in his lake, if it even was his lake, but he walked away, with the dog at his heels, and she realised that he probably hadn't got close enough to see her. And he wouldn't have expected anyone to be in there anyway, would he? That was a good thing. If it was his lake, what would she have said? It was all very well feeling brave about trespassing, but it was difficult to pass it off as an accident when the lake clearly belonged to someone. Perhaps this close call was a sign that she ought to seek permission from whoever owned it.

Having been interrupted, she'd spent too long in water that was barely more than a couple of degrees celsius. Swimming back on herself to the wooden platform, she felt for the bottom with her feet. With her back to the dock and her hands on the edge, she pushed out of the water and quickly pulled her neoprene socks and gloves off. Her kit was laid out ready and waiting so that she could get dry and warm as quickly as possible. Her frozen fingertips made this part tricky, but she was well practised and once the gloves were off, she pulled her swimming costume down, safe in the knowledge that there was no one else around to see anything, and dried herself vigorously with the towel. With the worst of the water away, she started dressing, pulling a dry bobble hat onto her head once she'd put her hoodie on. It was always hard to dry her legs enough to pull leggings and joggers on easily, and by the time she had, she was ready for a cup of tea. The last job was to wrap herself in her dry robe and pull her woolly socks on, then she sat cross-legged on the ground and poured a cup of hot tea from a flask.

Before today, the feeling that she was trespassing had been fading slightly with each visit. After all, what harm was she doing? She gazed out across the water, finding it incredible, as she always did, that she felt so compelled to jump into a lake when she found it hard to undress to get into a hot shower on a chilly day. But there was something addictive about it. Something that made it an enormously uplifting experience that always left her feeling invincible.

Nora had lived in landlocked Croftwood for a month, and just when she thought she'd go mad from missing the coast and her daily swims in the Clevedon marine lake, she'd found this lake. Her lake. Because until today, she hadn't seen another soul.

She'd stumbled across it when she'd taken the wrong path on a walk through the woods. She knew in time she'd know the place like the back of her hand, but now she was still finding her way around and was yet to experience glimpses of familiarity. The lake had been such a lovely surprise that she noted exactly which path she'd taken to get there. Crucially, she'd clambered over a ramshackle dry stone wall that was probably supposed to be the boundary to somebody's property. What may once have been a beautifully managed and manicured fishing lake had fallen into disrepair, and she intended to make the most of the fact that no one appeared to have any interest in it. A leisurely stroll around the perimeter, overgrown with reeds and sycamore saplings that had taken advantage of the fact that no one was watching, had informed her it was fed from a spring; not unusual since Croftwood was known for its natural spring water. And she could see just by gazing into its inviting depths that aside from the plant and leaf debris floating on the surface, it was as clean as a whistle.

So the very next day, she had decided she had nothing to lose by taking a dip. A frosty January morning might not seem the most appealing time for a swim, but Nora loved the cold. Not in general, but there was something about swimming outdoors in the cold water that made her feel amazing. In Clevedon, she'd been part of a group of women who met regularly to swim together, all finding that the cold water had some magical benefits. But here, for the moment at least, she was just happy to have found somewhere on her doorstep to satisfy her obsession, even if it was by herself.

Keen to see where the lake was in relation to her house, she reached into her bag and pulled out her phone. It took a minute for the maps app to load since the signal wasn't great. Nora peered at the screen until the blue of the lake appeared. She switched the view to a satellite image and zoomed out. Okay. So she wasn't just trespassing on farmland. She was on land belonging to Croftwood Court. Perhaps that was the lord of the manor who'd been out with his dog. She giggled to herself, not sure why it was funny. But from the lake for as far as she could see, there were fields. How big exactly was this estate? It was hard to tell from the map, but as she zoomed out further, it spread to the north of Croftwood by what looked like miles. Well, she thought with a smile, this was the first time in ten days that she'd seen anyone, so chances are she would still have the lake to herself without anyone knowing. Could she email the lord and ask permission? Of course she could, but she quickly decided that she wasn't going to, just in case the answer was no. Because what would she do then? Drive to Clevedon for a swim every day? She'd considered doing something like that before she'd discovered the lake. She'd swim, but she'd prepare something to say in case she got caught.

She finished her tea and packed up her things, deciding to walk a little further into the fields to see if she could glimpse the elusive Croftwood Court. From the map, it looked as if she'd be able to see it from the next-but-one field in front of her. As she walked, only now did her mind allow her to contemplate what the rest of the day might hold. And after the swim, it didn't seem nearly as overwhelming as it might have done an hour ago.

As she reached the end of the second field, she could see signs that the hibernating meadows gave way to more formal landscaping further ahead. Hedges that were the boundaries between the fields were now clipped into something more shapely than the natural hedgerows closer to the lake. Nora ventured even further still and saw that beyond the hedge lay lawns. Lovely striped ones, even in winter. And they led towards the most beautiful manor house she could have imagined. It was brick built but had a softness and elegance that came from the smoothness and colour of the bricks, which were a dark caramel. What struck Nora the most was the multitude of ornate, twisted brick chimneys that rose out of the gabled roofs and were topped with delicate chimney pots. She was desperate for a closer look.

Forgetting that she was hoping to stay under the radar, she walked across the lawns towards the house. The chimneys were works of art. The clever brickwork screamed out to be admired, but what Nora really wanted to see were the chimney pots. From the age of the house, she knew that they'd have been hand-thrown by a master potter and that the fun the designers had had with the chimneys would be echoed in their crowning glory.

She was so busy gazing up that it took her a moment to cotton on that someone was watching her from one of the large mullioned windows. It was the man with the dog, so presumably he actually was the lord of the manor. Crikey.

Turning on her heel but determined not to run, in case it made her look more suspicious, Nora walked purposefully back the way she'd come. Hopefully, he would think she'd just taken a wrong turn. And hopefully he wouldn't connect the fact that she was wearing a massive dry robe and a bobble hat with the fact that there was a lake in close proximity.

As mornings for Nora went, it had been eventful. By the time she emerged from the woods and had walked along the lane back to her cottage, she was ready for another cup of tea and a biscuit. She kept her dry robe on while she boiled the kettle and threw some logs into the wood-burner. Although the cottage was old, it had been refurbished so thoroughly that it was easy to keep it toasty warm without much effort at all. The old two-bedroomed cottage had been turned into a state-of-the-art one-bedroomed cottage with en-suite bathroom and dressing room just before Nora had bought it. Everything was fresh and beautifully finished. The walls were painted in a soft buttery cream colour and the exposed beams had been stripped back to the natural wood. The floors in the kitchen and lounge were large limestone flags, gently warmed by underfloor heating. Upstairs, the bedroom had a carpet that Nora's feet sank into and, although she felt a dressing room was wasted on her, she loved the touch of luxury it offered, even if it was mostly home to the boiler suits she wore for her work as a potter.

Before she settled next to the fire to check her emails, she unzipped her dry robe and hung it on a hook next to the back door. Tea in hand, she padded into the lounge, sat in her beloved vintage Ercol armchair, and opened her laptop.

Nora had always been a potter, something that had terrified her parents when she first announced that the hobby she'd pursued as a teenager was a passion she was going to turn into a career. Her mother'd had the same passion for art but had followed the safer path of teaching rather than pursuing her dreams, and she had worried for Nora taking what she saw as an enormous risk. Inevitably, it had taken a few years of hard slog before she found the balance between producing what she loved to make and what she needed to produce to be commercial. Now, she had made a name for herself and had two parts to her business; a mass-market model where she designed pottery and had it manufactured for her in Stoke, and her exclusive one-off piece production, which she sold to galleries and high-end department stores across the world. But it was a constant battle to give enough of herself to each part of the business so that it ran smoothly and that was one reason she'd moved. Worcestershire was that much closer to Stoke than North Somerset was and what she gained in time from not having to travel so far, she hoped to pour into the business. Over the next few years, she hoped she could become more hands off on the mass-market side and spend more time doing what she loved: throwing pots.

Discovering the lake on her doorstep had felt like the universe underlining that she'd made the right decision about moving to Croftwood. Whatever she told herself about it being a more convenient location for work, she still had doubts about whether she'd made a knee-jerk decision in moving away from the place she'd called home for twenty years. But the lake, along with how quickly she'd fallen in love with her little cottage, seemed to be willing her to settle in. She just had to hope she hadn't blown it by getting caught on the lawns of the manor house by the man in too much tweed.

2

Archie put his teacup onto its saucer and left the breakfast table to take a proper look out of the window.

'What are you looking at?' His mother, Constance, the dowager Countess, paused in her efforts to clean out the insides of her soft-boiled egg and waited for his answer.

'There's somebody on the lawn.'

'Is it Sebastian? Or one of the gardeners?'

Archie had to bite his tongue to stop himself from pointing out to her that he knew quite well what Sebastian or any one of the gardeners looked like. 'No. It's a woman I don't recognise.'

Lady Harrington left the table to peer out of the window herself. 'What on earth is she wearing?'

Archie smiled to himself because, although his mother was right, there was something endearing about the bobble-hat-wearing woman. Anyone who left the house wearing that hat, a voluminous coat and practical but unattractive boots was someone he already knew he would like. People these days were so hung up on what they looked like when, of course, that didn't matter at all.

'Ah,' he said, suddenly realising that she wasn't wearing a ridiculously oversized and shapeless coat after all. It was one of those new-fangled coats that people wore if they'd been swimming in the sea. 'It's one of those coats for outdoor swimming, Mama.'

'We're about as far from the sea as one can get. I hardly think she is wearing it for the practical purpose it was intended.'

'Perhaps not,' he said. 'Although when I took Tatty out earlier, she made a beeline for the old fishing lake and had a swim herself.' Was that why? Had the woman been in the lake and Tatty wanted to join in the fun? Perhaps he would have noticed if he'd gone closer. Surely though, she would have cried out if a dog had dived in next to her.

His mother sat down again and poured them both a fresh cup of tea, saying out loud exactly what he'd been thinking. 'You think the woman has taken a dip in the lake?' She laughed. 'Do you remember Papa suggesting you and Betsy swim in there?'

'Yes,' Archie said, smiling as he remembered him and his sister being terrified that a fish might bite their toes off and flat refusing to get in. 'To be fair to us, the carp were huge.'

'They were,' she agreed. 'I refused myself on the same grounds.'

'I remember Papa diving off the dock and swimming over to the island and telling us it was a desert island, thinking that would encourage us. But even that didn't work, and he ended up swimming back.'

'He was exasperated by your lack of adventurous spirit, Archie.'

'I'm adventurous,' he said defensively, feeling put out that his mother would say this now when he had no way of making amends to his much-missed father's opinion of him.

His mother laughed. 'Oh, Archie. If you're adventurous, I'm the Queen of Sheba!'

After breakfast, Archie headed over to the estate office,

with Tatty at his heels. Sebastian was due in for a meeting about the summer festival that would be held in Croftwood Park. Archie had given them the use of some of his land for camping last summer, and it had been such a success that they were hoping to increase the numbers this year. Sebastian was the mastermind behind the festival and had even organised an extremely successful Christmas market here, in the grounds of the Court, becoming the closest thing Archie had to a friend over the past year.

It was a lonely business being Lord of the Manor. For Archie, it all boiled down to the fact that he still lived at home with his mother. Of course, if he'd been lucky enough to meet the girl of his dreams a decade or so ago, everything would be perfect. He'd be living in the manor house with his family and his mother would be happily living in the dower house, which was a charming little house on the edge of the Estate, closest to the village. It had always been assumed that she would stay in the manor house until Archie found a match, but it had never happened. And now, at forty-one, it seemed unlikely. He had little to offer anyone; a money-pit of a house and a mother who would certainly be reluctant to be turfed out of her home of almost sixty years. And even if he was in the market, where was he likely to meet anyone when he hardly ever left the estate? No, Archie had resigned himself to the fact that that boat had sailed.

'Morning Archie!' Seb called from the doorway of the old stable where he kept most of his worldly possessions along with everything he'd accumulated over his years running an events management company.

'Morning! I'll boil the kettle!' It always lifted Archie's spirits when Seb was around. Since the Christmas market closed on Christmas Eve, he'd been around for a week in January to supervise the clean-up of the site but then he and his fiancée, Jess, took a well-earned break while it was the off-season for both of them. Now that the festival planning was underway, Archie hoped to see more of him.

'You haven't come across a woman in a swimming robe this morning?' he asked Seb once they were sitting in the office having a cup of tea.

'No,' Seb said, with a puzzled grin. 'Have you?'

'Tatty launched herself into the lake this morning. Then a woman in one of those coats wandered across the lawn while we were eating breakfast.'

Seb shot a look of respect at the dog who was dozing by the fire, looking like the least likely dog ever to decide to take a swim. 'I didn't know you had a lake.'

'It's on the far west side of the estate, used to be a fishing lake. It was my father's pride and joy. He ran a fishing club for the town. We didn't keep up with it after he died.'

'Well, I'm not surprised it's attracted someone. It's all the rage at the moment, cold-water swimming. You could turn that lake into something.'

Archie saw Seb's cogs begin to whir. He'd seen it happen before when they'd first had the idea for the Christmas market.

'You think so? Let people swim in there?'

'It's something to look into, definitely. Why don't you see if you can track that woman down? She might say it's a rubbish place to swim and don't bother wasting your time, in which case you know you're onto a winner because she's after keeping it to herself.'

Archie laughed. 'She's a brave woman. I wonder if she has any idea how big those carp might be by now?'

'See? There's an income stream you didn't know you had. We ought to get an expert in to assess the water quality. And if there are some whoppers in there, you might be able to sell some of them if you need a cash injection.'

'I always need a cash injection,' Archie said, thinking about the phone call to the roofer that he'd been putting off. The roof of the main house was a complex structure of many gables, ornate tiles and chimneys and that made even replacing a few broken tiles an expensive business.

'Seriously though, the lake could help you out, I'm sure of it. As far as I know, there's nothing else like that around here.'

'I'll do some research, see what I can find out.' Seb's excitement had sparked something in Archie and besides, he was keen to meet the woman who'd so brazenly walked across his lawn. 'Where are you up to with the festival planning?'

Seb put his mug down and sat back in the chair, resting his ankle on his knee. 'So, you remember last year we had the field that's adjacent to the park for camping? Well, this year, we'd like to expand and have a stage in that field too and extend the camping into the next field along.'

'That's no problem.' Archie said, happy to support the event in any way he could after the town supported the Christmas market so generously.

'Look, I know how things are financially and your generosity is amazing, but it shouldn't be at the expense of other things that are important. You know you can charge the festival for the use of your land?'

Archie waved a hand, hoping to put a stop to this conversation. It was one thing for Seb to know more than anyone else how tight things could be keeping the house up and running, but Archie had been brought up knowing that as well as keeping the family estate up to par, he had a responsibility to the wider community. The Croftwood Festival was a Community Interest Company, and all the profits went back into the town in one way or another, and he would never want to take away from that for his own gain. 'I won't accept payment, Seb. I'm happy to allow use of what I have left for the good of the town.'

After his father died, Archie had come to an arrangement with a national organisation and had given them the majority of the estate land in a trust. The trust had their own tenant farmers and paid the estate an income. It meant that Archie didn't have to manage the whole thing himself and also wasn't faced with selling off the land piecemeal to fund the ever-growing costs of running the house and gardens. And at least this way, it was still the Croftwood Court Estate that he had inherited, but after seeing the stress it had placed his father under, the income dwindling because they couldn't keep pace with modern farming practices, Archie had wanted to find a different way.

As part of the arrangement with the trust, he still owned the land closest to the manor house and a couple of other parcels, which were of no value for farming. This included the land next to the park in the centre of town. He employed a small team of gardeners who were also quite happy to do some of the simpler maintenance jobs around the estate.

'It's very good of you, Archie,' Seb said. 'It goes without saying that you and your mother will be on our VIP list again this year.'

'Thank you, although I'm not sure whether that's a blessing or a curse. She had one too many glasses of Pimms last year and decided she wanted to sleep in a tent. It took all my powers of persuasion to get her home. And poor Ursula had a terrible job getting her up the next day.'

'Feel free to offer Ursula and Mrs Milton tickets if they'd like to come and all the lads, of course.'

'Thank you, I'm sure everyone will appreciate that.'

'Oliver and I are meeting for a drink later, if you'd like to join us?' Seb said, standing and buttoning his jacket before he left.

'Ah, that's very kind of you, but I won't this time.' Archie had never accepted Seb's previous offers and had given up producing a reason why. Because there wasn't one other than he'd never done that. Never been to the pub with friends, at least not since he'd been at university. Being sent away to boarding school at thirteen meant his friends weren't local and those friends and the friends he'd made at university mostly lived in the south-east, having pursued careers in the City. Running an estate on a shoestring made it difficult for Archie to keep up with them, and he'd gradually grown apart from almost everyone. The only exception being his closest friend, James, who was in a similar position to him but in Scotland.

'Next time,' said Seb. Something he said every time, which Archie was always heartened to hear. Because it wasn't that he didn't want to go out for a drink with Seb. He enjoyed Seb's company immensely, but he didn't know Oliver terribly well and being out of practice, socially, it seemed a step too far.

So Archie nodded and stood to see Seb out.

'You know, I was thinking we ought to put aside some money from the next Christmas market to bring the rest of the courtyard buildings up to scratch.'

'Yes, I suppose we could,' Archie said, knowing that in reality there would be more pressing things to spend the money on. Aside from the money they'd stashed away to pay for this year's market, the profits from last Christmas had been sunk into a long overdue upgrade of the heating system in the manor house, and there hadn't been much change from that. He'd like to offer to freshen up the apartments that Ursula, the housekeeper and unofficial companion to his mother and Mrs Milton, the cook, lived in. It was the least he could do in return for their loyalty and the pittance he paid that they happily accepted. That was more important than tarting up the old stables for no good reason.

Seb waved a hand from the window of his truck as he

headed down the drive. Archie raised a hand and then turned, sighed and went into the office to tackle some paperwork. He settled at his desk, thinking that perhaps tomorrow morning he'd take a walk over to the lake again. Early. Before breakfast in the hope that the woman he'd seen was a creature of habit and might be there again.

3

The following morning, Nora was later than usual setting off for the lake. She'd made the mistake of responding to a text message from Neil, her kiln technician at the pottery. She had left several bespoke pieces in the drying room, and last night, when he'd come to fire them, the only kiln with the capacity to take these larger items wasn't working. There were very few kiln engineers to call on these days, but after years in the industry, Nora had contacts. She put a call in to an engineer who had recently retired and he agreed to go later that morning to take a look. She hadn't planned to visit Stoke today, but now she'd swim and then set off so she could be there when he arrived.

It was another beautiful, crisp day and Nora could feel the anticipation of the swim start to creep through her as she made her way through the woods to the lake. Even more so now that she'd had a relatively stressful start to the day. There was a deadline associated with the pots that were waiting to be fired. They were due to be shipped to New York the following week, and a delay to the firing meant a delay to her being able to make the final touches to them without having to rush. And she hated rushing.

She climbed over the collapsed wall and headed for the

dock, which had become her preferred place to enter the water. There were other, smaller wooden platforms dotted around the edge of the lake but this was the only one that extended out over the water. Already prepared with her swimsuit on underneath her clothes, she stripped off with abandon, not noticing that the man from yesterday was standing on the opposite side of the lake. The sun was behind him, so Nora wasn't looking in his direction. The first sign to her that there was anyone else there was the dog who trotted over to her, looking at her as if asking when it would be time to get in.

'It's you again,' she said to the dog, before scanning the shore for the owner. Feeling somewhat exposed, she pulled her dry robe on, wrapping it around her before she walked around the shore, heading for the man who was watching her. His dog at her heels.

'Good morning,' he said as she approached. He looked friendlier than she'd expected, given that she was trespassing and he was probably about to tackle her about that.

'Morning.' Was it better to leap in with an explanation or wait until he said something? She decided to wait and a long silence ensued while they stood facing each other, taking each other in.

Nora wondered whether he'd looked in the mirror that morning. He had curly hair which was too long and seemed to be allowed to do anything it liked. His brown corduroy trousers did something to dilute the allover tweed look he'd sported yesterday, but they were worn down to the cotton fabric at the knees and his tweed jacket was just as threadbare.

'Have you been in today?' he asked, nodding to the lake.

'No.' She'd almost said not yet, which might have sounded too presumptuous, or cocky even.

'But you come every day?'

Nora bit her lip. Was this a trick question? Was he trying to entrap her into admitting she'd done it lots of times before yesterday?

'I don't mind, if that's what you're wondering,' he said, smiling. Now, his face softened and Nora could see beyond his dishevelled appearance. He had kind eyes. Deep brown, kind eyes. 'Really,' he said, bringing her out of the trance she hadn't realised she was in.

'Oh, well, thank you. I do come most days, actually.' Despite what he'd said, she was sure he would mind, and there was a cautious tone to her voice as she admitted it.

'And how does it shape up? Do you have anything to compare it to?'

He seemed genuinely interested, and for some reason, he put Nora at ease with his relaxed tone.

'I used to swim in a sea pool so it's very different to that, but I think the water quality is good and it's wonderfully tranquil here.'

'It is,' he agreed, reaching down to stroke his dog's head. 'Are you new to the area?'

'I've lived here about a month.'

'And how's it been so far?'

'It's pretty good,' she said, grinning. 'The lake helps. Do you ever go in yourself?'

'Goodness no. I'm not saying this to scare you, but the carp in that lake were huge twenty years ago.'

'I don't mind fish. I haven't noticed them yet, so I expect they're steering clear of me.'

'Ha, I expect so. Well, please don't delay your swim on account of me.' He gestured to the lake.

'I'm assuming you own this place?'

'I'm sorry, how remiss of me not to introduce myself. I'm Archie Harrington.' He held out his hand.

Nora took it, noticing how warm it felt and enjoying the

fact that she was making contact with him more than she would from a handshake with anyone else. 'I'm Nora Hartford. Nice to meet you, Archie.'

He still had her hand in his. Then the dog jumped in the water, splashing them both, and they sprang apart.

'Tatty! Out!'

'She seems to enjoy a swim,' Nora said, as they both watched the dog, who looked as if she was smiling, paddle to the shore and heave herself out.

'Oddly, she's never launched herself in before yesterday. She is rather old to start surprising me now.'

Nora wondered whether perhaps the dog wanted her as a swimming buddy.

'I'm with Tatty. It's an extremely inviting lake.'

'Even in January?'

'Especially in January. And at the moment, it's not too cold, and not too warm.'

'It's been lovely to meet you, Goldilocks,' Archie said, failing to mask his pride at making a pretty good joke.

Nora grinned at him. 'Nice one. I'll see you again.'

Archie fixed his eyes on hers for a moment, nodded, and then turned and walked away, his hands clasped behind his back like an old man. Tatty ran to join him and trotted devotedly at his heels.

Nora walked back to the other side of the lake and watched Archie until he was out of sight. So that was Lord Harrington. Perhaps she should have called him that instead of assuming that first-name terms were alright? But he hadn't seemed to mind, and she was pleased to have his blessing to swim in the lake. How easy had that been?

After her swim, she bundled herself up, not having time for a leisurely cup of tea on the dock after being waylaid by Archie and Tatty. Instead, she sipped at it on her way home through the woods. As always, the rest of the day had melted into insignificance while she was swimming and only now did the anxiety over getting the kiln fixed come back into her thoughts. If Ken couldn't mend it, she had no idea where she could get the pieces fired before next week. But until she knew it couldn't be fixed, she wouldn't waste her time and energy tracking down the nearest alternative kiln, because that's what it would come to. No, she'd go up to Stoke and hope for the best. On the bright side, she could catch up with her production manager and see how the samples for the Christmas range were coming along. They weren't due to be ready until next week, but they always built some contingency into the schedule, so she had high hopes that Val would have something ready for her to see.

While Ken was dismantling the controls for the kiln, convinced that a loose wire could be the problem, Nora headed upstairs to the production floor to find Val. The place was a hive of activity and Nora felt a lump in her throat, as she always did when she walked through the pottery. The sense of pride knowing she'd built this and that all these people were part of her success, as well as depending on it, was sometimes overwhelming.

'Hey, Val,' she said, knocking gently on the open office door.

'Nora! It's great to see you!' Val got up from her desk and hugged Nora. 'Nightmare about the kiln, though.'

'I know. I thought I was ahead of the game with that order, but never mind. Let's just hope the kiln gods are on my side once I get that far.'

'Talking of kiln gods,' said Val, 'we've had the first firing of the Christmas samples. Want to see?'

'I was hoping you'd say that!'

'Let's grab a coffee to take with us.'

They headed to the compact kitchen, which had a small table and chairs and so often was a good place to sit and chat.

'So how's the new place?' Val asked as they waited for the kettle to boil.

'I love the house. It's gorgeous. Tiny but luxurious compared to my old place.'

'And you're not lonely? Being in a new town must be weird.'

'It's a bit strange,' Nora agreed. She wasn't going to let on that Archie was the first person she'd spoken to since she'd moved in. Being on the outskirts of town along a country lane meant she hadn't come across any neighbours yet. She hadn't ventured into town because she'd been busy getting the house straight and had been back and forth to Stoke, finishing the bespoke order, picking up a grocery shop at the big supermarket at the motorway junction on her way back. 'I did meet the lord of the manor this morning.'

'The lord of what manor?'

'Croftwood Court. He introduced himself as Archie, but I'm pretty sure he's Lord Harrington.' It said a lot about Archie, in her mind, that he hadn't introduced himself as such.

'Ah, he owns the lake you told me about.'

'Yes, Miss Marple.'

'So he caught you in the act?'

'Almost,' laughed Nora. 'I hadn't got in, so at least it was a level playing field.' And she'd have missed out on shaking hands with him. Why that stuck in her mind, she wasn't sure. It was probably just because she was on her own now, and didn't have the most basic level of physical contact with anyone very often.

'And what was he like? He doesn't mind you sloshing around in his lake on a daily basis?'

'Thankfully not. He's young for a lord, I think. Similar age to us.'

'Eligible?'

'No idea. Shut up.'

Val laughed. 'That's all I need to know. Come on.'

The Christmas samples were in their best room, in that it was one they tried to keep nice for entertaining buyers and so wasn't dusted with clay like the rest of the place. Nora made a beeline for a ceramic bauble which was decorated to be a very fat robin. There was also a snowman, a Father Christmas and an angel.

'I love these!'

'I knew you would. I'm not sure the angel works, so we're coming up with a reindeer option instead.'

'Mmm, I probably agree about the angel. Could we do a Christmas pudding as well? Just in case.'

'That's a great idea,' Val said, making a note on her phone.

They went through the other samples, which were a mixture of decorations and gift items like mugs and candle holders. There were things Nora loved, and things she didn't. Things she didn't hate, which might be an idea for another year, or something that could be tweaked for another collection. They chatted through the cost versus possible selling prices to make sure they had the right mix of price points and a range that all kinds of retailers could stock, from the small to the biggest. And by the time Ken came to find her with a kiln update, they had made all the important decisions.

'You're up and running again,' Ken said with a huge smile on his face. 'It was touch and go.'

'It always is. That kiln's an old lady now.'

'That she is. A word of warning though, it wasn't a loose wire, it was a faulty element. I've repaired it, but it could go again and with the age of the thing, you won't be able to replace it. That'll be it.'

'Oh god, really?' The thought of having to replace the kiln was a headache she didn't need.

'You could use one of the old brick ones?' Val suggested.

Nora shook her head. 'Not controllable enough. You think it'll be alright for this firing? I can't risk anything going wrong.'

'My best guess is it's fixed for another couple of firings. Might be more, but you never know. If I were you, I'd be on the look-out for a plan B,' Ken said.

'Okay, I suppose at least I know what I'm dealing with. Thanks Ken, you're a lifesaver.'

'Here, look at the robin again,' Val said, shoving it into Nora's hands.

'I'm not sure even he's going to cheer me up. A new kiln isn't what I was hoping to hear.'

'At least you should be alright to get this lot fired now. When's your next order due?'

'I've got another month before I'll need to use that kiln again, and even then, it's a batch of smaller pots that I could put through the production kiln if I had to.'

'There you go then,' Val said soothingly. 'There's time to sort it out. And you'll have a fancy new kiln to look forward to.'

Nora smiled, but she didn't want a fancy new kiln that she'd have to faff around with doing loads of test firing. She wanted her old, trusty kiln. Why did everything have to change at once?

4

While Nora was at the pottery, Michelle from the sales office had popped her head around the door and asked Nora if it was Croftwood that she'd moved to.

'We've just signed a new account. A retailer called Candles and Cushions. Do you know it?'

Nora shook her head, beginning to feel ashamed of her lack of interest in exploring the town so far. 'Why don't you put together some samples and I can pop in and introduce myself.'

'Really? That'd be amazing. They haven't placed their first order yet, so it might encourage them.'

And so, Nora sat in her car in the only car park she could find, which was behind the church, plucking up the courage to go and be friendly and smiley. Not that she wasn't naturally a friendly, smiley person, it just took more effort these days. Since Julian had called it a day on their almost twenty-year relationship, she'd slightly lost her confidence in all aspects of her life, except her work. Her work had ultimately been the reason he'd left, unable to cope with her success and not able to keep his feelings to himself that he deserved that kind of success more than she did.

She paid for an hour's parking on the app, picked up the

pretty paper bag that Michelle had packed the samples into, and headed past the church towards what looked like the centre of town. On the opposite side of the road was a coffee shop. It was trendy, with a kind of hipster vibe that made Nora fully expect to come across a man with a well-groomed beard as part of the staff. It was tempting to stop off there now, but it was better if she had that to look forward to after she'd got the work part out of the way.

Candles and Cushions was further up the road on the same side of the street as the coffee shop. Its window lifted Nora's spirits because she could see immediately that she'd find things in this shop that she'd want in her own home. It was a great fit for Hart Pottery to be stocked here.

A bell gently sounded as she pushed the door open. The lighting was soft. Bright enough to shop by but dim enough to make you feel cosseted in the warm hug of the shop, as if no one was watching you. Candles were dotted here and there on shelves that were otherwise empty of stock — presumably so that the cushions didn't go up in flames.

'Hi there,' said the woman who appeared behind the counter. 'Give me a shout if you need anything.' She smiled and sat down, going back to whatever it was she was doing.

Nora loved that. No pressure at all. Exactly what she wanted, so before she announced herself, she wandered around having a good look and picked up a couple of candles and a new lampshade for her bedside light.

'That's such a lovely choice,' the woman said when she stood up as Nora placed her things on the counter.

'Believe me, there were several I could have chosen. I'm sure I'll be back once I finish unpacking properly.'

'Oh, you've just moved here?'

Nora wondered if she'd live to regret sharing that information, but this woman seemed like the kind of person who was easy to open up to. 'Yes, about a month ago.'

'I moved here about a year ago and I've still got boxes I haven't unpacked. It's never ending, isn't it?'

Nora felt her shoulders drop. 'Yes, I'm never moving again.'

'Me neither! I'm Hilary. Lovely to meet you.'

'I'm Nora. Actually, I popped in because I work for Hart Pottery and once they realised this is where I moved to, they asked me to bring a couple of samples in. They're complimentary since you've just opened a new account with us. You've sidetracked me with your lovely wares.'

Hilary laughed. 'You're Nora Hartford? Oh my god! Sorry, I'm going to fangirl for a sec. I absolutely love your pottery. I'm thrilled to be a stockist and thrilled that you like my shop!'

This kind of thing happened sometimes. It was exactly what Julian hated. If he'd been with her he'd have stalked out of the shop at this point. But Nora tried not to think about that.

'That's so kind of you.' Nora handed over the bag and Hilary delved in straight away.

'I can't believe you've moved here. I don't suppose you'd consider doing some sort of meet and greet thing one evening? No, sorry. I shouldn't be putting you on the spot. Ignore me.' Hilary put the samples aside and began wrapping Nora's purchases. 'These are on the house.'

'Absolutely not. I'll never be able to come here again if you do that,' Nora said.

'But you've given me stuff for free,' Hilary protested.

'Because you're a new client. You must get free samples from other suppliers. Let's keep the business side of things… professional.'

'Right. Of course. You're right.' Hilary seemed a little flustered, and Nora hoped she hadn't offended her because Hilary might be the first friend she made in Croftwood. Aside from Archie, she was certainly the first person she'd spoken to.

'What time do you close? Maybe we could grab a coffee or something?'

Hilary brightened. 'I'd love that. Shall I meet you in Oliver's in half an hour?'

As Nora could have guessed, Oliver's was the hipster coffee shop she'd seen on her way to Hilary's shop. She pushed the door open and the aroma of great coffee hit her, followed closely by an eyeful of the most tempting looking cakes. Her stomach grumbled reminding her that a slice of toast and a banana probably hadn't been enough for lunch.

'Hi there,' said the young man with a big smile who was behind the counter. 'What can I get you?'

'I'll take an oat milk latte and a piece of whatever that chocolate slice is.' She pointed to a traybake that looked like it might be solid chocolate.

'It's healthier than it looks,' he said, reading her mind. 'It's got lots of dark chocolate in it and is at least half dates. Great choice.'

Nora paid, and the barista said she could take a seat and he'd bring it over. The place was buzzing. There were a few people engrossed in their laptops, interspersed with other people taking time out of their day to have coffee with a friend. Nora chose a table for two where she could keep an eye on the door for Hilary coming in, and while she waited, she checked her phone for messages.

There was an email from Julian to let her know he had a box of her stuff that had got mixed up with his during the move. Had it really taken him a month to realise? He was suggesting it would be too expensive to post since it was mostly books and had said he could drop it round to her in a couple of weeks when he would be passing. That was the last thing she wanted. She needed her house to remain a Julian-free zone, untainted by him and with no memories of any kind made there with him, good or bad. She replied and said she'd collect them at the weekend since she was planning to visit a friend and swim in the sea pool. Not a lie. She'd just have to arrange it.

She and Julian had ended things relatively amicably. The ending had been the most amicable part of the last few years, and Nora was surprised to find that she wasn't lonely living by herself. If anything, it was relief not to be walking on eggshells all the time, worried that the wrong remark about how her day had been, or her side of a telephone call could trigger a major sulk from Julian that would make a couple of days at a time unbearable. As her star had risen, his had stayed where it was. He tried to disguise his jealousy as a belief that she was selling out, thinking that he was staying true to his craft and she wasn't. But it was the challenge that Nora loved, in her work and in the business side of things, and that fed her creativity, spawning more ideas and avenues that she wanted to explore. And they could have done it together. When she thought back to their days at college and then as struggling artists, finding it hard to pay the rent, she remembered those days with affection because their relationship had been so much easier then. The moment she made more money than Julian, even though she was happy to share everything with him, he began to shut her out. And that had been the beginning of the end. So what she didn't want was to give him any opportunity to criticise the new life she was building. The days of her putting up with that were over.

She looked up from her phone at the moment Hilary walked in. She waved and Nora left her jacket on the chair and her empty plate and took her cup over to the counter.

'Hilary, let me get these.'

'Absolutely not,' Hilary said sternly. 'Would you like the same again?'

'That'd be lovely, thank you. Oat —'

'Oat milk latte?' the barista said at the same time.

'See? You're a regular already,' Hilary said. 'Flat white for me please, Jack.'

'I started making it when I saw you,' he said. 'Take a seat and I'll bring them over.'

Hilary followed Nora over to the table, waving at a man who was smiling at her from behind his laptop. He had headphones on and age-wise was somewhere in between herself and Hilary.

'That's my partner, Toby,' Hilary said. 'I mean, he's my boyfriend. It's so ridiculous at our age, you don't know what to call it.'

'What does he do?'

'He's a barrister. He gives online legal advice.'

'Wow. Useful person to know.' Even though she and Julian hadn't been married, they'd been together long enough for their lives to have been intertwined to the degree where they'd needed a solicitor. The house had been in joint names and there had been some back and forth over the finances involved in that. Nora had paid off the mortgage once her business had reaped dividends, and her solicitor had wanted her to fight for a bigger share of the house. She'd decided to split it fifty-fifty with Julian and he'd been so disdainful about it, she wished she'd listened to her solicitor. But she wasn't about to tell Hilary all of this when they'd only just met.

'Whereabouts do you live?' Hilary asked.

'Off the Worcester Road, down a lane near Croftwood Court.'

'Oh, really? That's such a nice area. Some friends of ours live down that way. Their garden backs onto the woods. Great for walks.'

'I've been walking in the woods every day.' Again, it felt

too soon to admit she'd been swimming in the lake, but she was interested in finding out what Hilary might know about Archie. 'Do you know much about Croftwood Court?'

'Lord Harrington, Archie, helped with the Croftwood Festival last summer. He lent some of his land and a huge marquee. I think he's doing the same this year.'

'Does he have a family?'

'He and his mother live in the manor house. I don't know much about him, but I've always assumed he's single. Isn't that awful of me?' Hilary said with a shocked expression. 'Jess would know. Her partner, Seb, is friends with Archie.'

'And whereabouts do you live?'

'A couple of streets behind the church. Toby and I live on the same street and we're sort of living between each other's houses. I feel too old to start thinking about going all in with someone again. I like my independence and I think Toby likes that too. Having said that, we hardly ever spend a night apart.' She grinned and sipped her coffee, her eyes darting over to Toby. 'How about you?' She put her coffee down, looking worried. 'I'm finding it hard not to think of you as Nora Hartford, famous businesswoman. I'd never ask Nora Hartford about her personal life. You don't have to tell me anything. I won't be offended.'

'Look. Can we pretend I didn't walk into your shop unannounced today because I'd much rather be friends with you than sell you any pottery.'

Hilary beamed. 'Okay. In that case, tell me everything.'

And Nora did. Everything about Julian and the slow rot of their relationship and how she felt the same way as Hilary about living with someone again.

'So you're not on the lookout for a man?'

Nora laughed and shook her head. 'Not at all. I can't think of anything worse!' But at the exact moment she said the words, the image of Archie in his threadbare woollen jumper and tweed trousers, looking at her with his soulful brown eyes popped into her mind and she wondered whether she was telling Hilary the truth.

5

Nora wasn't sure that Hilary was being entirely honest when she said that the date-with-a-book club was nothing to do with actually dating. But then, Hilary was with Toby and yet still going to this book club, and that was why Nora gave her the benefit of the doubt.

Although it seemed like a lot of trouble compared to her Bristol book club, Hilary had insisted it would be worth it to be in the 'best group' since that meant the book club meeting was at Oliver's.

Nora had parked her car behind the church again, having found that it was a handy spot for getting almost anywhere in the town. She headed to the library where she was hoping to sign up to the book club. Doing it via the library was apparently the 'in' to being in the right book club group. The library was at the opposite end of the high street to Candles and Cushions and was separated from the road by railings and then a garden with plenty of benches that might invite someone to sit and read, if it were a warmer day.

As soon as the wooden doors swung open, Nora was flung back in time to her childhood and the visits to her own local library. The smell was almost exactly the same and she immediately loved the fact that Croftwood Library had managed to survive any kind of modernisation that might have changed that. The library of her childhood had closed years ago so it was heartening to find that the same fate hadn't touched this one.

'Morning,' said the woman from behind the desk that dominated the entrance. She had brown curly hair and was wearing some dungarees with a Liberty print blouse underneath, both of which Nora loved.

'Morning. I was hoping to sign up for the book club.'

'Wonderful! These are the book choices for this month. We always have a romance, a crime or thriller and a biography or historical non-fiction. Most of the copies are out on loan apart from this one.' She pointed to Unruly by David Mitchell which was the history of all the Kings and Queens of England. 'I think people are overwhelmed by the idea of that much information in one book. Most people have gone for the thriller this month.' It was The Housemaid by Freida McFadden.

'I've been meaning to read that, so perhaps that'd be the best choice,' said Nora, keen not to have to tackle anything too taxing.

The librarian checked her computer. 'I don't have any in at the moment but I've got a handful due back in the next couple of days. I could put you on the waiting list. Do you have a library membership?'

'I'll need to join, please. I've only just moved to Croftwood.'

'Ah, welcome to the town! I'm Lois. I live in Worcester but obviously spend quite a bit of time in Croftwood.'

'Nora. I can't believe this library, it's just like the one I used to go to as a child.'

Lois beamed. 'I know, isn't it gorgeous? We had to fight to keep it from closing a couple of years ago. It was a bit tired and neglected but this book club is actually what helped save it.'

'Now that you've said that, I remember hearing the story on the radio. Didn't you win an award or something?'

'We were Library of the Year. It was pretty amazing. Do you have any ID on you? I can take your details off that if you have something like a driving licence.'

Nora rooted around in her purse and found her driving licence, then wandered over to browse the shelves while Lois sorted out the membership. She tended to read thrillers most of the time but she loved a really thick book now and again having grown up stealing her mum's Jilly Cooper novels. Polo was a particular favourite and she had a very battered copy that now she thought about it was possibly in the box that Julian had because she didn't remember unpacking it.

She was flicking through a book called 'Wild Swimming' when Lois came over and handed her the membership card.

'I love the idea of wild swimming,' Lois said. 'Not that I've ever tried. It's just got a strange appeal.'

'I used to live near the sea so I swam most days. It was a sea pool, so not exactly wild but I think it's a similar experience and you definitely get the same benefits.'

'You must miss that now you're living the furthest you can get from the sea.'

'I've found a lake so I've been swimming there for a couple of weeks.'

'Oh, fantastic. So not an organised thing? That's quite brave.'

'I suppose I know what to look out for after so many years, and it's definitely a high-quality lake, not a stagnant pond or anything.'

Lois laughed. 'Where is it?'

Nora's heart sank. She should have anticipated this.

'I'm not sure exactly, I came across it when I was on a walk. I don't think I could find it any other way.' It wasn't an outright lie. If she hadn't seen Archie and Tatty the other day, she'd never have ventured further than the lake itself, and would never have known that it was in the grounds of Croftwood Court.

'Lucky you. That sounds idyllic.' Lois didn't press for any more information, and Nora was grateful for that. She'd be more careful about what she said from now on. 'So we'll give you a ring when the book's in and I'll add you to the book club list for next week. Will you get through it before then?'

'I should think so,' Nora said confidently, 'And the meeting is at Oliver's?'

'Yes. We have so many people in the book club now that we have three venues and only people who book through the library can go to the meeting at Oliver's since that was our original meeting place. We have meetings at the Courtyard Café for anyone linked to a library other than Croftwood. We get a lot of people from Worcester,' she explained. 'And then there's a meeting at Croftwood Cinema for anyone who just wants to join in and isn't a member of the library but actually it's become overspill for the entire club. It's been huge since the summer. We had to start that one after the Croftwood Festival because there was so much demand.'

'That's incredible. Running a book club on that kind of scale must be a lot of work.'

'It's the biggest part of my job now,' Lois said. 'Luckily we have a great team here so Linda and Rosemary manage the library day-to-day, and I run the book club. Today's my regular day to cover for both of them and I love working on the desk. Except on Saturdays. It's total chaos.'

'Well, thanks for enrolling me,' Nora said. 'I'll pop back as soon as I hear from you.'

'And I'll see you at the book club for your date.'

Nora went cold. 'I didn't think that it was actually going to be a date. Do you mean it's a date with the book?'

'Sorry, I should have explained,' said Lois, smiling and unaware of Nora's dread that she might have signed up for some weird speed-dating involving books. 'We just match you up with someone else who's read the book. Not like romantic dating, although we have had a few successes in that department. It could be anyone, and usually once you've had a chat about the book with your date,' she air-quoted, 'it turns into more of a group thing. The idea behind it was to be less intimidating so that individuals feel more comfortable joining in. Saves having to find a friend who's interested in coming.'

'Ah, okay. That makes sense.' Nora laughed with relief. 'I guess it's a good way to meet other people from the town.'

'Exactly! And the group that meets at Oliver's is almost all locals. It'll be great,' she said reassuringly.

Feeling pleased that she'd finally done something to involve herself in the community, Nora left the library and headed to Oliver's for a chai latte. She could see Hilary's partner, Toby, sat at the same table he had been at the other day. He smiled and raised a hand when she went in. She waved back, feeling odd that they kind of knew each other without having spoken. She was sure Hilary would have shared their conversation with him, and she didn't mind that, but it might take a while to get used to that small-town thing where everyone knows everyone and their business.

Today, the barista was a bearded man, similar to her age rather than Jack from her last visit.

'What can I get you?' he asked.

'An oat milk chai latte, please.'

'Drinking in?'

'Yes, thanks.'

'Take a seat and I'll bring it over.'

Nora paid with her phone and took a seat at a table tucked in the corner behind some open shelving that was chock-full of trailing foliage. While she waited for her drink she replied to a text from her friend Liz, who she used to swim with regularly at Clevedon. Liz was free to meet on Saturday, so Nora suggested late morning which would give her time to pick up her box from Julian's and then wash the whole experience away with a lovely cold swim.

'One oat milk chai latte,' said the barista. 'Are you a new regular?' he asked with a lazy smile, leaning against the shelves with his arms crossed and making no move to go back to the counter.

Nora gave him an uncertain smile. 'Why would you say that?'

'I saw you wave to Toby. And I had a text from my girlfriend Lois who I think you just met? So I put two and two together.'

She desperately wanted to make some quick-witted comment but couldn't think of anything. And besides, it was nice that everyone was so welcoming. Or it would be once she got over the weirdness of it.

'Hey, Oliver. I hope you're not going to need legal representation when Nora has you arrested for harassment.' Toby called over. He'd pulled his headphones down so they were looped around his neck, and he looked amused.

'I'm not harassing her, I'm making friends with a new customer,' Oliver objected.

'I'll vouch for him and reassure you that it starts out like this but develops into something that seems more normal once you get to know him,' Toby said.

'Good to know,' said Nora, grinning. 'I'm not used to a town on this scale. I've moved here from Bristol,' she said to Oliver.

'As owner of the best coffee house in town, allow me to formally welcome you to Croftwood.' He held out his hand and Nora shook it, noting that it didn't have the same effect on her as when she'd shaken Archie's hand, and making a mental note to wonder more about why that might be later on.

Toby came over and stood next to Oliver. 'Nice to say hello properly,' he said with a reassuring smile. 'I think word has spread that Nora Hartford has moved to town so this isn't the last time you'll come across people being odd around you. Hilary's mortified about the other day.'

'I'm not being odd!' Oliver said, looking offended.

Nora laughed. 'She shouldn't be. I was the one who took her by surprise. I should have made an appointment instead of turning up unannounced.'

'You made her year,' said Toby. 'She's been singing your praises to everyone. I imagine that's how Oliver ended up coming across like a stalker. He's probably been hyped up by Hilary. No offence, you're not a Hart Pottery lover are you Oliver?'

'I like a bit of crockery as much as the next man,' said Oliver. 'But I have to admit I googled you about two minutes before you walked in here, after Lois texted me. She was pretty excited.'

Nora was baffled. She was hardly a celebrity, but the demographic of people who bought her mass-produced work was thirty- to fifty-year-old women, so perhaps she shouldn't have been surprised that other people in Hilary's friendship group had heard of her.

'Well, I've signed up for the book club and this is a pretty good chai latte so I probably will be a regular. Despite the overly attentive proprietor.'

Toby barked out a laugh and slapped Oliver on the back. 'That's what you'll come to love about this place, Nora. Oliver's a mine of information about everything and everyone in Croftwood.'

'So get used to it?'

'Ha! Nora, we're going to love having you here,' Toby said, heading back to his own table.

'Well, it's nice to meet you,' Oliver said, looking abashed. 'Next time you come in, it's on the house.'

'That's okay,' Nora said, smiling.

'Lois'll kill me if she knows I let you buy that one, so you'd be doing me a favour.'

Nora strolled back to her car with a smile on her face. Maybe she ought to be wary about making friends with the first people she'd met. She didn't want it to end up like when she went to college, having to avoid people for the next three years because she'd misjudged who she might get along with. But she was older and wiser now and they seemed like genuinely nice people. Normal people, with jobs and partners. Could it really be that easy to make friends? Probably best to be cautious, just in case. But she already got on with Hilary. At least she could pump her for information about the other people she came across. Weed out the weirdos.

6

Nora drove to Clevedon on Saturday morning, via Julian's house, with a mixture of trepidation and excitement. It had been over a month since she'd seen him, and her stomach was in knots at the thought of it. She'd put him out of her mind further than was probably healthy, and knew she hadn't been allowing herself to process the fact that the relationship had ended. Coming to terms with the fact that twenty years of her life had been spent with a person who didn't love her enough to support her through some of the best times of her life was hard. And if he couldn't be there for her during the good times, what would it be like in the bad? She knew that if she let herself think about it properly, it might turn into grieving of sorts. Grief for the years she'd lost. But she wasn't in love with Julian anymore and it felt stupid to be upset about the end of everything when she wasn't actually heartbroken.

She passed Gloucester services and made a mental note to call in there on the way home for something delicious for dinner, and concentrated on looking forward to seeing Liz at the pool. One of the best things about the people she knew from the pool was that they were friends at the pool, but not really outside of that. Their small group knew everything about each other's lives in some detail but they all knew that what was said at the pool stayed at the pool and it had been a lifeline for Nora when everything with Julian had started to fall apart. Liz and the others knew what she'd been through because they'd been there for her, and now that she was out the other side, she wanted to tell Liz how much it had meant to her.

Once she got to the outskirts of Bristol, she had to follow the maps app to find Julian's new place. Of course she'd googled it when he told her the address and she was surprised to see that it was in Clifton. He'd have struggled to afford anywhere in that postcode on half of the proceeds from their house, but then, it was a few years since they'd shared the ins and outs of their finances with each other, so perhaps he was better off than she imagined.

She pulled up at the side of the road a few houses away from Julian's and took a deep breath. She could do this. If he was normal and friendly, it would be fine. What she couldn't deal with was the surly, distant man that she'd been living with towards the end. Hopefully, the few weeks of space they'd had might have helped on that front. And anyway, once she collected this box, they need have nothing to do with each other again.

Nora pulled the sun visor down to check herself in the mirror. She applied some extra lip gloss and smoothed her hair, annoyed with herself for caring what she looked like, but it mattered. She wanted to look better than he might remember her. Like she was living her best life, which of course she was.

Julian's new place was a town house. Tall, skinny and painted in a fresh blue shade to complement the other brightly coloured houses in the area. Considering they used to both insist they'd never live in a house more modern than a Victorian one, this was about a hundred years newer than that. It made Nora smile and somehow settled her nerves, knowing that he'd compromised his idealism in this area at the same time as accusing her of selling out. She rang the bell, forcing herself to smile in readiness for when he opened the door.

'Nora! You're early.' He leant in and gave her a flustered kiss on the cheek, which took her aback. She'd been expecting a frostier welcome, so this was good. He smelled freshly showered. His hair was damp and arranged in the style he favoured to disguise the fact he was balding and receding. Why he didn't lean into it with a hairstyle that didn't look like it was covering something up – literally – she had no idea.

'It was quicker than I thought it would be to get across town,' she said.

'Come in,' he said, standing aside to let her pass. 'Straight up the stairs.'

Nora climbed the stairs and emerged into a bright open-plan living room and kitchen with double doors that led onto a tiny balcony and overlooked the Avon gorge.

'This view is amazing,' she said, walking over to look out of the window.

'It is,' he agreed. 'Coffee?'

'Yes, please.'

She turned and took in the rest of the space, having been too drawn by the view to notice at first. Some of the furniture she recognised, more of it she didn't. In particular, the old G-Plan sofa they'd had for years, that he'd insisted on having, was missing, replaced by a modern L-shaped slouchy thing covered in more cushions than she'd ever seen on one sofa before.

'You've got a new sofa.'

'The old one wouldn't fit up the stairs.'

How the old one wouldn't fit up the stairs if this mammoth

sofa-cum-double bed did, she had no idea. She wanted to say that she would never have agreed to him having the sofa if there was any possibility he was going to get rid of it. Out of all their shared possessions, it had been one of the most contentious and now it appeared he hadn't wanted it that badly anyway. But she fought the urge to say anything because she was glad not to have too many reminders of that life in her new one. If he gave her the sofa now, all she would remember was the time they bought it and all the times they'd laid out on it together. Times when they'd been happy. There was something about a sofa that held more memories – good and bad – than say, her favourite armchair, a chest of drawers or a table.

'Shame. That was a good sofa.'

He did at least look guilty for a second and looked like he might be about to apologise, which, after all the arguing over the past few months, was a rare thing. But he didn't say anything. He brought the coffees over to the sofa and put them down on a wooden board perched on top of one of those trendy massive footstools that was so big it would take up most of Nora's lounge.

'So how's the new place?' he asked.

'Good, thanks. Still finding my way around the town, but it seems nice. How about you? This place is amazing.'

He looked guarded, and Nora had the feeling that she was missing something. 'Yes, I mean it's not ideal…'

'It's not what I expected, if I'm honest. You used to hate houses like this.' It still niggled her about how he could have afforded it. A part time art teacher's salary, even topped up with sales of his pieces through local galleries, didn't add up to this.

'I have something to tell you. I didn't tell you before because… well, we had a lot going on, with the house sale and everything. I've met someone else.'

Nora sat in silence for a minute, doing the maths. Even if she counted back to when she'd first suggested perhaps things weren't working any more. Back to that time when she realised the problems they had were insurmountable after all. That wasn't more than six months ago. He'd met and moved in with someone else in six months? After coming out of a twenty-year relationship?

'You were seeing her before we split up,' she said.

He gave her the same look he had a few minutes ago. Guilt mixed with a startled look that said he hadn't expected her to work it out.

'Nora —'

'It's fine. It's nothing to do with me anymore.' She gulped the coffee down and stood up. 'I'd better go. Have you got my box?' It wasn't because she was upset. But she suddenly felt like an intruder. This was someone else's house, and she didn't want to be part of any of this.

Julian stood up and put a hand on her arm, which she shrugged away from, stunned that he would think she would find that comforting.

'Nora. She's not here. Anyway, she knows you were coming. She's fine with it.'

'I'm sure she is, Julian. She has all the information available to her to make an informed decision about what she's comfortable with, whereas I feel a little blindsided.'

Julian stood up and stood in between Nora and the top of the stairs. 'I know how it looks.'

'How does it look?' she retorted. 'Because if you think it looks like you've moved on before the dust has settled on our twenty-year relationship and that you got rid of our sofa because of someone else, then yes, that's what it looks like!'

'The sofa wouldn't fit up the stairs,' he said weakly.

'Oh, shut up about the bloody sofa! Give me the box so I can get out of your life, Julian!' She was yelling now. All the feelings she'd been so careful to control over the past few months when she'd been aware that it was she wanting to end things. Feeling that she had no right to be the injured party when all the time, Julian had been seeing someone else. If she hadn't called time on their relationship, what would have happened? Would he have been cheating on her? Had the relationship started before she had wanted to end theirs? Is that what had sent them into the downward spiral that spelled the end? These were all things she was desperate to know, but too proud to ask. She wouldn't give him the satisfaction. As it was, she had come here for a box and was leaving with a whole lot more.

Julian gestured down the stairs. 'The box is in the hall,' he said.

Nora ran down the stairs and picked the box up, hoping to stick it under her arm and leave as quickly as possible, but it was too heavy to make a fast or graceful exit.

'Let me give you a hand,' Julian said, heaving it off the floor.

She stalked out of the house and opened the boot of her car, then sat in the driver's seat while he put the box in the boot and closed it. Then, just as he was about to come to her window to have a last word, she drove away. She could see him in the rear-view mirror, holding his hands in the air in exasperation.

Until now, she thought she'd come to terms with the feeling that she'd wasted almost twenty years of her life with someone who didn't love her the way she'd hoped. Hadn't loved her enough to support her in the good times, let alone through anything bad. But now it looked like Julian had moved on long before she'd noticed. Long before she'd realised that he didn't love her anymore, and long before she'd stopped loving him. And that made her so angry.

Because she'd thought it would take longer at Julian's,

Nora was early for meeting Liz at the sea pool, so she took a walk along the beach first. She needed to organise her thoughts and calm down. She wanted to enjoy the swim and at the moment was feeling too full of rage and indignation for that to happen. After she parked the car in the marine lake car park, she walked along the length of the pool until it gave way to the beach. Since it wasn't a particularly sunny day, and the forecast was for rain later, there weren't too many people around. Nora loved the feeling of having the beach to herself. Luckily, the tide was out, but there was a keen wind coming off the sea, making some big waves. It was the best kind of day for a swim because you felt like you were in the sea, yet were protected in the pool from the ferocity of the waves – until later when the tide came in and the sea would over-top the dividing wall. You had to be careful swimming in those conditions even in the pool, in case you got pounded into the wall. By the time she had walked up and down the beach, taking lungfuls of sea air, she felt better and was looking forward to seeing Liz.

'He's moved in with someone? Who is she?' Liz was exactly the right amount of incredulous to make Nora feel justified in having felt so angry.

'I don't know. I didn't ask. I didn't want him to think it mattered to me. I doubt I'd know her anyway, but whoever she is, she's got a very nice house in Clifton overlooking the gorge.'

They swam side by side to the far end of the pool, then stopped at the edge for a breather, which was just an excuse to carry on chatting.

'The thing is,' Nora said, 'I don't really mind that he's moved on so quickly. If anything, it confirms to me that I did the right thing because I know I don't love him anymore. The thing that makes me angry is that he must have been seeing her when he was giving me a hard time about me wanting to split up.'

'You think so?'

'Yes!' said Nora, feeling as if she was having an epiphany. 'And even if I give him the benefit of the doubt on the timeline, it's still only four months from me initiating the conversation about the fact things might be over between us, to him living with someone else. Four months.'

'At least you can forgive yourself. He was gaslighting you, making you feel bad for wanting to end things when that must have been what he wanted too,' Liz said.

'It sounds so dramatic, but you're right. And I have been feeling guilty.'

'But not anymore.'

'Not anymore!' Nora shouted into the wind.

They began swimming back. Nora felt lighter. As much as it hurt to think that Julian had been that manipulative, she could let go of the feeling that it all ended because of her.

'You know, if you hadn't been selling the house, things probably wouldn't have happened that fast with him and his new woman,' Liz said. 'Your place did sell incredibly quickly.'

'True. Well, good luck to her.'

'That's the spirit. Sod them!' Liz shouted, startling a couple of people nearby.

'Sod them!' Nora shouted, laughing.

'Come on, let's get out before we turn to ice.'

Nora had forgotten how much more fun it was swimming with someone else. Perhaps she ought to ask Hilary if she'd be up for it next time she saw her. It might be nice to start a little community around swimming in the lake.

7

Archie stood looking up at the roof, his hand shielding the sun from his eyes, as he watched the man from the roofing company assess the latest batch of repairs that were needed. He'd been hoping to delay it until later in the summer, but a deluge of rain the night before last had resulted in one of the bedroom ceilings bowing with the weight of the water in quite an alarming way. Luckily — or unluckily — it was his mother's room so they had realised fairly quickly. If it had been one of the unoccupied rooms, they may have been dealing with a ceiling collapse which would have been a much more costly repair. As it was, he'd had to go up into the attics himself and scoop the water into a bucket using a dustpan to avoid that happening.

Simon the roofer stood in a gully between the points of the roof and called down to Archie. 'I don't know if you've seen, but you've got a couple of broken chimney pots up here. I'll take some photos, show you when I come down.'

'Thank you,' said Archie, although why he was thanking the man for adding to the eventual bill, he didn't know. His manners were automatic though, even when he felt far from being polite. And obviously it wasn't this chap's fault, but it didn't help that Archie knew he was mentally rubbing his hands in glee at the prospect of handing over an inflated bill just because of which house it was.

While he waited for Simon to be escorted down through the house by Ursula, Archie shoved his hands in his pockets and paced the lawn. Each determined stride helped the stress ebb away slightly, but these days he never felt relaxed. There was always something new to be worried about.

'Some missing tiles, is it?' Archie asked optimistically when Simon joined him.

'And then some! You've got some flashing missing from one gulley. Looks like it's been nicked.'

'We had some of the lead stolen a few years ago and it was replaced with something else.'

'Mmm. Inferior materials. Probably been blown off in a storm. They should have replaced it with lead since this place is listed.'

Archie nodded. 'We always intended to replace it properly when funds allowed.'

'You want the whole thing sorted now, or do you want a patch up job?'

'Whatever you can do that isn't going to bankrupt me.'

Simon laughed, assuming Archie was joking.

'And here are the pots you might want to sort before next winter.' Simon pulled up a photo of the damaged chimney pots on his phone. 'If you leave them, the rainwater will get in the cracks and they'll shatter.'

'That's rather dramatic.'

Simon shrugged. 'That's what happens with terracotta.'

'If you could let me have a quote for the bare minimum, please. And a separate one for the chimney pots because they might have to wait.'

'No problem, mate.'

Archie walked Simon back to his van which was parked outside the estate office, waved him off and went to find Seb who was doing something or other in his side of the courtyard.

'Seb?'

'Up here!' Seb was standing on one of the rafters that ran across the roof. The roof space was open and he was planning to turn part of it into a mezzanine.

'This roof is in better shape than the one at the house, apparently.'

'Ah, you've seen Simon?' Seb lowered himself down onto the top of a stepladder, which wobbled precariously until he had both feet on it.

'Yes,' Archie said glumly, perching on top of an old tea chest. 'Looks like that's where the profit from this year's Christmas market will end up. It's depressing that I've spent the money before we've made it.'

'This Christmas, the market will be bigger and better than last, so at least you have an idea of what to expect.' Seb sat down on an exercise bike and leant forward on the handlebars, all his attention on Archie. 'Have you thought any more about opening the house?'

Seb had suggested the idea of opening some rooms in the manor house to the public. There was enormous interest locally, driven partly because during the Second World War it had been planned that the young princesses, Elizabeth and Margaret, would have been sent to the Court if they'd had to evacuate London. There were rumours that all the things that had been sent to prepare for their visit were still stored in the cellars.

'I haven't found the right time to ask Mama yet.' Because he knew what she would say. It would be a firm no. And he didn't want to share with her how bad the finances were because he didn't want her to worry. If she knew the truth, she'd give in and allow the public to visit, but he knew she'd see it as a failure on his part as well as a violation of her privacy and something unbecoming of the family name.

'What about the swimming lake idea?'

'I went down to the lake and met the woman. Her name is Nora.'

'And what did she say? Does she know much about it?'

'I'm not sure I asked,' Archie said, casting his mind back to his brief conversation with Nora and finding that he couldn't remember much other than how lovely she'd looked bundled up in her swimming robe, smiling and chatty once she'd realised he hadn't been about to evict her from the lake. 'She did say it was a very inviting lake, and she didn't seem to mind that there are fish in there.'

'So you didn't exactly milk her for information.' Seb said, shaking his head but grinning.

'It wasn't the right time. She was about to get in the water and I was holding her up.'

'It's your lake and she was trespassing.'

Archie winced. 'Well, I hardly think it counts as trespassing, Seb. But I take your point. I'll pop along with Tatty and see her on another morning. She swims every day.'

'Does she? Perhaps I should come with you armed with a list of questions if it makes you uncomfortable to ask her.'

'No need,' Archie said, feeling that Seb's presence might spoil the moment. Because now that he'd met her, she was forefront in his mind and he wanted to see her again. He certainly didn't want to scare her away with an interrogation. 'But if you could give me an idea of what may be useful to ask, I'm happy to.'

'What's she like then?'

'Oh. I imagine she's around our age. Pretty.'

'I see. Pretty.' Seb smirked. 'And very friendly? You like her.'

'I do like her,' Archie said, missing Seb's emphasis on the word *like*. 'She was lovely.'

'Arch. If I were you I'd go down there in the morning in my trunks. How often do you meet a woman who you could ask out?'

'Hold on there. I'm not propositioning her, I barely know her. She'll be married, I'm certain.'

'Well at least find out before you write her off. It's about time you had some fun. If I can't drag you to the pub with me and Oliver, perhaps she can tempt you out of the grounds once in a while.'

Archie was well aware that his social life was a tragedy. He told himself that he didn't have time to socialise. That it wasn't fair to leave his mother alone when Ursula and Mrs Milton were off duty. She was quite capable of looking after herself, but with him out of the house during the day, he liked to keep her company in the evenings. But the reality was that his mother went out more than he did and he was desperately out of the habit of maintaining friendships. Seb was the first person he'd had a proper friendship with for years and Archie loved chatting to him. He enjoyed hearing Seb's ideas, his mind constantly whirring with plans. If he could have sat in a pub with Seb, he'd feel quite comfortable that they'd have a pleasant conversation. But bring anyone else into the mix, like Oliver who Archie had only met a few times, who was confident beyond belief, successful and also friends with Seb, Archie knew he would feel small. He was protecting himself from it becoming obvious that he was the less interesting friend.

'What were you doing up there?' Archie said, changing the subject.

'Just trying to get a good look at the space. I dumped everything in here in such a rush in the summer, it needs a good sort out. I was wondering whether to use the mezzanine for storage or for an office. What do you think?'

'I think we might need to speak to someone at the Council

if you're thinking about having an office here,' Archie said. 'We'd need to apply for change of use.'

'Let's get a planning officer down here. See what's possible because we could do something with the building on the other side of the courtyard too. It needs repairing but it's wasted using all this space as storage. It could be another income stream if we put our minds to it.'

Seb would make a far better estate manager than he did. Archie blundered from one day to the next, feeling he had no time to look beyond what each day presented to him. 'That's a good idea. I don't know why I didn't think of it.'

'It'll take some sorting out and you've got enough on your plate worrying about the roof of the house, let alone the roof of an empty stable block.'

Archie nodded gratefully at Seb. 'I'll start looking into the lake idea properly,' he said. It was the least he could do when Seb was taking care of so many other things for him. And it was the excuse he needed to see Nora again.

That evening, his mother was heading out to her usual book club. She had a standing arrangement to share lifts with two friends and because she didn't drive, Archie acted as taxi driver every third month, which he didn't mind at all. But not tonight. So he was planning to light a fire, pour himself a whisky and do some research on swimming in lakes.

'I do wish you'd come to the book club, darling,' his mother said over dinner. 'I thought you'd enjoyed it after we did it at the festival in the summer.'

This was a standard conversation he had to sit through once a month on book club evening. Actually, he had enjoyed the festival enormously, but the idea of accompanying his mother to a book club seemed desperately tragic. Almost a confirmation of what his life had come to: tagging onto his mother's social life.

'I did enjoy it, but I never have time to read. Anyway, at

Seb's suggestion I'm doing some research tonight.' Dropping Seb's name in would give some credibility to what he was doing. His mother loved Seb.

'Researching what, exactly?'

'You know we saw that woman on the lawn the other morning? I bumped into her again and as it happens, she swims every morning.'

'In our lake?' his mother said indignantly.

'Yes. I don't think it matters,' he said weakly, knowing that she wouldn't agree.

'Of course it matters, Archie.'

'Seb thinks we could use the lake as a swimming lake,' he said, not sure whether in this instance, even dropping Seb's name in would help. 'Charge people to come and swim.'

'Well, I suppose if the woman's swimming anyway, the least she can do is pay. Surely there's no call for swimming in a lake. There's a perfectly good municipal pool in Croftwood. And do we want to encourage people traipsing around the estate?'

'The people who traipsed around over Christmas bought our new heating system, Mama.'

'Don't be impertinent, Archie,' she said, suppressing a smile.

'I'm only looking into it at this stage. Seb and I won't do anything on the estate without talking to you first.'

His mother laid down her knife and fork and dabbed at her mouth with a cloth napkin. 'Archie. You must run the estate as you see fit. It's of no consequence what I think.' She laid a hand on his and squeezed it. 'I'm just a cross old woman.'

'Mama…'

'I must go. Penny will be here any minute.' She kissed his cheek on her way past and left him to finish his dinner.

8

Nora was surprised how much she was looking forward to the date-with-a-book club meeting. She'd finished reading The Housemaid and was excited about discussing it with whoever she was partnered with.

Hilary had suggested that since it was Nora's first time at book club, they should go together. She said she remembered being intimidated by the sheer number of people the first time she went and had almost bottled out before Lois had spotted her loitering outside Oliver's and encouraged her inside.

So, even though it wasn't far from her house, Nora was using her map app to navigate to Hilary's house in a part of town she hadn't discovered yet. The street was a leafy — well, it would be except that it was barely spring — tree-lined avenue with Victorian houses of various sizes on either side of the road. Hilary lived in a substantial semi-detached house which, even from the outside, oozed taste. The pathway to the door was paved with blue bricks and the smart front door was painted navy-blue and had two panes of leaded glass in the top half and a knocker in the shape of a giant pinecone. A pair of standard bay trees stood sentry in pots on either side of the door.

Nora rapped the knocker and waited, desperate to see whether Hilary had the original encaustic tiled floor in her hallway.

'Come in!' Hilary said, opening the door and then hurrying back into the kitchen. 'I am ready. I just need to finish sending an email.'

Nora closed the door and took a moment to look at the floor, which sadly, was a reproduction, but looked the part nevertheless.

'Oh, I know. Some idiot had ripped the original floor up,' Hilary said, coming back into the hallway and taking her coat from a cupboard underneath the stairs. 'You'll have to come to Toby's sometime. He's got an original Minton floor in his hallway. His house is much fancier than mine. Ready?'

'Your floor still looks amazing. I love your lounge as well. The wallpaper's beautiful,' Nora said, glimpsing it through the door to the right as she went out.

'This house is the first place I've ever lived that is just mine. So I did it exactly how I wanted. All the things I'd seen in my years of working with interiors and loved, all of that went into this house. And I loved every minute of it.'

'My house is a bit of a blank canvas,' Nora said. 'I really like it, it's very cosy but the decor is so bland compared to yours. I think I need some wallpaper.'

'If you need any advice, I'd love to help,' Hilary said. 'As an arty person, you can't live in a house with white walls.'

'No, but I think I've only just realised that I can have it exactly how I want.'

Hilary laughed. 'Welcome to the best thing about being single.'

'You're not single.'

'True. Welcome to the best thing about living alone. As much as I love Toby, I don't ever want to see the end of us having our own places.'

Nora enjoyed the walk to the coffee house, along streets she'd never been down before. This side of town was very different to where she lived, but although it was more built-up, it felt spread out and roomy. They walked around the edge of the park, past Croftwood Cinema, where there were quite a few people queuing.

'They let you know who your partner is when you get to the door,' Hilary explained.

'Do you ever end up with Toby?'

'We hardly ever read the same book,' Hilary said. 'This time, he chose that massive book about the kings and queens. I don't know how he found the time to finish it.'

As they approached Oliver's, they could see a couple of people queuing outside, but they'd gone in by the time they'd reached the door.

An older woman with her hair drawn back into a tight bun peered at Nora over her glasses. 'Name?'

'Nora Hartford.'

The woman ran her pencil down the list. 'You're meeting Constance. She's the lady over there.'

'This is Rosemary. She works at the library. Rosemary, Nora has just moved to Elderbrook Lane,' Hilary said.

'Welcome to Croftwood,' Rosemary said. 'Enjoy your evening. Hilary you're with Sam.'

Nora headed over to where Rosemary had pointed, where an elegant lady with her hair in a Princess Anne style up do was sitting at a table for two. It seemed they were lucky to have a table to themselves. The place was thronging with people, and chairs were crammed into whatever space was available.

'Hello there, are you Constance?'

'I am. You must be…'

'Nora.'

'Nora, yes. Do take a seat. I'm desperate to hear what you

thought of the book. I've never read anything that gripped me like this did.'

Nora sat down opposite Constance, who was absentmindedly rolling the stem of her wineglass in her fingers. Before she could answer, Oliver came over. 'Coffee or wine?' he asked.

'Oat milk chai latte, please.' Nora tapped her phone on the small card reader he held out to her.

'Be a couple of minutes,' he said with a smile before he was off to the next table.

'He looks after us marvellously,' Constance said.

'Do you usually read psychological thrillers?' Nora asked.

'No. I'm a romance reader through and through, but this time Lois warned me that the romance book was rather steamy. That was how she put it, and apparently these steamy books are quite different to the racy books I used to enjoy. You know, Jackie Collins, Jilly Cooper, that sort of thing.'

'I love those books. I used to sneak them out of my mum's room and read them when I was a teenager.'

Constance threw her head back and laughed. 'Wonderful!' she said. 'And do you read this new steamy romance?'

'I've come across it,' Nora said, thinking that Lois was probably right to divert Constance away from anything that might have more than a chapter or two of smut. 'It actually gets quite boring to read after a while.'

Constance raised an eyebrow. 'Oh, really? In what way?'

Nora took a breath. Was she really going to explain how one novel she read had a blowjob that lasted more than a chapter? 'Oh, I suppose it just gets a bit samey, hearing about how a man can curl his fingers and hit a G-spot the woman never knew she had.'

'Good lord! How graphic.'

'Sorry,' Nora said, 'I mean, it gets more graphic than that, so perhaps Lois was right.'

'Quite. Thank goodness for The Housemaid.'

They had a very enjoyable discussion about the twists and turns of the novel and especially whether either of them had guessed the twist at the end, which they hadn't.

'Are you new to the town?'

'Yes, I moved here just over a month ago from the Bristol area.'

'Not somewhere I'm familiar with. I grew up in Hampstead before I came here. And what brought you to Croftwood?'

'I wanted somewhere closer to my work, which is in Staffordshire, but there are great rail links to London from here and that's handy for visiting my family in Surrey.' It had been a while since Nora had visited her parents. They were retired teachers who spent most of their time travelling around Europe with their caravan. She made a note to plan something in before they went off on their usual trip to the south of France.

'Any significant other?' Constance asked unashamedly.

'No. Just me.'

'I have a son about your age,' she began.

Nora's heart sank. The last thing she wanted was for this evening to turn into dating after all.

'He's been single forever only because he finds it difficult to meet women.'

He sounded like a real catch.

'I'm very recently out of a long-term relationship,' said Nora, hoping this would stop the conversation in its tracks.

'Oh, no. I think best to get back in the saddle at your age. As I said, my son is desperate to meet someone. Perhaps you'd like to come for dinner one evening?'

'I don't think that would be a good idea.'

'No, of course not. Better if I ask him to give you a call?'

Thankfully, at that moment, Hilary came over and there

was no need for Nora to tell Constance that in no circumstances was she interested in dating her desperate son.

'Do you two want to come and join us? We've commandeered the big table by the window now that there's a bit more space.'

'Yes, lovely,' Nora said, standing up straight away, hoping that she wasn't coming across as desperate to get away from Constance as she was.

'I'm going to sit with Linda. We've got some catching up to do about knitting,' Constance said. 'Lovely to meet you…'

'Nora. Lovely to meet you too.'

Nora gave her biggest smile, one of relief, and followed Hilary over to the window. There was no opportunity to milk Hilary for information on Constance or her son because they were drawn into the group conversation as soon as they sat down. Nora happily listened to Hilary introduce her to Patsy, Jess and Penny and by the time they'd all heckled Hilary and interjected with thoughtful anecdotes about each other, she'd forgotten all about Constance's son.

'So what's the best thing about Croftwood so far?' Patsy asked her, shifting along the bench to make room for Lois who had just arrived.

'This. The book club, obviously,' said Lois, accepting a kiss from Oliver as he whizzed past delivering wine to another table.

'It's definitely a contender,' Nora said.

'The cinema's the best thing,' Patsy said. 'Hey, are you all coming to the fortieth anniversary showing of the Breakfast Club?'

'I never understood the appeal of that film,' said Penny, who was in her fifties.

'Penny! It's a classic!' Patsy protested. 'The Brat Pack films are the best.'

'Overrated.' Penny said, emphatically.

'I loved Andrew McCarthy,' said Hilary with a sigh. Along with Penny she was the only one of the women around the table who would have been alive forty years ago.

'If it was Pretty in Pink, I'd be there like a shot,' said Lois.

'That's not forty until next year,' Patsy said. 'You'll have to wait. Anyway, Molly Ringwald is in the Breakfast club, too. What more do you want?'

'Do we get to dress up like the 1980s?' Jess asked.

'Yes! And we're having classic 1980s food and drinks.'

'The only food I remember from the 1980s are Alphabites and Findus Crispy Pancakes,' said Penny.

'We used to have Mini Mac sausages every night when I was a child,' said Hilary, making everyone laugh.

'Well, it won't be that kind of food,' Patsy said. 'But it'll be amazing. And most importantly, Long Island Iced Tea was all the rage.'

'I'll come,' said Jess. 'And not just because of the cocktails. I've always wanted to dress up as Madonna in her Like a Virgin era.'

'Madonna wasn't in the Breakfast Club,' said Penny.

'It's general 1980s, not just Breakfast Club-specific dressing up,' said Patsy.

'Count me in,' said Nora, thinking that this was the most fun she'd had in a long time. In fact aside from her group of swimming friends from Clevedon, she couldn't remember the last time she'd had a group of friends like this.

'Yes, Nora!' Patsy said, smacking her palm on the table and making them all jump. 'See? Nora's into it.'

'We're all coming, Patsy,' Lois said, grinning at her friend. 'The theme nights at the cinema are always a good laugh and I quite fancy seeing Oliver in a long tweed trench coat.'

'You're not going to encourage him to go for the Emilio Estevez look and wear a vest top?' Jess asked.

'God no,' Lois said, laughing. 'Let's leave that for someone who actually has some muscles to show off.'

By the time Toby joined them and it was time to leave, they'd all settled on who they were going to dress up as, even Penny.

'I chose the wrong book,' Toby said, as they strolled back to Hilary's house. 'The chap I was talking to was irritated beyond belief that it had an edge of comedy to it. What did he expect when it was written by David Mitchell? He was bitterly disappointed. But honestly, I'd never have got through it if it'd been a dry old boring history book. That's why I chose it, because it seemed like a good opportunity to finally learn some history but have some fun with it.'

'Oh, love,' Hilary said, consoling him. 'You can't win them all. Did you tell him you enjoyed it?'

'I tried. He didn't want to hear it.'

Hilary and Nora couldn't help giggling at how glum Toby was about the evening.

'I know what will cheer you up. We're going to the fortieth anniversary showing of the Breakfast Club at the cinema. We're dressing up.'

'Ha! No I'm not!' Toby said.

'Oh, spoilsport. I bet you'd look just like Rob Lowe if you had the right clothes.'

'No thank you. Presumably I'm allowed to attend in my own clothes?'

'I don't know if you are. Isn't that right, Nora?'

'Honestly, I'm not sure,' Nora said, diplomatically, but amused by their banter. 'But you probably want to avoid anyone thinking you're dressed up when you're not.'

Toby laughed. 'Good point. In which case, I'll think about it.'

'I could buy you a Frankie Says Relax t-shirt,' suggested Hilary.

'We'll see.'

'Thanks for a great evening,' Nora said when they got to Hilary's and she dug her car keys out of her pocket.

'Glad you enjoyed it. You did enjoy it, didn't you?'

Now wasn't the time to debrief Hilary on the conversation with Constance. She'd save that for another day. 'It was brilliant. Really good fun.'

9

A couple of days later turned out to be one of those days where Nora had to force herself to the lake. Not because she didn't want to swim, but because the pressure of everything that she had to do for the rest of the day made her feel as if she didn't have time to fit it in. Dawn was breaking when she left the house, and by the time she'd walked through the woods, she was greeted by a spectacular sunrise, its orange and pink hues reflecting on the surface of the lake. The moment that she lowered herself off the dock and into the water, she felt the tension ebb away. Because the water temperature was still low, she made sure her breathing was under control before she pushed off, gliding through the still water, feeling as if she was the only person in the world. One loop of the lake took her about fifteen minutes and in that time, the sun rose, lost its beautiful colours and settled into producing a bright late winter day.

Nora dried off, dressed, and wrapped her dry robe around her. She'd brought her flask, but since there wasn't time to linger, she planned to sip her tea on the way home. As she was about to clamber over the wall, she heard a splash and turned to see that Archie and Tatty had arrived at the other side of the lake. He raised a hand, and she waved back, waiting while he made his way around to her, all thoughts of the next part of her day forgotten.

'Morning!' he called when he got closer.

'Morning.'

'You've already been in.' He sounded disappointed. 'How was it today?'

'Wonderful. The sunrise was amazing.'

'It certainly was,' he agreed. 'Starts the day off on a good footing.'

'Would you like some tea?' It seemed only polite to offer, given that perhaps he had come to see her.

'Ah, no —'

'I have an extra cup.' It was a habit from her days at the sea pool when inevitably someone would be grateful for it.

His face brightened. 'That would be lovely if you have time. You were about to leave.'

All the things that had seemed so important earlier suddenly didn't seem pressing at all. 'I have time,' she said, smiling. His eyes did something to her insides, and she had to try not to stare at him. 'Shall we sit on the dock?'

The dog was still in the water, happily paddling back and forth before she hauled herself out on the island and settled down for a doze.

'Daft dog,' Archie said affectionately. 'I hope she won't mind getting in again when she realises she's marooned on the island.'

'You might have to go and fetch her,' Nora teased him, handing him a battered enamel mug half-filled with tea.

'Thank you. That won't be happening, I can assure you.'

Nora felt a thrill that Archie had expected her to be here. He'd come at exactly the same time of day, as if he'd come especially to see her. But then, she'd told him she was swimming every day, so perhaps not that surprising. 'Do you always walk her in the grounds?'

'Always. Convenience, I suppose. Tatty is running around after me all day, anyway. I'm not really walking her.'

'More for yourself?'

He looked at her and Nora lost herself in his eyes again for a moment before he looked away. 'A good walk seems to help with most things. Same as the swimming, I imagine?'

'Definitely. Especially today. I have a million things to do and none of them are fun. But at least now I feel like I'm ready to tackle it all. Coming here has made me take a breather before all of that starts, otherwise I'd be halfway up the M6 by now, all stressed out with my shoulders up around my ears.'

'You work that far away?'

'I'm a potter. I work out of a pottery in Stoke. I don't have to go in every day. A lot of the admin can be done remotely, but that's where my kiln is. Was,' she added, with a sigh.

'What's happened to it?'

'It's old and unreliable, so I had to buy a new one and now I have to do a load of test firings before my next batch of work can be fired. The window for making sure it's firing perfectly is tiny. I need to try and pin it down this week, otherwise I'll miss my next deadline.'

'It sounds like a lot more than I envisaged a potter having to cope with. Where do you sell your work?'

'The stuff I'm worried about is sold mostly to department stores or galleries. Here and overseas.' She was usually more reserved with information she gave when someone asked something like this, but Archie was a lord and unlikely to be after her money. And as such a new friend – if she could even call him that – it was better to start out with no misconceptions. 'And I have a production line that produces pottery for the mass-market.'

'Goodness me. I can understand why it's important to take some time for yourself.'

'I love it all, but not today. Making friends with a new kiln is a tricky business.'

'Lots of gods involved, as I understand it,' he said.

Nora laughed. 'You've been watching that pottery competition on television.'

'My mother loves the chap on there.'

'He's brilliant,' Nora agreed.

'I don't suppose you know anything about chimney pots?'

'I've made a chimney pot or two in my time but it's been a while, and nothing as ornate as the beautiful chimneys on your house.' Realising that she had just admitted she'd taken a wander further into the estate, she blushed. 'I'm sorry, I —'

'No need to apologise. We're friends now. In fact, I was hoping to pick your brains a little more about the swimming.'

Nora relaxed. 'Fire away.'

'My friend has suggested that cold-water swimming is all the rage these days and that opening the lake might be something to look into.'

The prospect of the lake being commercialised excited Nora because she'd love other people to experience the beauty of the place. But it was her lake. 'I can see that working,' she said. 'I mean, you could easily have twenty or so at the same time without it feeling crowded.'

'Really? As many as that?'

'I think you'd need to make it worthwhile. The first step is to have the water tested, just to make sure. And in the meantime, I could ask some friends if they'd like to try it? Get you some early consumer feedback?' Hilary and the others might like to come.

'That sounds wonderful,' said Archie. 'You know, if Tatty and I hadn't come across you here, I'd never have thought the lake was useful.'

'Happy that my trespassing has helped,' Nora said.

Archie laughed. 'It's hardly that now.'

'And the chimney pot. If you give me the measurements, I'm happy to see what I can do.'

'I can't ask you to do that,' Archie said.

'It'd be a welcome challenge. The clay will cost next to nothing. It's the least I can do in exchange for my morning swims.'

'In that case, I accept. Thank you. I'll jot down the size and pop down one morning.'

'Lovely,' said Nora, pleased that he had a reason to come back. 'I had better go.' She stood up and gathered her things.

Archie gulped the rest of his tea, stood up next to her, and handed the cup back. 'Thank you for the unexpected refreshment.'

'No problem. Perhaps I'd better make extra for next time I see you.'

They faced each other, not more than a footstep between them. Archie shoved his hands in his pockets and began moving from one foot to the other, as if he had something else to say.

'I look forward to seeing you soon, Nora,' he said. It sounded slightly formal, and perhaps not exactly what he was hoping to have said. If he was feeling anything like she was, he was hoping the next time they saw each other would be the following day, but Nora didn't want to assume anything. Perhaps he just had such good manners that he put people at ease. Found it easy to befriend people. And perhaps she had so few friends here she was clinging to the idea of Archie becoming one of them, when really, if she hadn't been caught in the lake, their paths would never have crossed.

'Me too, Archie. Bye.'

Later that day, after throwing endless pots on her wheel for the never-ending test firings, Nora finally reached the quota she'd set herself. Breathing a sigh of relief, she stood, stretched, and went in search of Val.

'I've finished,' she said, as if she was telling her mum she'd finished her homework.

'Fab. Come on then, let's get cracking.'

The kiln technician, Neil, helped them carry the pots into the drying room, exchanging them for pots that had been thrown the week before. They needed to dry out for at least a week before firing, so Nora had been throwing for the past seven days to make sure there was an ample supply for all the tests. They'd decorate them like they did with the mass-market lines and sell them as seconds if any of the firings were successful.

They carried the next dry batch downstairs, then Neil and Nora decided on the settings for the first run.

'Let's go with the suggested settings for a bisque firing,' he said. 'If it goes well, brilliant, and if not, we've got something to work on tomorrow.'

Neil sounded hopeful, but they all knew that there were so many variables involved; the thickness of the pots; how many pieces they loaded; whether there was any moisture left in the clay when it went in. And it was hard to control all of those variables at once. But that was what they were trying to do.

'Can you fix me up with some terracotta clay?' Nora asked Val while they were grabbing a coffee in the kitchen.

'What are you dabbling in?' Val said. They only used porcelain clay in the pottery, both for the production line and for Nora's bespoke pieces.

'I want to make a chimney pot.'

'Oh, times are so desperate that you need to throw your own chimney now?'

Nora laughed. 'You know Lord Harrington? Archie? He asked me if I could. It's ridiculous really. All of his have those beautiful twisted, ornate pots and I'm not sure I'm up to that standard, but I fancy having a go.'

'Funnily enough, we haven't got any on hand, but I'll get

some added to the next delivery. Look at it as a reward for getting the new kiln sorted out.'

'Anything that isn't throwing boring test pots is a reward.'

'Are you staying tonight?'

Nora sometimes stayed in a local hotel if she had a late finish and an early start, but it wasn't as far to go home and back as it had been before she moved. And she wanted a swim in the morning.

'I won't. There are enough pots for the tests now, so I don't need to be here first thing. And who knows, the kiln might fire perfectly tonight and I won't need to worry.'

'We can but hope. Do you want to get dinner before you go?' Val asked.

'I'd love that. Give me ten minutes to clean up.'

They went to the pub round the corner that did wonderful homemade pies. They chose mushroom and Stilton with chunky chips and mushy peas and had non-alcoholic beers since they were both driving.

'So you've seen the lord again?'

'I saw him this morning. I shared my flask of tea with him, which is why I was late.' Nora didn't mind sharing all the details with Val. They'd worked closely together for years and were friends as much as colleagues.

'Does he swim?'

'No, but he probably should. He seems quite anxious, but I think he's scared of the fish.'

Val laughed. 'Until you said that I had visions of him wading out of the lake like Colin Firth's Mr Darcy!'

'He's definitely not Mr Darcy,' Nora said, feeling disloyal as she said it. 'But he's lovely. You could get lost in his eyes.'

'Oh god,' Val said. 'You've already fallen for him.'

'Of course I haven't,' Nora said breezily, waving a hand at Val. 'I barely know him and I'm just out of a long-term relationship. All I'm saying is he has nice eyes. Lots of people do, and I don't fancy all of them.'

'Just the lord?' Val teased.

Nora grinned, not minding.

'You ought to be careful. He might only be after you for your chimney pots.'

'If I manage to make anything remotely resembling a chimney pot, it's the least I can do in exchange for all the free swimming I've done. Actually, he mentioned he's looking into opening it to the public.'

'And your days of having your own private lake will be over,' said Val.

'You should come and stay the night sometime and have a swim.' Nora knew what Val's response would be. It wasn't the first time she'd tried to get her in the water.

'If you were offering me a hot tub or a sauna to jump into afterwards, I'd happily join you, but I can't do with being cold.'

'Do you know? That's something I might suggest to Archie. I don't know whether he's thought beyond the swimming, but last year when I went to Dorset, they had a wood-fired sauna on the beach and it was absolute bliss after a swim.'

'That's what I'm talking about,' said Val. 'Get him to buy a sauna and I'll come and try it out for you.'

The pies arrived golden and crispy, accompanied by a huge mound of chips that Nora thought she wouldn't possibly manage, but always did.

'I'll see what I can do,' she said, taking the pastry top off her pie to let the steam out.

The sauna idea was brilliant. But before she mentioned it to Archie, she'd do as she promised and try to get some locals to try the lake. It was important to find out whether it was likely to appeal to other people the same way as it did to her.

10

'I don't know whether I mentioned this, darling, but I had the most enchanting partner at book club last week,' Constance remarked over breakfast.

'Really?' Archie said, hoping that the inevitable wasn't about to happen.

'Yes, she's about your age. Very pretty. Now, what was her name? She's a friend of Hilary, you know, from the candle shop.'

'Mmm hmm.'

'I think she'd be lovely for you, Archie. If you'd like, I can ask Hilary for her number and you could give her a call.'

Archie could think of nothing worse than cold-calling whoever this poor woman was, who had already suffered an evening with his mother and probably knew far too much about him to start things off on an even footing.

'No need, thank you, Mama.'

'It's so unusual for a man your age to be unattached. Let me do what I can to help.'

He hated that she thought he was a charity case. Hated that she hadn't cottoned on that he was too old to be an attractive prospect for anyone.

'Really, Mama. It's very kind of you, but I've arranged to

go out for dinner with someone, so there's no need for you to worry about me.' He could hardly believe how easily he'd blurted out something that wasn't remotely true, without even thinking about it.

His mother couldn't hide her astonishment. 'Whomever have you asked?'

'She's only recently moved here, so I doubt you'd know her.' Although it was an outright lie to tell his mother he'd asked someone out, he had thought that perhaps, at some point, he might ask Nora. He was still convinced she must be married or attached to someone. Why wouldn't she be? But he could ask her under the guise of wanting to know more about the lake swimming. So even if she had a partner, it's not as if it had to be strictly a date or anything like that.

'Oh, darling. Well done.'

Somehow, it made him feel even worse that his mother was a well-mannered step away from jumping up and down and cheering. That the idea of him taking a woman out for dinner should be cause for celebration was yet another mark on the tragic tally that was his life.

'Thank you,' he said, tightly.

'When is the big night?'

Oh god, he hadn't thought this through at all. 'Next week sometime. I forget now.' He patted his breast pocket, and looked around the table, pretending to have lost track of his phone.

'You must let me know so that I can tell Mrs Milton not to cook for you that evening.'

It was starting to feel like the butterfly effect; a tiny fib was beginning to blossom into a web of lies he already knew he was going to struggle to keep track of. The best thing he could do now was to actually arrange something for an evening next week, even if it was to take Seb up on his ongoing offer to go to the pub.

'I will. Right, I must be off,' he said, more to put an end to the conversation than because he had anything pressing to do. 'What are you doing with yourself today?'

'Penny is picking me up. We're going to the pictures.'

'In the park?'

'Yes. It's a special showing of Singing in the Rain and we can knit while it's on.'

'That sounds… fun.'

'It will be. Bye darling!'

Since the Croftwood Festival the previous summer, his mother's social life had blossomed. Joining the book club and a sewing circle, which Seb's fiancée Jess ran, had given her friends she could have fun with instead of the stiff-upper lip crowd she used to socialise with before his father died. Losing her husband at a relatively young age had isolated her. No longer part of a couple, the invitations fell away, and she had become lonely. Archie's father had been brought up to keep up a benevolent yet arm's length relationship between the Court and the town and it was only recently that Archie and his mother had ventured into becoming part of the community by becoming involved in the festival. Both planning and attending had been wonderful experiences for the pair of them.

Archie was hoping that Seb might be around when he went to the estate office, but he wasn't. He looked at his watch. He'd almost certainly missed Nora this morning, and anyway, he had been uncomfortable with the idea of seeing her two days in a row in case it frightened her off. But the impending evening out was pressing down on him as if he were carrying a sack of potatoes across his shoulders so he rang Seb.

'Seb, I wondered if you were on the estate somewhere.'

'I'm in town. I popped into the council offices to see if I could make an appointment with the planners and now I'm having a coffee. Have you got time to come and join me?'

Archie was about to say no, then he stopped and wondered why not? A coffee was not as bad as having to go to a pub and if he was thinking of becoming friends with Nora as well, he ought to get some practice in. Although why Seb would pay for a coffee when he could have a perfectly satisfactory one in the estate office, Archie couldn't fathom. 'Where are you?'

Seb gave him directions to Olivers, a café he'd driven past numerous times but never been into.

'I'm on my way,' he said decisively and with a small thrill that he was doing something very much out of the ordinary.

Oliver's wasn't very busy. Archie supposed it was between the breakfast rush and elevenses.

'Archie!' Seb raised a hand and pointed to the two cups on the table, indicating that he'd already bought Archie a coffee.

Toby, who Archie had met a few times while they'd been organising the festival licensing, was sat at a table engrossed in something on his laptop but otherwise, Archie didn't recognise anyone. It wasn't a surprise but it made him feel a little sad that even though he'd lived in Croftwood his whole life, he was that much removed from the town.

'I got you a cappuccino,' said Seb, pushing the cup towards him.

'Thank you.' Archie took a sip and realised straight away that this coffee was in a different league to what could be produced from a jar.

'I've arranged a meeting with the planning officer for Friday morning at the estate office. Does that suit you? I mentioned that we're looking for change of use to offices, maybe retail. We'll just pick their brains about what's possible.'

'Great,' said Archie. 'Might we ask what they think about the lake?'

'I think it could be too soon. We need to do some research first so we're clear what we're asking for when the time comes.' Seb drank his coffee. 'Speaking of which, have you seen any more of Nora lately?'

'Yesterday.' Archie took a moment to consider how to share his current predicament with Seb. 'Do you think it would be odd if I asked her out for dinner?'

'Not at all! Good for you!' Seb reached over and gripped Archie's forearm. 'Where are you going to take her?'

Needing to take a step back, Archie said, 'How do I know whether she's free to come out with me?'

'Well, you could ask her.'

Archie shook his head.

'Come on. You must have an idea already about whether she's with anyone. If you've had a handful of conversations with her and she hasn't mentioned anyone, you're probably safe.'

It was true. He would have remembered if she had. And surely when she talked about moving to Croftwood, it would have come up naturally in conversation, and he didn't remember her saying 'we' rather than 'I'.

'Right. So perhaps I'll go to the lake tomorrow and ask her.'

'There's no need to be nervous, Arch. Are you feeling a bit rusty?'

'More than a little,' Archie admitted. 'It's a long time since I did anything like this.'

'So what's prompted it? You don't sound that keen. Is it just the nerves, or something else?'

'My mother is trying to set me up with someone. I ended up telling her that I had arranged a date with someone myself to try and get her to back off,' Archie said, trying to keep the panic out of his voice.

Seb stifled a laugh with his fist. 'Oh god. That's a nightmare. Sorry, I know it's not funny. But now I see where you're coming from. Presumably you'd like to ask her out for dinner, just not right now.'

'I thought about suggesting you and I go out, but I'm having enough trouble lying to Mama without adding another layer of lies when she inevitably gives me the third degree about my evening out.'

'Good point. Look at it like this. You like her. You need to go on a date to make your mother happy. This is win-win.'

Archie wished he could see it like that. He already knew that once he got the asking part out of the way, all the anxiety he had around that would be replaced by the anxiety around not only the date but what she would think of him. 'It's ridiculous,' he said quietly. 'I have nothing to offer her. It seems wrong to suggest that I'm interested in a relationship when the reality is that she won't want a man of little means.'

'How do you know what she wants? And why shouldn't you have some fun? Don't overthink it. I know that's difficult if you like her as much as I think you do, but give yourself a chance. What if I'd thought that when I met Jess? I was basically homeless and squatting in the flat upstairs,' he said, pointing to the ceiling. 'You're not quite at rock bottom, you know. And also, this isn't the nineteenth century, so your means shouldn't matter to anyone. But can I give you one tip?'

'Please.'

'You need a haircut. And not the kind your housekeeper gives you. A proper one. Go to the barber's shop by the traffic lights and ask for Andy.'

There was no time like the present. Perhaps a new haircut would give him the confidence he needed. Maybe he'd feel like a different person. Someone Nora would be proud to be seen with. He also needed to think about what he was going to wear, but that could wait until he'd asked Nora.

In the event, when he ventured home with the coolest

haircut he'd ever had, his mother pounced on him. She was in the drawing room with piles of clothes draped across the back of one of the sofas. When he walked in she had her back to him.

'Oh, Archie,' she said, when she heard him come into the room. She was holding a man's jacket in each hand, 'I asked the gentlemans' outfitters to drop a few bits off for you to try. Good lord!' She turned and saw the new haircut.

'Do you like it, Mama? It was Seb's suggestion.' To be fair to his mother, it was rather radical. His mop of curly hair that Mrs Milton trimmed on occasion, had been cropped on the top, along with a short back and sides. The front had been left long enough so that it could be swept back, as it had been expertly by Andy the barber, who'd taken the time to show Archie how to achieve the same look himself.

His mother stood, taking it in, her shocked expression gradually softening. 'It's wonderful, darling. You look very dashing. I imagine this is in preparation for your… date?'

'Well…'

'We are thinking along the same lines.' She thrust a jacket at him. 'Try this one.'

'I don't need new clothes. I'm sure I have something in my wardrobe that will do.'

'Archibald Harrington. You cannot possibly hope to find anything smart enough within your current wardrobe,' she said in a tone that made Archie feel about eight years old. 'It's my treat.'

'Mother,' he began, about to put his foot down, until he met her eye and saw that it would do no good. 'Thank you.'

He shrugged on the jacket. It was a chestnut tweed that even to his inexpert eye didn't seem attractive.

'No, that's not your colour at all,' his mother said. 'Try this one.'

After half an hour of shucking jackets on and off, she

declared victory with a dark navy blue tweed that had tiny flecks of colour in it. Archie went into the hallway to take a closer look in the ornate gilt-framed mirror that hung over the fireplace, handily tilting forward from its hook so he could see himself quite well. It was remarkable how the well-cut jacket, aided by the haircut, made him look at least ten years younger and instantly smartened him up.

'Reluctantly, I have to agree,' he said, smiling affectionately at his mother when he went back into the drawing room. 'This is a very nice jacket.'

'Now. Let's start on the slacks.'

'I will not be wearing slacks,' he said, holding up a hand, as if that was likely to stop his mother when she was on a roll. 'I will be wearing jeans.' He'd already settled on this since he had a newish pair that didn't look that different to the jeans that Seb would wear. And they were dark enough to look smart.

'You cannot wear…jeans!' Constance exclaimed in horror.

'Honestly, Mama. Jeans are considered acceptable these days. I think a nice shirt, perhaps the floral one that Jess made for me, would go well with this jacket and a pair of jeans,' he said firmly.

'Perhaps I am old-fashioned. I only want you to look your best because it's been so long since you've courted anyone.'

Archie walked over to her, took the trousers out of her hands and took her hands in his. 'I'm grateful that you take an interest. And thank you for the jacket.' He kissed her cheek, and then she reached up and cupped his cheek with her hand, giving his face a gentle tap.

'Go on with you,' she said. 'Hang that jacket up before it creases.'

11

Nora had the whole day to herself. It was her first proper day off in eight days, and she planned to enjoy it. She lay in bed, savouring the warmth and noticing that the sun was peeking around the edge of the curtains enough to tell of a bright spring day outside. She picked up her phone and blinked, bleary-eyed, at a WhatsApp message from Hilary inviting her out to lunch. She tapped out a quick reply and they exchanged a couple more messages arranging to meet at Oliver's. It would be a good opportunity to see if Hilary fancied joining her for a swim sometime.

Nora threw back the duvet and pulled on her swimming costume, followed by sweatpants, a hoodie, and some woolly socks. She padded down to the kitchen and put the kettle on for her flask and a cup of tea to savour while she scrolled through some social media. All of this meant that she arrived at the lake later than usual and was sorry to see Archie walking away towards the manor house.

She cupped her hands around her mouth. 'Archie!' She started laughing because it felt so odd to be bellowing across the fields. Nora couldn't even remember the last time she'd shouted so loudly.

Archie spun around with a big grin on his face and began

striding back.

'Good morning,' he called across the water, beaming at her.

She waved and waited for him to walk around to her. He'd had his hair cut. She'd never seen such a dramatic transformation. His curls had been tamed, and what was left of them were closely cut on the top of his head with a forelock that had fallen, rather attractively, across his forehead. The cut had revealed sideburns that had presumably been lost in the curls before now, giving his jaw a chiselled look.

'I like your new hair,' she said.

'Oh. Thank you,' he said, running a hand across the back of his head self-consciously. 'You're later this morning.'

'I've got the day off, so I've had a leisurely start.'

'Good for you.'

'No Tatty today?'

'My mother is meeting a friend for a walk this morning, so she will take Tatty with her.'

Nora began to strip down to her costume.

'I'm holding you up,' Archie said, taking a step backwards.

'No, it's lovely to see you.' Nora was taken aback to realise she didn't want him to leave. 'If you don't mind waiting for me, why don't you stay and we can have a cup of tea afterwards? I'll only be fifteen minutes or so.'

'That would be wonderful.'

They stood, grinning stupidly at each other for a moment until Nora remembered what she was doing and finished undressing. She sat on the edge of the dock and lowered herself in, allowing her breathing to become regular before she pushed off.

'How cold is it?' Archie asked.

'Really not too bad.' The chilly water felt like tiny needles pricking at her bare skin, but she loved that feeling. And she was so used to it she knew that in a couple of minutes, her skin would begin to feel warm, at least until she got out and then it would be so cold that she'd barely be able to feel whether the towel was drying her off or not.

He began strolling around the edge of the lake as she swam, keeping pace with her.

'We had the results of the water test back,' he said.

'And?'

'It's perfect. Couldn't be cleaner.'

'I knew it,' Nora said.

'I was wondering whether you'd like to go out for dinner with me.'

It was so unexpected, that Nora turned to look at him, interrupting her stroke and resulting in her splashing around for a moment until she got back into the rhythm. She'd rather not have been swimming in the lake when he'd asked her, but she realised Archie had probably only got up the courage to ask because she wasn't looking right at him. The same way as the best conversations they'd had so far had been sitting side-by-side on the dock.

'I'd like that,' she said, once she'd recovered herself, smiling as she noticed out of the corner of her eye Archie stop and grin before he started walking again.

'Amazing,' he said. 'Should I book somewhere? How about Friday?'

'That would be lovely. I'm sure you know more places than I do. I haven't ventured further than Oliver's coffee shop yet.'

'I'll have a think about where we might go,' he said.

Archie kept pace with her as she looped the lake, and then offered her a hand up from the dock when she climbed out.

'Good god, you're freezing!'

Nora laughed. 'It's the best feeling in world. Sorry, do you mind? I need to get my costume off.'

'Of course.' He turned his back and walked away, taking an interest in the tumbledown section of wall that Nora climbed over every day.

Nora dried herself in record time, struggling as she always did to pull her clothes on over her cold, damp skin. Her dry robe was last, cosseting her in its warming fleecy layers.

'I'm done!'

Archie came back over and suggested they find somewhere drier to sit, so they walked to one of the wooden platforms further along the lake edge, and sat together with their legs dangling over the water. Nora pulled the flask out of her bag and handed Archie the cups to hold while she poured the tea.

'Thank you,' he said, wrapping his hands around it. 'So, how did your kiln testing go the other day?'

Nora was touched that he remembered. 'It went better than I expected, to be honest. It only took two test firings and then another just to check. So I'm back in business.'

'That must be a relief.'

'It definitely is. I've got an order I need to start working on this week and I'd started to think I might have to move the deadline. I hate doing that. It's so important to me that we deliver when we say we will.'

Archie nodded and they sipped their drinks.

'So, going out to dinner. Is it a date?' She'd been wondering since the moment he'd asked. It seemed like the only explanation, but she wanted to know for sure.

'Would it be alright if it was?'

'I should tell you that I'm quite recently out of a long-term relationship. That's not to say I don't want to go on a date. I do. I suppose all I'm saying is that it wasn't part of the plan.'

'It's been a long time since I've been on anything remotely resembling a date. We don't have to think of it like that. I'd like to be friends, if nothing else. Shall we call it a first foray into our friendship for now?'

'Okay.' She turned and smiled at him, catching his eye before he looked back at his drink, smiling shyly. 'I'm glad you asked. I don't have many friends around here and we're almost neighbours after all.' She leant into him gently, feeling his arm stiffen briefly against hers before she pulled away.

After a lazy rest of the morning, having showered and dressed in something appropriate for a lunch date with Hilary, Nora set off for town. She parked at the same place as before and walked through the churchyard to the high street.

Hilary had bagged them a table and gave a wave when Nora walked in, beckoning her out of the queue.

'Have a look at the menu board and then save the table while I order,' said Hilary.

After a quick to and fro about who was going to pay, Nora backed down, chose a tuna melt panini and sat at the table. There was no sign of Toby today which after a handful of visits where he'd always been there, seemed unusual.

'Where's Toby today?' she asked Hilary when she came back to the table carrying their drinks.

'He's gone to America to visit his children. They live in LA with their mother and her husband. He goes over every couple of months if he can. Plus, he has business in New York so it's easy for him to do that at the same time.'

'Blimey, he's a bit of a jet-setter, then.'

'Mmm, he is. He used to do a lot more of it from what he says, and he doesn't miss it. If it wasn't for the children, he wouldn't be. A lot of the business can be done online these days, but he likes to show his face every so often.'

'Have you been to New York with him?' Nora had always wanted to go, but once she had the money to afford it, Julian wouldn't accept the fact that she'd be paying for him, and so they never went anywhere that he couldn't afford to pay for himself. To start with, she'd thought that was quite a noble stand to take, but now she felt differently; he had been a martyr, trying to spoil her fun.

'No, but I want to. He only ever goes for a couple of days

on his way to or from LA, and there hasn't really been a good time so far. We've not been seeing each other that long, really. We had a holiday to California planned at Christmas, but we had to postpone it, and then Laura brought the children over here instead.'

'I've always wanted to go to New York,' Nora said, dreamily. 'I love the idea of seeing all the places that are in the films, especially Sleepless in Seattle.'

'Don't you sell your work over there? It could be a business trip.'

'I do. It'd be more fun if I didn't have to do any work or networking, but it'd be cool to browse the shops where they sell my stuff.'

'We ought to go on a girls' weekend. It'd be much more fun going with you than with Toby. There's no way he'd want to go shopping.'

Nora laughed. 'You're on.' It was one of those things that she knew would probably never happen, but if it ever did, she'd be up for it. Hilary was definitely shaping up to be a good friend. 'I've been meaning to ask whether you think anyone would be up for swimming at the lake? Archie's thinking about opening it to the public and I said I'd gather a few people to get a feel for whether it's a goer or not.'

'How cold is it?' Hilary looked less than keen.

'I don't know exactly, but it's got to be almost ten degrees by now I would have thought.'

'Ten?'

'Honestly, once you're in you'll feel amazing. I was going to ask Lois as well. She seemed keen when I told her about it.'

Hilary sighed. 'If there's one thing I hate more than a cold lake, it's missing out on the fun in a cold lake. I'll come. Do you want me to ask Jess and Patsy? See if they can rustle up any other takers?'

'Perhaps that's enough for now. We probably ought to keep

it quiet for now in case anyone objects.'

'No problem. I'll make a WhatsApp group for us and we can decide on a day.'

'Great, thanks.' Nora took a sip of her elderflower lemonade, and decided now was the time to share about the book club. 'Have you been to the library to choose the next book for book club yet?'

'No, have you? You are going to come again aren't you? Did you enjoy it?'

Nora laughed again at Hilary's barrage of questions. 'I loved it. It was so refreshing to be able to chat to a total stranger about the same book we'd both read rather than to people you know who might be a bit judgy.'

'That's definitely the beauty of it. Of course, in the end you'll know all of us and you'll never be with a stranger but the judgy thing never really happens anyway. I think because you've both made the choice to read that book out of the options, it's not like the book is ever forced on you like a normal book club.'

'Do you know, I never thought of it like that, but you're right. We both picked the thriller because we preferred that over the others, so it's a much better starting point.'

'And you got on with Constance.'

'I did, she was so funny. Kind of old-fashioned but she was easy to talk to. The only thing was she was trying to set me up with her son.' Nora rolled her eyes.

'You know who her son is?' Hilary said, with a glint in her eye that put Nora on edge. Because who did she know here? She'd guessed almost before Hilary could say, 'Archie Harrington.'

'Oh god, really? That's so awkward.'

'Why? It's not like you're going to go out with him.'

Nora looked sheepishly at Hilary, whose eyes nearly popped out of her head.

'No! Oh my god, that's so funny! She was trying to set you up and he's beaten her to it!'

Nora couldn't deny that it took some of the magic out of being asked out now that she knew Constance's — in her words, romantically hopeless son who hadn't had a girlfriend for the last fifteen years was Archie. She groaned and put her head in her hands.

'Tuna melt and a roasted veg?' Oliver said. 'Having a bad day?'

'Not until about thirty seconds ago,' Nora said while Hilary giggled. 'Thank you.'

'Thanks, Oliver,' said Hilary. 'She'll be fine in a minute.'

He gave them a bemused grin and went back to the counter.

'I can't go out with him now. Constance is going to think I feel sorry for him or something. What if he finds out I was with her at book club and thinks I only said yes to the date because of his mother?'

'It's so unlikely that he knows you were her date-with-a-book. I mean so many people are called Nora. It could be any one of them.' Hilary giggled again. 'Sorry. But I doubt she went home and said, Archie, your love life is so tragic I asked a lovely girl called Nora if she'd go out with you. Did she?'

'I bloody hope not.' Nora sighed. 'Am I overthinking this? I actually got on well with Constance if you leave aside her sales pitch, which by the way, wasn't obvious that it was Archie.'

'She didn't lead with him being a lord?'

'No, she didn't mention anything about either of them being titled. Presumably she's Lady Harrington.'

'I think technically, she's the dowager Countess, if my recollection of Downton Abbey is correct,' said Hilary. 'I think it's nice that she doesn't flaunt that.'

'I do too. Archie hasn't told me he's Lord Harrington in so

many words.' And Nora liked that too. She was starting to see how his unassuming nature was Archie through and through.

'So you're going on the date?' Hilary asked, taking a bite of her panini while waiting wide-eyed for Nora's answer.

'I'm going on the date.'

12

The day they'd arranged to meet at the lake was unfortunately not the best day to introduce people to wild-swimming. Nora pulled open her bedroom curtains and groaned. It was a grey day and the cloud had settled low. It looked like it may even be drizzling.

She checked her phone, expecting to see a raft of messages from the others saying that they couldn't make it after all, but there was nothing. After she'd dressed and had a quick cup of tea, she set off for the lake, glad that it wasn't actually raining after all, but getting dripped on by the trees, nevertheless.

Nora climbed over the wall, hoping that she'd be the first to arrive, but found Jess already there and warming herself next to a blazing fire pit which had appeared from nowhere.

'Morning!' Nora called.

Jess grinned and stood up from where she'd been sat on a fold-up garden chair. 'Morning!'

'Wow, this is a treat,' said Nora, standing close to the fire, feeling its warmth against her face.

'Seb suggested it. He had these fire pits for the Christmas market and thought it'd be a good idea. I have to admit, I'm not itching to get in,' Jess said, inclining her head towards the lake. 'I grew up by the sea and I could never bear to go in unless the sun was out. It didn't matter if it was winter or summer. I just need the sun.'

'It's a game-changer on a day like this,' Nora agreed. 'So you're used to going in the cold water?'

'I used to be. Bit out of practice these days, but I love an excuse to wear my dry robe.'

'Hey! How do we get in?' Patsy called from behind the hedge.

'Walk along a bit further,' Nora called. 'There's a gap.'

Patsy and Lois emerged from the hedge, followed by Hilary who was wearing about three coats.

'I want to be supportive,' Hilary said, 'but I can't go in.'

'It's okay. You don't have to. It's not for everyone, especially on a day like today,' Nora said, understanding completely. It was always less enticing on a grey day. 'You can be our lifeguard.'

'Oh god. I'm telling you now, I won't be jumping in to save any of you but I'm happy to watch you from here.' She sat herself down in the chair that Jess had vacated.

'Come on then, let's do it,' said Nora. 'I don't want to tell you what to do if you know, but I always get my stuff ready for afterwards before I get in.'

'No, carry on,' said Patsy. 'We don't know anything, right?' The others nodded, so Nora carried on.

'So, I have my towel ready to grab and then my clothes in a pile in the order I'll put them back on. Once you're out, the most important thing is to get your wet stuff off as quickly as you can and get dried and dressed quickly, so you don't get too cold.'

They stripped off down to their swimming costumes. Nora had given them a list of basics that they might want to bring if they had them to hand. She'd suggested neoprene gloves and socks, although the water wasn't so cold now that they were essential, and they wouldn't be in for that long today.

Nora lowered herself into the water from the dock and stood up. 'It's not that deep here,' she said, the water coming to just below her waist. 'It's a good place to get in and out.'

'Here goes,' said Jess, lowering herself in next, and managing it with little more than a sharp intake of air.

'Oh god, is it freezing?' Lois said.

'Of course it's freezing,' said Hilary. 'Look at it.'

'It's actually not that bad,' said Jess. 'It's warmer than the English Channel on Christmas Day.'

'Oh, well in that case,' said Patsy, laughing. 'Christ!' she shouted as she lowered in with a splash. 'It's bloody freezing!'

Lois dipped a toe in, her eyes widening in shock. 'It is!'

'You just have to get in,' Jess said. 'Do it in one go or you'll never do it!'

Lois took a deep breath and lowered herself in in one swift move. 'Arrggghh!'

They all laughed, including Lois.

'Okay, put your hands in. Getting your wrists acclimatised will help you get used to the temperature before we go any further,' said Nora.

Apart from Nora, they all had their arms crossed but they reluctantly dipped their hands in the water.

'When you feel ready, bend your knees and dip yourselves in up to your shoulders.'

Jess went first and seemed quite happy. Lois, still on a roll from when she got in went next and to everyone's surprise just started swimming. 'I just need to swim,' she called as she headed off.

'Come on, we'd better stick together,' said Jess.

Patsy rolled her eyes, dipped herself down, swore loudly, making Hilary roar with laughter, and the three of them set off after Lois.

'Everyone feeling alright?' Nora asked after a minute.

'I'm actually starting to feel warm,' said Jess. 'Not in an "I've got hypothermia way", though.'

'Good! It's actually not as bad as I was expecting,' said Patsy. 'How far are we going to swim?'

'Not too far today. We'll turn round when we get to that wooden platform with the rope tied on,' Nora said.

Lois screamed. 'There's something by me!' and started splashing around, which caused Patsy to panic and do the same.

'It's just a twig,' said Jess calmly. They all roared with laughter and Nora had to stand up because she went all weak from laughing too much.

'You can stand up!' Patsy said, doing the same, which for some reason just made them laugh all the more.

When they climbed out a few minutes later, they all had big smiles on their faces.

'You actually look as if you enjoyed yourselves,' Hilary said, handing them their towels which she'd thoughtfully warmed by the fire.

'I feel amazing,' Lois said, looking surprised.

'Me too,' said Patsy.

'It's so different to swimming in the sea but I realised how much I miss that,' Jess said.

'I feel like a right wuss now,' said Hilary. 'I'll come in next time.'

'We'll hold you to that,' said Nora, already pulling on her clothes while the others were still drying themselves.

'How have you got dressed so quickly?' Lois said.

'Practice.' Nora took her tea flask out of her bag, and a packet of custard creams she'd bought specially. Hilary had popped open some more garden chairs that had been thoughtfully provided by Seb, and they both took a seat while they waited for the others to dress. The fire pit was wonderful. This was probably the worst weather that Nora had encountered so far in her almost daily swims. She'd been very lucky. If Archie did open the lake, something like this would be just the thing. Not only did it help warm people up, it created a nice community atmosphere. Even if someone came to swim alone, they could be sure that there would be a warm welcome and good conversation from others around the fire pit if this group were anything to go by.

'No sign of Archie this morning,' said Jess. Nora wasn't sure whether it was a question, but with everyone's eyes on her she felt she had to say something.

'I didn't think we'd want an audience,' she said.

'Too true,' said Patsy. 'Is it going to be women only if it's open to the public?'

'I doubt it, but I think it appeals more to women. Certainly where I've swum before, there are usually way more women than men.'

'Nora's going on a date with Archie,' Hilary blurted out.

'Hilary!' Not that she minded people knowing, it seemed unnecessary to announce it quite so publicly.

'Seb said he might ask you,' Jess said, smiling. 'I think it's lovely.'

'It'll be interesting to see what he turns up in, said Patsy. 'I've never seen him wear anything but very old tweed.'

'There's nothing wrong with that,' Nora said, feeling the need to defend Archie, even though on some level she really hoped he wasn't going to wear double-tweed on the date.

'Nothing,' Lois agreed.

'Easy for you to say when your boyfriend is immaculate at all times,' Patsy said.

'Matt always looks alright.'

'I've put a lot of work into getting that to happen,' Patsy said, which sent them all into fits of giggles again at how serious she was.

'I could get Seb to have a word,' Jess suggested.

'No, please don't,' Nora said. She would hate for Archie to feel that she cared at all about how he dressed, because she didn't. It was obvious to her that he wasn't exactly flush and she would hate him to feel any pressure to spend any money on clothes for her benefit.

'Hitting it off with Constance is quite helpful though,' said Hilary. 'Constance tried to set them up, not knowing that Nora and Archie were already friends.'

Nora was beginning to think that being friends with Hilary was a double-edged sword. Clearly, nothing was sacred. She seemed happy to share Nora's personal life with everyone.

'Hilary, do you think perhaps Nora ought to tell us this sort of thing herself?' Lois said.

'You don't mind do you?' Hilary said, looking confused that it might even be a problem.

'I suppose not,' Nora said with a sigh. 'I'm not used to living somewhere where everyone knows, or is even interested in what everyone else is up to.'

'Best that you realise now,' Patsy said.

'It's not really like that,' said Jess. 'At least not all the time. We're just pleased that Archie is going out with someone as lovely as you. He deserves some happiness. And Constance can be a good laugh. Just keep her away from the Pimms.'

'She got tipsy at the festival last summer and insisted that she wanted to stay the night in one of the glamping tents. She got so cross with Archie for making her go home. He shoved her into the back of a taxi which she wasn't happy about at all,' said Jess. 'Poor Archie didn't hear the end of it for weeks and he only put his foot down because he knew she wouldn't normally stay anywhere that didn't have a flushing toilet.'

'You know, he's letting the festival use his land for free again this year,' said Hilary.

'Seb's tried to persuade him to charge but he won't hear of it,' said Jess. 'It's so kind of him, but I'm not sure he can afford to be kind.'

'Do you think this swimming lake is a good idea?' Nora asked them.

'I love it,' said Lois. 'I've wanted to try cold-water swimming for ages but I can't be bothered to travel to the other side of Worcester to do it. I haven't got time. If this was open, I'd be able to come before or after work. I'd come as often as I could. I'm on a high, even if I can't quite feel my toes yet.'

'I'd come,' said Jess. 'I'd forgotten how much I miss the feeling of swimming outside. The rush you get from being cold and then feeling invincible when you get out. It's amazing. Count me in.'

'You've all convinced me that I've missed out,' said Hilary. 'I'd like to think I'd be a regular.'

'Me too,' said Patsy. 'I spend so much time indoors, and in five minutes this has totally invigorated me. I can walk here too, which is brilliant.'

'Great!' said Nora. 'Honestly, I think there's a market for it but I was worried that I'm biased. I didn't want to set Archie off on something that'll never work.'

'Seb thinks it's a great idea too, and he's got an expert eye for what works,' said Jess.

'Same time tomorrow then?' Nora teased, laughing at their faces when they thought she was serious. 'Same time next week?'

There were a chorus of yeses which gave Nora a fuzzy feeling inside. She'd found her new tribe. And whether or not the lake ever opened to the public, she hoped this group of women would continue to enjoy it regardless.

'I'm off to buy a dry robe,' said Lois before she disappeared through the hedge.

'See you next week!' Patsy called, following her.

'Should we douse the fire?' Nora asked Jess.

'Probably. Seb said he'd come back to collect the chairs, but I reckon we could leave them here. Why don't we fold them and put them under the dock? We could put a couple of stones from the wall in front of them to stop them from rolling into the water.'

Jess went to collect the stones while Nora pushed the chairs underneath, then dipped her cup into the lake and threw a cupful of water on the fire.

'It's like a proper swimming lake now, with the fire pit,' said Nora.

'You don't mind that you'll end up sharing it?'

'Not at all. Today has been brilliant.'

She couldn't wait to tell Archie what a success it had been, and she couldn't wait for the same time next week to do it all again.

13

Archie had no idea where he was going to take Nora so, as he did with most things, he enlisted the help of Seb.

'If it was up to me, I'd choose the pub every time,' he said. 'It's relaxing and the food's good, so it really depends.' He plonked himself down in the chair next to the fireplace in the estate office, and scratched Tatty's head while Archie made the tea.

'On what?' Archie asked, feeling as if he ought to know the answer.

'What's the end game? Are you pumping her for info about the swimming lake idea, or is it the first date?'

Archie opened his mouth to answer, but Seb carried on.

'I know you like her because whatever you think, you haven't asked her out just to make good on the fib you told Constance, so I'll help you out and suggest it's a first date. But how good an impression do you want to make?'

Archie mulled this over for a moment while he poured the tea. If he discounted the lie he'd told his mother and the fact that he was quite interested in finding out more about wild-swimming, he realised that neither of these things were more of a reason to have asked Nora out than the fact he actually liked her. He liked that she was brave enough to venture into his lake without knowing, or caring, who it belonged to. He liked that she was self-aware enough to know that swimming was something that helped her state of mind, and she wasn't afraid to admit that she actively gave time over to looking after her mental health. He admired she had her own business, because it felt almost like something they had in common, and from what little she'd told him, she was successful. And these things added up to the biggest and best reason of all to have asked her out: to get to know her better.

'Where did you take Jess on your first date?' he asked, hoping it would be the perfect thing to copy.

Seb shook his head, realising what Archie's game was. 'No, that won't work because I was stupid and stubborn and skint, so we never went on a proper first date. It was more of a slow realisation for us by which time our first date had passed us by without either of us noticing. We had a takeaway in the flat above Oliver's.'

'Ah. Yes. Not the right tone.'

'But that's a start. And if it's the right tone you're after, I'd go for the Italian on Priory Lane. The food is amazing, and it's a traditional kind of place, you know, candles in bottles on the tables, that sort of thing. It's relaxed but intimate. It'll go perfectly with your new hair.'

'Thank you,' Archie said, grinning. 'It sounds perfect. I'll book a table.'

'If it goes well, we could do a foursome sometime.'

'One step at a time. But yes, I'd like that.'

After Seb had left, Archie booked a table at Ciao Croftwood, then texted Nora to let her know.

I've booked a table for us at Ciao Croftwood. Shall I pick you up at 7.30? A

That sounds lovely! I'm at Woodside Cottage on Elderbrook Lane.

I know it. I'm very much looking forward to seeing you.

A

He read the last message before he pressed send. Was it too much? In the end he settled on something more restrained.

Wonderful. See you then. A

'I don't think you told me the name of the girl you're taking out,' Constance remarked over dinner that evening.

'Her name's Nora,' he said, patiently.

'Nora. Unusual name, isn't it? Although I've heard that name recently. Where was I?'

'You're out and about so much these days, it could have been anywhere, Mama.'

'As it happens, I will be out tomorrow evening as well.'

'Will you need a lift?' Archie said, warily. He wouldn't put it past his mother to have invented a reason to need to come with him when he picked Nora up.

'No, Linda from the library is going to collect me.'

'That's good of her.' Archie worried that Constance took advantage of her new group of friends, all of whom seemed happy to ferry her around, aside from when Archie took his turn for the book club evenings.

'It's on her way, darling.'

Croftwood Court wasn't on anyone's way to anywhere but he wasn't about to start interfering in his mother's arrangements.

'Where are you off to?'

'The knitting at the pictures the other day was so much fun, Linda reminded me about the knit and natter group at the Croftwood Haberdashery. It's a lovely chance to chat to everyone rather than getting on with any knitting, so she knows I'll enjoy it.'

This sent Archie into a panic. Seb was sure to have mentioned his date with Nora to Jess, who owned the Croftwood Haberdashery, and who might comment on it to Constance. And he could only imagine the kind of conversations that might stem from that.

'Nora is the woman who has been swimming in our lake.' There was only so much subterfuge he could stand. It was going to come out at some point, so there was no reason to hide it, although in what context his mother had heard Nora's name, he wasn't sure.

'You have asked out the woman with the swimming coat?' Constance asked, her voice rising in surprise. 'How on earth did that happen?'

Reminding himself to be patient, Archie said, 'I thought it was worth introducing myself to her, purely to find out what she was up to. She's very interesting, easy to talk to, you know,' he carried on, feeling a little flustered.

'I hope she's not going to take advantage of you. Does she know who you are?'

'Yes, Mother, she knows. If anything, she ought to worry about me taking advantage of her. She's a very successful businesswoman.'

'Why is she interested in swimming in a lake, then?' Constance seemed genuinely perplexed, but presumably wasn't up to speed with the phenomenon of cold-water swimming.

'She finds it therapeutic. A way to relax.'

'Well, you're old enough to know what you're doing, darling.'

'Thank you,' Archie said, relieved that the conversation seemed to be over.

The following evening at seven o'clock, Archie was attempting to tame his forelock like Andy the barber had shown him. It wasn't working, but he had no intention of using Andy's failsafe suggestion of hairspray. Instead, he put a little more wax on the tips of his fingers and ran his fingers through his hair, trying to knead the product in, willing it to look how he wanted. It didn't, but it would have to do. He tipped some ancient aftershave into his palm and slapped it on his face, gasping as it stung his freshly shaven skin, but judging that it smelled alright, if a little old-fashioned.

Thankfully, Constance was eating dinner and wouldn't have wanted to be disturbed so he was able to leave the house unhindered. Earlier in the afternoon, he'd turned over the engine on his father's Jaguar XJS, which had been his pride and joy, to make sure the battery wasn't dead. It was the one thing Archie was thrilled to have inherited, even though he didn't drive it very often. And it was perfect for tonight.

Although as the crow flies, Nora didn't live far away, it was a good ten-minute drive to get out of the estate and onto the country lane that led to her house. Dusk was well and truly falling but thankfully there was enough light to see the names of the houses on the gates along Elderbrook Lane.

The gates to Woodside Cottage were open, so Archie pulled the car into the gravelled driveway that ran down one side of the house before he climbed out and brushed his hands down himself to iron out the non-existent creases in his jeans. The cottage looked welcoming from the outside, slightly overshadowed by trees on the far side, and the glow from the small windows made him long to be inside, next to a cosy log fire. It looked as if all of its corners had been smoothed away, and the walls disappeared into the low overhang of the roof, all contributing to make it exactly the kind of house that he thought suited Nora perfectly.

He rapped the large circular knocker on the front door and almost immediately the door opened and Nora was there, smiling. Instantly, he felt himself relax. She looked beautiful. Her hair was swept back, and gathered low at her neck. Tendrils of hair escaped and gently waved around her face and shoulders. She was wearing a grass green coloured dress that reached almost to the floor but it was cinched in at the waist and had lots of tucks and things across the top and fitted her perfectly.

'You look wonderful,' he said, leaning in and kissing her cheek. It was how he'd been brought up, so there was nothing more to it than good manners as far as he was concerned, and he didn't give it a second thought, but he noticed Nora blush slightly.

'You look very good yourself,' she said. 'I love your shirt.'

'Thank you. Do you know Jess from the haberdashery? She made it for me.'

'Gosh, that's incredible. I'm terrible at sewing.'

'Well, I'm not sure how Jess's pottery skills are.'

'Speaking of pottery, I have something to show you. In the garden,' she said, gesturing for him to step back outside. She locked the door, then led the way around to the back of the house. There was a little patio next to the kitchen door. 'Here. I made these.'

There, bathed in the glow from the outside light, were two chimney pots.

Archie was speechless. She'd actually made him chimney pots for his house.

'I know they're quite plain. I really just wanted to get the feel for making them, and to find out whether they'd even fit. So try them out and if they're okay, I can have a go at something more ornate.'

'Nora,' he said softly. 'They're incredible. Thank you so much.' He turned to look at the car, which as his mother had constantly pointed out to his father, was the epitome of style over substance, since it didn't have a back seat and the boot space wasn't huge. 'I think I'd better collect them in a more suitable vehicle, but I can't wait to pop them on the roof.'

Nora was grinning. 'I'm so glad you're pleased. It at least makes me feel that I'm paying you back in some way for the use of your beautiful lake.'

'There's no need for you to worry about that but I'm all for a bartering system. I wonder if my roofer is into cold-water swimming?'

'You never know,' Nora said, laughing.

Archie grinned, feeling more relaxed with every moment he was in her company. 'Right, we'd better go.' He walked to the car and held open the passenger door, waiting while Nora climbed in and settled herself before he closed it and went around to the driver's side. It felt amazing to have her beside him. He couldn't quite believe how he found himself here.

'This car is wonderful,' she said as Archie reversed out of the driveway and headed along the lanes to town. She ran her hand over the polished walnut dashboard.

'It was my father's. Apparently, it's entirely responsible for my parents ending up together.'

'I can understand how the car might help if you were trying to woo someone.'

He chanced a glance at Nora to see whether there was anything to this comment other than an off-the-cuff remark. She flicked her eyes towards him before going back to looking out at the road ahead, but he thought he could see her suppressing a smile. It was hard to see now that it was dark.

'You think I'm trying to woo you?' The darkness, and Nora's easy company made Archie feel bolder. For once, he wasn't stifling what he wanted to say for fear of what the answer might be. Perhaps because he felt confident he wasn't about to be rejected.

'I do. I think you're a surprising man, Archie, and I'm glad we're friends. I'm looking forward to getting to know you better.'

'Likewise.'

They stuck to safer topics for the rest of the ten-minute

journey, with Archie pointing out local landmarks, and Nora interested, asking questions about everything.

'This is the park where the festival was held last year,' he said, pointing it out, not that you could see an awful lot in the dark.

'What's the building over there? With the festival lights in the trees?'

'That's Croftwood Cinema. It had been derelict since I was a child, then Oliver from the coffee house, and his business partner, Patsy, renovated it. It's very versatile now. They hold all sorts of events there. My mother went to see Singing in the Rain the other day, a special showing where they left the lights on so people could knit.'

'How fantastic. I love it when people are innovative like that. It's so inspiring.'

'And they held part of the Croftwood Festival in there too. They had the book club during the day and music in the evening.'

Archie parked the car on the side of the road outside the restaurant and came to open the door for Nora, offering his hand as she climbed out of the low-slung seat.

'Thank you,' she said.

He smiled and put his hand on the small of her back, guiding her inside, feeling like the luckiest man in the world.

14

Nora had never experienced such chivalry, and she was absolutely charmed by it. She could tell that it was Archie at his most natural, rather than a show being put on for her benefit. From the moment they left the car and she felt Archie's hand on her back, to the way he held her chair out. All of it made Nora wonder why she had ever thought she might not be ready to explore a relationship with this man.

'Would you like the dessert menu?' the waiter asked as he cleared their plates.

Archie raised an eyebrow in question and after Nora confirmed with a nod, he said, 'Yes, thank you.'

'I don't have room for pudding,' Nora admitted, 'but that pasta was so delicious, I bet they do an amazing tiramisu.' She wasn't ready for the evening to end and being too full seemed like a small price to pay to extend it.

'Our cook, Mrs Milton, makes the best sticky toffee pudding in the world but I don't think she's ever turned out a tiramisu.'

'I'm not sure how trendy it is these days but it was the only pudding you could get in the Italian we used to go to as students. We used to share a portion between us.'

'Where did you got to university?'

'I went to art college in Bristol. And then I stayed in that area afterwards.'

'It must have been a big decision to leave there after such a long time. Brave.'

'I don't think I was being brave. On some level it was more like running away, trying to leave the past behind. I wanted a life that was mine, where I didn't have to consider anyone else. I wanted things on my own terms. Gosh, that makes me sound so selfish.'

'I've never had a relationship for anywhere near as long as yours was, but I imagine that when it ends, it's important to find yourself again. Get used to being an individual again. That's not the same as being selfish.'

'The thing is, I always felt as if I'd kept my identity. I've built a career for myself and although Julian would take the credit for helping with that, as soon as I became vaguely successful, he was resentful. Not massively at first, but it built over the years and it took me a while to notice.'

'What does he do?'

'He's a potter too. That was part of the problem. I suppose he didn't understand why my stuff started selling better than his. He still doesn't,' she said with a soft laugh.

'It sounds like jealousy as much as resentfulness.'

'Mmm. I think once I realised that, it was probably over.'

'I'm not sure someone who loves you would ever feel like that. I'd imagine you'd be each other's champion, wanting the best things for each other. Always.'

'That's what I think too, but perhaps that's idealistic.'

The waiter came back and Archie ordered two tiramisus and coffee to follow. Nora would never normally drink caffeine after lunchtime, but tonight she didn't think the caffeine would make any difference to whether or not she slept. She knew her mind would be full of tonight. Running over what they'd talked about and thinking about Archie.

'How about you? Has anyone broken your heart?'

'Not for a long time. I had a girlfriend a good few years ago, before my father died. We met at university and ambled into living together afterwards. We'd decided to marry, but in the event she didn't want to be stuck on the estate in the middle of Worcestershire when I had to take over.'

'You mean when your father died?'

He nodded. 'The inevitable consequence. It was always going to happen, but I was young and thought there was more time for a life before that responsibility became mine. Clarissa wasn't ready.'

It didn't sound as if Archie had been ready either, and Nora was stunned that something as devastating as losing his father was the catalyst for a breakup.

'What was your plan before your father died?' she asked, intrigued.

'We still had a family house in London at that time, so we'd based ourselves there. Most of our friends were there, and I was managing the family's small property business. Clarissa liked the lifestyle, but once my father died, there were so many debts. We had to sell most of the London property, save for a couple of small flats which weren't suitable for us to live in, she said. The idea of moving into the Court with my mother appalled her, so that was the end of it.'

'I'm so sorry. That must have been an awful time.'

'It was. But it worked out for the best. Better to have discovered her disdain for the idea of living in Croftwood before we married rather than later down the line. Imagine the complication if we'd had a family.'

The tiramisu arrived and they tucked in, rolling their eyes in delight at each other as they took a first taste.

'How does this stack up against the sticky toffee?' Nora asked.

Archie tilted his head to the side, carefully considering his answer. 'It's absolutely delicious but I think the sticky toffee pudding is too ingrained in me to be beaten.'

Nora laughed. 'Fair enough. I'd like to try that sticky toffee sometime.'

Archie's eyes sparkled. 'I'd like that too.'

After some back and forth about splitting the bill or not, Archie paid and they strolled back to the car. It was chillier than Nora had expected, and she wrapped her shawl tightly around her shoulders before she took Archie's arm.

'I've so enjoyed tonight,' she said, briefly squeezing his arm in the crook of her elbow.

'Enough to do it again?'

'Definitely.'

When Archie pulled into the drive at Nora's cottage, he turned the engine off and climbed out of the car, reaching Nora's door just as she'd opened it. He offered his hand, helping her out.

'Thank you for a lovely evening.' She leant towards him and kissed his cheek.

'Nora. You're wonderful company.' For a moment she thought he was going to kiss her. Properly. But he kissed her cheek which was almost as good. 'Might I see you at the lake in the morning?'

'Of course. Do you think you would join me for a swim?'

He gave her a shy smile. 'Perhaps not. But I can bring the tea.'

Nora went to the door and unlocked it, then paused to watch Archie back down the drive, flashing his lights in a last farewell before he turned out onto the lane. She put the kettle on, and went upstairs to put her pyjamas on. Although it was late, she lit a fire because she wasn't ready to turn in. She curled up in front of the television with a cup of tea and mindlessly watched a couple of episodes of Virgin River while her mind worked overtime.

The shy man she'd met at the lake had turned her head tonight. It was as if the fact that she'd accepted the date, accepted him, had built his confidence. He'd been relaxed, funny, absolutely charming, and she felt as if she'd known him for years rather than only a couple of weeks. And although the fact that he'd spruced himself up was in his favour, that wasn't what made Nora feel differently about him. She was falling for his soul.

The following morning at the lake, Archie ambled along with Tatty just as Nora was climbing out of the water. It was excellent timing and he busied himself with making the tea while Nora dried and dressed herself.

'You're outclassing me in the tea stakes,' Nora teased him as he fished the teabags out of two china mugs.

'Only because I had to ask Mrs Milton for a flask and she insisted I bring hot water and do it properly. But the upside of that is that she also insisted I bring cake.'

'For breakfast?' Nora pretended to be shocked but she wasn't averse to cake this early in the day, especially if she'd been swimming.

'It's an apple crumble cake so perhaps better than chocolate cake at this hour?'

'Technically the last thing I ate was cake too,' Nora said, thinking of the tiramisu, and accepting a sizeable slice of cake on a plate, that she was quite sure was Royal Worcester porcelain, accompanied by a cake fork. She had to suppress a smile. It was so comical, using delicate crockery and silver cake forks at the lake's edge.

'You know, I had planned to pump you for information last night. Everything you know about cold-water swimming and whether you think it could work here.'

'And why didn't you?'

'There were better things to talk about,' he said simply.

'I don't know how much help I can be, other than to tell you what I think and what the others have said about it. Whether it's anything to do with actual regulations, I wouldn't know.'

Nora proceeded to tell him what she understood of the capacity of the lake, how the entry system worked in other places and how it might work here, and what else he might need to think about in terms of his offer to swimmers.

'Some places have saunas or fire pits to help people warm up afterwards. You might need to think about providing some sort of shelter for people to change in with somewhere to leave their things. In the winter people bring a lot more kit. And you probably need to think about access, parking, that kind of thing.'

'There's a lot more to it than I thought.'

'Did this lake used to be open to the public when it was a fishing lake?'

'Yes. My father used to run the local angling club from here.'

'I wonder where they used to park? Patsy and Lois parked on the road and climbed over the wall, then came through the hedge over there,' she said, pointing.

'Ah, perhaps that's the closest access point.' He set his mug down and stood up, pushing his way through the undergrowth towards the hedge, and peering through it. 'Yes!' he said triumphantly, turning to face Nora with a grin on his face. 'I can see the road through here. There's an old brick toolshed on the other side of the hedge where a mower was kept just for the area around the lake.' He came back to sit next to her. 'I don't think that hedge is ancient or anything. It looks like self-seeded hazel and sycamore that's out of control. We could take that out and make an entrance.'

'That sounds like a plan. And you won't mind people driving through the estate?'

'Actually, I'm sure that years ago there was a gate over this side of the estate. Perhaps we could look into reinstating it? I don't think it would be too much trouble. It would probably come out fairly close to the lane you live on.'

'That would be better for people coming here from town.' Of course Nora had driven past the gates to the Court out of curiosity. 'It will be quicker than coming through the main gate and would mean people weren't driving past the house.'

'I think Mama would be happier with that. She does worry about lack of privacy.'

'I can understand that,' Nora said, licking her finger to pick up the last crumbs of cake. 'It's her home.'

'There's a fine line between using it as a resource and having it as a family home, and I understand that. But it's getting ever more important to generate cash from it. It's so expensive to run. The quote I've had for repairing the roof is eye-watering and that's just for a patch-up job. I seriously doubt we will ever be in a position to repair it properly.'

Nora reached for Archie's hand. 'Do you talk to your mother about any of this?' She already knew what his answer would be. There was no way he would burden her with these things that he felt were his responsibility, in the same way as they were his father's.

'It's not for her to worry about.'

'You shouldn't have to deal with it on your own.' Nora said, wishing she could offer something more helpful than stating the obvious.

'But I am on my own. Seb's fantastic about putting his ideas into action. We might have already lost the house if it weren't for him bringing the Christmas market to life. But a cash injection in December isn't going to be enough this time.'

'Hilary mentioned that you give the use of your land for free to the festival. If you charged for that would it make a difference?'

'No,' he said firmly. 'It's important that we do what we can to help the town. I can't charge for use of the land and then ask the same people who are paying me for that to come to my Christmas market, or pay to use my lake. It has to be give and take.'

'I can understand that,' Nora said squeezing his hand. She might not agree with him but she needed him to know that she was on his side. That these things were his decision, but that she was willing to help him if she could. 'If we write a proper business plan for the swimming lake, you could try and get a bank loan,' she suggested, having financed her production line in exactly that way. 'It wouldn't need to be very much and you'd have it paid back in no time. Everyone who came the other day to try it loved it, and they all said they'd come regularly if it opened. We can get up and running before the summer, and literally make hay while the sun shines.'

'I can't take out a loan. It isn't right.' Archie said.

'Why?' Nora asked gently, wanting to understand. 'Because it's not something that's happened in your family before?'

He nodded. 'And we do have assets. We still have the London flats.'

'Could you sell those?' It felt cold-hearted to suggest it, but better that than him losing the Court. 'Surely that would pay for the roof and the development of the lake and more.'

'They're the last of our assets. The one flat gives Mama an income and the other we keep for the family to use. My sister, Betsy, lives there at the moment.'

It seemed to Nora that Archie was fighting to keep everything as it was for his mother and sister and they, probably unwittingly, were taking advantage of him.

'Could your sister pay rent? Then that would be an income for your mother and you could then sell at least one flat.'

Archie shook his head. 'I can't ask her to do that when I live here rent free. It wouldn't be fair.'

'Archie, it's hardly free. You're paying your way by being the one who's holding all of this together. For them. And that might be okay in the good times but these are tough times for you. You need to be honest with your family and ask them to help you. I'm sure they would if they knew what the alternative was.'

'That's just it. The alternative is unthinkable. That we might lose the estate on my watch is unthinkable. It's my solution to find. I just haven't thought of it yet.'

When he looked at Nora, the desperation and sadness on his face made her heart ache for him. 'I'll help you. At the very least, let me help you get the swimming lake up and running. Let's have a meeting with Seb and we'll make a plan. We should aim to be open by the first week in June.'

Archie frowned. 'I don't think we can. If the planners are involved it'll take some time.'

'Best that we get started now then.'

15

'Seb's free for a meeting today, if you're available,' Archie said the next morning as he strolled around the lake, keeping Nora company as she swam. It had very quickly become a habit. One that he looked forward to immensely. Every day he watched for signs that Nora might be tiring of him, and even though he wasn't terribly confident about what form a sign like that might take, he didn't think there had been one.

Tatty's morning swim was over, and she was asleep on the island while she waited for Archie. The dog still hadn't cottoned on that perhaps it'd be better to sleep on the shore and avoid the need to get wet again.

'Brilliant,' Nora said, looking up at him and smiling. 'I can't wait to make a proper plan. It's so exciting.'

Archie wished Nora's enthusiasm would rub off on him a little. He was struggling to imagine his fortunes turning that quickly. And the investment he knew would be required; he had no idea where that was going to come from, because while he knew Nora was simply biding her time until she broached the subject of a bank loan again, it wasn't something he could bring himself to undertake. It would be another bill to pay. Another debt weighing him down. He had to find another way.

'Mama asked me whether you've chosen a book for the book club yet?' It had come as a shock that Nora had been the woman his mother had tried to set him up with. He discovered it from Nora, rather than his mother, who hadn't remembered the name of her delightful book date, but was thrilled that she and Archie agreed Nora was the perfect match. Archie tried not to think about that. He liked Nora too much to be put off because his mother had recommended her to him and vice versa, and it wasn't ideal for Constance to think she had played any part in it.

'I'm going to the library after this,' Nora said. 'Well, after I've showered and warmed up. What time shall I come back for the meeting?'

'Would eleven be alright? In the estate office?'

'Yes. That's through the main gates?'

'And follow the road around until you get to a courtyard on your right. It's the old stables. You can't miss it.'

Once Nora was out and dry, they shared her flask of tea; they'd started taking it in turns. And even though the chairs were underneath the dock now, they preferred to sit in their usual place, feet dangling over the water, side by side.

'It's starting to feel warmer in there now,' Nora said, nodding towards the lake. 'And look, everything's starting to grow again around the edges. I think we'll have to do some clearing up around the perimeter. Get the dead leaves and grasses cleared so that it looks smarter.'

'I could ask the gardeners to spend a day down here,' Archie said. 'They'd have it shipshape in no time.'

'We'll need to build some steps into the water as well. It's better if people can get in slowly rather than having to launch off the dock.'

'I think they could probably help with that, too. They can turn their hand to just about anything.' If he could use the gardeners, who he was paying anyway, it would save money.

'Do you think they'd be able to clear that hedge if we needed to?' Nora asked.

'They could. And we have an old wood chipper in the sheds. We could make paths with the chippings.'

'Good idea. See? It's all coming together and we haven't even had the meeting yet.'

'Are you sure you have time for this?' Nora was busy. She'd been in Stoke every day this week and he thought it odd that by fortunate coincidence she had today free.

'It's one of the perks of having my own business. I'm between commissions, all the decisions about the Christmas lines have been made and we're in production. There's nothing that can't wait.'

'You know my mother has been to Hilary's shop and bought up most of her Hart Pottery stock.' He grinned as he watched Nora's reaction. He'd predicted exactly how she'd react and he'd been right.

'Oh, that's so awkward. I would have given her anything she wanted. And what happens if —'

'If what?'

She looked at him with a tortured expression. 'I was going to say, if we break up.'

Archie was sure the silence that descended meant that Nora was contemplating as much as he was, that she'd just defined them as being in a relationship. They simply hadn't discussed what this might be since they'd been out for dinner and she'd said it would be as friends. But he felt they'd moved on from there. They spent time with each other every day. He knew she looked forward to seeing him as much as he did her. They'd begun confiding in each other and although they hadn't moved on from kisses on the cheek, they'd taken to holding hands. They were more than friends, but were they in a relationship?

'If we break up, I'll throw the pottery in the lake and be

done with it.'

Nora laughed and leant against his arm. It felt like the most natural thing in the world to reach his arm around her shoulders and pull her to him. She rested her head on his shoulder. It was the most wonderful thing and almost took his breath away.

'I think we're more than friends,' she said.

'I want to be more than friends but if you're not ready, I'll wait,' Archie said, rubbing the top of her arm with his hand as he gazed across the lake, soaking in every moment of the closeness.

'We don't need to wait,' Nora said. 'Archie.'

He turned to face her and could see in her eyes that she wanted him to kiss her. He'd wanted that since the moment he'd dropped her home after their dinner date. That night, he'd helped her out of the car and wanted more than anything to drop a kiss onto her perfect lips. But although it had felt like the right time to him, he'd been mindful of Nora saying she wasn't looking for anything other than friendship. He hadn't been confident that the magic he'd felt between them in that moment had been something she'd felt too.

But now, he could see that magic reflected in her eyes and he leant down, tipped her chin gently towards him with a finger and thumb, closed his eyes and kissed her. He went in tenderly, but it was followed quickly by an overwhelming desire to kiss her deeply, as if that would somehow sate the desire building in him. Nora shifted around, grounding herself so that she could press closer to him. He did the same, their lips never leaving each other. Her hand moved to his face, caressing him, which was distracting but wonderful at the same time. Then her weight was pushing him to the ground, and they were lying next to each other on the dock.

Neither of them registered the splash as Tatty made her way back across from the island but excited by the pair of them laughing and kissing, she came to join in the fun.

'Get away, Tatty!' Archie said, trying to keep the wet dog at arm's length while Nora, snug in her dry robe, laughed at him. Then, of course, Tatty shook herself dry while she was still right next to them, making Archie cry out as he got showered with cold water.

'Are you alright?' he asked Nora, although she looked perfectly dry, unscathed by the dog shower.

Nora smiled and bit her lip which was enormously attractive, making Archie want to dive back into a kiss. 'I am,' she said. 'You look a bit damp.'

He grinned, because despite ending up cold and damp, he'd had one of the best mornings of his life. 'I'm grand,' he said, standing up and reaching a hand down to help Nora up. He pulled her straight into his arms.

'Do you want to warm up in here with me?' she said. 'I bet there's enough room.'

'Nora, you have no idea.' He leant his forehead against hers, then pulled back and kissed her again, hardly able to believe that this could make him feel so delightfully happy.

After what seemed like a lot more kissing, and yet not enough, Nora pulled away. 'As much as I don't want to leave, I'll never make our meeting later if I don't go home and shower. And you'll catch a chill if you don't get dried off.'

He sighed, wishing that real life didn't have to interfere.

'Would you like to come back with me?' she asked.

'I'd love that more than anything, but I ought to get back. Take Tatty. You don't want a wet dog in your house.'

Nora laughed. 'I wouldn't mind that at all. But perhaps another time.'

'Another time,' he said, giving her one last kiss. He touched her bottom lip with his thumb, then stepped back and clasped his hands behind his back. 'I'll look forward to seeing you later.'

'Me too.' She gathered up her things and clambered over the wall into the woods.

Archie watched until she disappeared into the trees and then began the walk back to the house. 'Come on Tatty,' he said. 'Let's get dried off.'

Seb was early for the meeting and was sat in his usual spot by the fire in the estate office, talking about something that Archie was struggling to follow, because his head was full of Nora. Though barely three hours since they'd seen each other, he was desperate to set eyes on her again. And lips too, if he was honest. And it was mildly annoying that Seb was going to be there, unwittingly putting a stop to anything like that happening.

'So what do you think?' Seb asked.

Archie had no idea what he was supposed to comment on so looked at his friend blankly as he went through the possibilities in his head. 'I think that sounds…good.'

'Do you?' Seb raised an eyebrow and looked at him with a lazy grin. 'You think it's good?'

'Fine. My mind was elsewhere. Sorry.'

'Is everything alright?'

'Fine,' Archie said again. He wasn't about to divulge the morning's events to Seb. 'Start again. I'm listening.'

Seb launched into a repeat of what he'd been saying before, which now that Archie was listening, turned out to not be good.

'That's awful. So the council will only allow the festival area to be in the park, not where we had the camping last year?'

'See? Not good. We thought we'd be able to expand by having the extra field off you, but I'm not sure we'll be able to now. Still, if it's the same as last year, it's brilliant. It's a shame not to build on it, that's all.'

'And this has come from Helena?' Archie asked. Helena

was the licensing officer for the council who had been tricky to deal with at first, but once Seb won her over, was a real champion for the first Croftwood Festival.

'Not directly, she's been keeping me up-to-date on the mutterings from above.'

'I can't imagine anyone from above having much say in it if Helena's willing to sign it off. She's very fair, does everything by the book.'

'Morning!' Nora stuck her head around the door, accompanied by Tatty who must have snuck out to greet her when she heard the car pull up.

Archie was thrilled to see her. She looked beautiful. Her hair was piled in haphazard manner on the top of her head, odd bits of it falling out here and there, and she was wearing denim dungarees and a pair of boots that were obviously old favourites. 'Morning,' he said, getting up and kissing her on the cheek, but taking her other cheek briefly into his hand.

'Hello, Nora. How are you?' Seb also got up, an amused look on his face as he looked from Nora to Archie.

'What?' Archie said.

'Nothing,' Seb said, giving him a knowing look that was lost on Archie. He offered Nora the chair he'd been sitting in, which was widely known to be the best spot in the office.

'Thanks Seb,' she said, sinking into the chair while Tatty settled herself in front of the fire at Nora's feet.

Archie made tea for them all and they began talking about the plans for the lake, Seb interjecting with questions around safety and protocols, some of which Nora knew the answers to and some which needed some research. As they chatted, Seb scribbled on a notepad and by the end of the meeting had produced a timeline for them.

'First things first. Arch, we need to check the estate plans as we may be able to reinstate that entrance without needing permission,' said Seb. 'In which case, all we need is to get planning permission for the lake to become a swimming lake and to check that the council are happy with the access.'

'All we need? Do you think it'll be that straightforward?' Archie said.

'No, I doubt it. This is the council we're talking about, but if we come from the angle that it's providing an amenity that will benefit the local community, show that there's demand around here for something like this, spin it as if we're doing them a favour, I think that's the way to go.'

'That sounds like a good start,' Nora said. 'I'll do some market research into the most local competitors. I think that would be useful for us in terms of how to price it and to get a feel for how they're operating it day-to-day. The places I've been before have been heritage lidos and sea pools which run similarly to traditional swimming pools. We're not going to have the lake open twelve hours a day or anything like that, and having had a quick look, most other lakes don't do that either.'

'Brilliant. So Nora, you're on market research. Arch, you're on landscaping and finding the estate plans. Presumably they're in this pile somewhere.' Seb gestured to the ridiculous heaps of paper on the desk opposite Archie's. 'And I'll liaise with the council. Right I'm off. Leave you lovebirds to it,' he added with a grin.

'Why did he say that?' Archie said, going over to Nora and pulling her out of the chair so that he could kiss her.

'I think he noticed that we're desperate to do this,' Nora said, kissing him back. 'It's written all over your face.'

'It's not,' Archie said, grinning. 'It's written all over *your* face.'

16

Nora was in Stoke to oversee the firing, or more accurately, the end of the firing, of her latest pieces for a department store in London. Her latest collection was statement vases. Each was unique in its shape and decoration and yet unmistakably Hart Pottery. This was the first batch to be glazed in the new kiln after two successful bisque firings, and numerous test firings, so it was a nerve-racking time. Neil, the kiln technician, seemed confident it would be okay, and Nora clung onto that, trying not to spiral into what-ifs. Her chief concern being, what if the glaze didn't perform as it should? It was all very well making bespoke pieces; you could pass off the odd imperfection as artistic intent, but not if they looked totally rubbish.

To keep the nerves at bay, Val had ushered her into the kitchen, tempting her with a lemon drizzle cake that was covered in crunchy sugar topping. It worked.

'Neil will come and get you as soon as they're ready to come out,' Val said soothingly. 'Come on, what have you been up to lately? How's the lord?'

Thinking about Archie was a welcome distraction. 'He's fine. We're seeing each other.'

'Well, I didn't see that coming,' Val said, laughing. 'No,

pointing her fork at Nora.

'You're up.' Neil popped his head around the door and then disappeared. Nora abandoned her cake and sped after him, Val's words spinning in her head. Was she in love with Archie?

All thoughts of Archie were abandoned as she and Neil carefully unloaded the kiln. The glazes looked spectacular.

'I should have bought a new kiln years ago,' she said to Neil.

'They look tidy,' he said, picking one up and turning it around in his hands. 'Very tidy.'

'What a relief!' Aside from meaning that this shipment would be on time, it meant that Nora had a whole other batch she had made, just in case. Now, that could be glazed and kept on hand for another order. She'd never been in the position of having any of her bespoke pieces on hand as stock before. It had been a slog to make the extra pieces, working every day in Stoke for the past few weeks, but it meant she could reap the rewards and take her foot off the gas a little.

She spent the rest of the afternoon cleaning and finishing the pieces ready for being packed and shipped. It was one of her favourite things to do, aside from throwing the pots in the first place. Making sure that they were perfect, sending them on their way and saying goodbye to them. It sounded strange, but it was an important part of the process for her. Every piece she created was part of her in a small way.

Her phone buzzed in her pocket. It was a text from Archie.

Would you like to come to the Court for lunch tomorrow? A x

He didn't say that it was lunch with him and Constance, but Nora knew that was what lunch at the Court meant.

I'd love to. What time? Should I bring anything? xx

Noon would be perfect. I'd like to show you around before lunch. No need to bring anything. A x

seriously. I could see it coming a mile off,' she said when Nora looked confused. 'And I know you're stressed out today, but you've looked happier than I've seen you in years.'

'Really?' Nora said, feeling pleased. 'You don't think it's too soon?'

'Why? I might be talking out of turn, but I don't think you and Julian had been in love for a while. You needed time to get used to being by yourself, but that's not the same as needing time to get over someone. I don't think you needed to do that, did you?'

'No.' It was true. She simply hadn't been heartbroken. She'd settled into life in Croftwood and the new routine of travelling up to Stoke from there, pretty quickly.

'So what's it like going out with a lord?'

'You have to stop calling him that, Val. It's weird. I don't think of him like that at all.'

'Really? I thought that was part of the appeal. You know, in Bridgerton. Anthony, Lord Bridgerton. He's so commanding. Doesn't Archie have that going on?'

Nora laughed because the thought of Archie being commanding was quite funny. 'No, he doesn't have that going on. He has the deepest soul. It makes my heart ache to look at him.'

'Oh my god,' Val said, putting her hand on her chest. 'You're in love with him.'

'No,' Nora said, frowning and delving into her slice of lemon drizzle cake. 'It's too soon to be talking about love.'

'You are,' Val insisted. 'I've known you a long time, Nora Hartford, and this is a Nora Hartford I've never seen.'

'You're so dramatic.'

'I'm right. And you'll look back on this moment and marvel about how right I am. You haven't admitted it to yourself yet. And I get that. It's a big step. But there's no denying what's staring me straight in the face,' Val said,

Nora was considerably more excited about seeing the inside of the Court than she was about the prospect of lunch with Constance. But she couldn't wait to see Archie again. Since kissing at the lake, they'd been kissing a lot. All the time. She'd wondered whether kissing might persuade Archie to swim with her, because as yet, he still hadn't ventured into the water. She also wondered when they might progress from kissing. Travelling to Stoke every day this week had been tiring, but aside from that, it seemed too calculating to invite him over to her house without offering him dinner or any other reason to visit, apart from it being a blatant booty call, and she hadn't had time for that.

When she'd finished with her pots, she went to find Val again.

'What have we got that I can take to impress Archie's mother? Something she can't buy from Cushions and Candles in Croftwood.'

'You'd better check with Michelle what they've ordered, or you could take something from the Christmas collection. Nobody's got that yet.'

'That's probably impressive enough,' said Nora.

'Actually we have a handful of Christmas candlesticks where we didn't have the glaze mix quite right. They look a lot less Christmassy and we won't be able to sell them except as seconds.

The rejected candlesticks were actually very pretty. The Christmas green had come out as a sage colour and the red as a dusky pink. There was also a gold shade which had fired perfectly and went very well. Unless you knew what they were supposed to look like, they were lovely and entirely suitable as a gift for Constance.

The following morning, Nora went for a swim and was surprised when there was no sign of Archie. They generally didn't arrange to meet every day, but now that he wasn't here, Nora felt disappointed. Perhaps it was that it was a slightly murky, drizzly day, and he didn't fancy sitting out in the rain. As it was, she enjoyed a swim alone, letting her mind wander. The sound of the rain pattering onto the water was soothing, although she wished she'd worn a hat because it was making her head cold.

When she got home, the hot shower was very welcome, and she made an effort to blow-dry her hair rather than let it dry into its usual waves. Although she knew Constance a little already, this lunch date felt like some kind of landmark occasion. Maybe it was a test. And in case it was, Nora wanted to prepare for it.

She picked out one of her favourite day dresses. It had long sleeves which were full, but elasticated at the wrist. The bodice was fitted, and the skirt was full and came to mid-calf. The dark pinky-burgundy colour suited her and paired with her favourite black suede wedge-heel boots, she felt good. She pulled a pretty crochet shawl from the blanket chest where she kept all her scarves and gloves, and wrapped it around her neck like a scarf but with the pretty edge across her collarbones and the ends draping down her back.

Now that she had a better feeling for where her house was in relation to Archie's, she knew that if she walked down her road, there was a spot where the estate wall had fallen into disrepair, much like the wall she climbed over near the lake. It wasn't ideal to clamber over in her dress, but it saved a very long walk around to the main gates, or a very muddy walk through the woods to her usual entry point by the lake. Driving was out of the question because she was hoping Archie would have some Dutch courage on offer, and she wanted to take full advantage of that.

When she was safely over the wall, she smoothed her dress down, adjusted her shawl and tucked her hair behind her ears. Clutching the prettily packed parcel of candlesticks for

Constance, she headed along the estate road, approaching the manor house a few minutes later. It looked very different from this side. The side that faced the lawns was more opulent, whereas this was the back of the house and the disrepair that Archie spoke of from time to time was more obvious.

'Miss Hartford?' A willowy woman in jeans and a sweater came out of the back door.

'Yes.'

'Come this way. We've had a bit of a morning.'

Nora went over to the door and into a boot room which was stuffed to the rafters with waxed jackets, tweed coats and wellies and boots of various sizes and colours.

'I'm Ursula, the housekeeper. Sorry to bring you in this way. Archie said you wouldn't mind.'

'I don't mind at all. Please call me Nora.'

'Right you are.'

Ursula led the way along some dark corridors before taking Nora up a short flight of stairs and through a door into a huge hallway. It was dominated by an ornate fireplace with a huge gilt mirror hanging above it. A galleried landing overlooked the space and a wide staircase led up to it.

'He asked that you wait in the drawing room,' Ursula said, leading the way into a bright room that overlooked the lawns and had about ten sofas dotted around it and almost as many windows. 'Don't worry, her Ladyship won't be down just yet,' Ursula said with a smile, as if reading Nora's mind about perhaps getting ambushed by Constance before Archie appeared.

She set her package down on the table and walked over to the largest window. From here, she could see within the walled garden, something that no one could see from the lawns. The area nearest the house had a patio with a large round table and chairs and it was surrounded by shrubs and succulents. Everything was about to spring into life now that the weather was improving. The rest of the walled garden must have been a proper kitchen garden in its day. The beds were still there, tidy and laid out as they would have been, but there was no sign that anything was being grown.

'Nora.' Archie came into the room, beaming but looking tired. 'It's wonderful to see you.'

They took a moment to kiss, although Nora couldn't help but feel odd. It was strange to see Archie here. He seemed different. Not in a bad way, but she couldn't put her finger on it.

'Is everything alright?' She cupped his cheek in her hand, and he closed his eyes for a moment.

'The rain last night caused a bit of bother. I should have had the roof repaired by now. It's made it worse by putting it off.'

'You look tired.'

'I was up until the early hours. Well. You'll see.' He raked a hand through his hair. 'I'm sorry I missed the swim this morning. I overslept.'

'It's okay,' Nora said, wanting to take him back to her house, tuck him into bed with her and let him sleep. 'It was raining. Well, you know that. So not much fun to sit on the dock today.'

He smiled and took her hand. 'Come on. Oh, would you like a drink?'

'What are you offering?'

'Tea, coffee, wine, beer?'

'Would it be awful to have a glass of wine before lunch?'

'You're nervous,' he said. 'There's no need. But of course you can have a glass of wine. I'll join you.'

Archie produced a bottle of red and two glasses from a cabinet in the room next door, filled them halfway, and handed one to Nora.

'To be perfectly honest,' he said, 'I feel nervous myself. This is uncharted territory. Who knows what Mama's going to come out with?'

'Thanks for the reassurance.'

Archie laughed. 'Here's to us.'

'To us,' she said.

Archie led the way through the rooms on the ground floor, which was really the first floor since the kitchens and what have you were downstairs, where Nora had come in.

'This is the best part of the house. We try to keep it as it was. All of these things are handed down from generations ago. A lot of it was brought over from France after the French Revolution.'

They walked through room after room. Nora wondered why it wasn't an option to sell the odd painting or twenty to raise funds. Surely Archie and the family must have considered doing that to take the pressure off. But it didn't seem like the right time to ask, so instead she concentrated on admiring everything.

In one room, there was a row of cabinets with glass fronts that held all sorts of china. Everything from dinner services to serving dishes to commemorative ware. Nora was drawn to it, remembering that even the plates Archie brought to the lake had been Royal Worcester porcelain. And there, in the cabinet, mixed in amongst all sorts of vases and jugs, looking as if no one knew what it was, was something that she knew might be the answer to Archie's money worries.

17

Nora peered into the cabinet. The light was awful. The heavy curtains weren't drawn back very far, stopping the weak spring sunshine from reaching very far into the room.

'Look at that vase,' she said, pulling out her phone and shining the torch into the cabinet. 'It's Royal Worcester.'

'Most of this is, I think,' Archie said, clasping his hands behind his back and leaning in for a closer look.

'I think it could be worth something.'

He shook his head. 'I doubt it. We had everything valued when Father died and anything of note wouldn't be in here. We have all the best pieces on display.'

'Honestly, Archie, I think it's a Donaldson vase.'

A gong sounded from somewhere and Archie turned to leave the room. 'Lunch is served,' he said, smiling at her.

The nerves had abated, overtaken by excitement at seeing what she was sure was one of only a few surviving examples of the eighteenth-century painter John Donaldson's work for Royal Worcester. She turned her phone torch off, picked up her almost empty glass of wine and followed Archie out of the room. She'd pick this up with him later. For a vase like that to be languishing amongst all sorts of run-of-the-mill crockery was a crying shame. But the lunch gong seemed to signal that everything else had to wait by the speed Archie was heading for the dining room.

Constance was already there, pouring herself a sherry from a decanter on the sideboard, but abandoned it to welcome Nora, giving her an air-kiss on each cheek.

'Welcome, Nora. Lovely to see you,' she said. 'Archie, pour the sherries. I had Ursula sound the gong early so we might enjoy a quick apéritif before lunch. Although I see you've started without me.' She raised a disapproving eyebrow.

'A sherry would be lovely,' Nora said. 'Archie would you mind fetching the gift I brought for your mother? I left it on the table in the drawing room and I'm not sure of the way.'

'A gift?' Constance said, looking thrilled. 'How lovely.'

Archie handed Nora her sherry and inclined his head, checking she was happy for him to leave her for a moment. She returned an imperceptible nod.

'Come, Nora,' Constance said. 'Let's take a seat in the smoking room.'

She led the way next door into a room that was a smaller version of the drawing room, with many sofas and chairs. The decor was darker and heavier than some of the other rooms, with thick burgundy velvet curtains at the windows and flocked wallpaper. Constance perched on a window seat that overlooked the gardens and patted the cushion next to her.

'This is one of my favourite spots in the house,' she said. 'When I was first married, it wasn't the done thing for the ladies to venture into this room. It was men only, if you can believe that.'

'It feels quite masculine compared to the other rooms,' Nora said.

'It reminds me very much of my husband so I'm not inclined to change anything about it,' Constance said with a smile.

Nora smiled back, but thought that nothing in the house looked as if it had changed an awful lot in the last hundred years anyway, let alone this room.

'This is very unusual,' Constance said. 'It's been years since Archie brought a girl home, and he's plumped for you.'

Nora wasn't sure whether Constance thought that was good or bad.

'He's a lovely man,' was all she could think to say.

'He's besotted with you, and I must admit, that wasn't my intention when I suggested the match. But here we are.'

'Look, Constance,' Nora began, immediately wondering whether she'd made a huge mistake by not addressing her as your ladyship. 'Archie and I don't know what the future holds for us. To be honest, we haven't discussed it much. We're enjoying getting to know each other, that's all. But I can assure you that I am not after anything.'

Constance gave a small laugh. 'Forgive me if I find that hard to believe. I know you're not after his money. You're probably bright enough to realise that there isn't any, but a title is something money can't buy.'

Nora almost laughed at the idea that being Lady Harrington might be something she'd covet. But what she couldn't understand was why Constance had suggested she go out with Archie at the book club if she was worried about her intentions.

'I thought you wanted him to find a partner?'

'Well, yes, but not someone like you. You're the type of woman who can turn his head. He's already so taken with you, his attention isn't on the estate in the way it should be.'

'Someone like me?'

'Someone who will turn him against me.'

'Here you are,' Archie said, arriving with Nora's gift.

'It's just a little something to say thank you for inviting me,' Nora said, wishing that she could have had a moment longer with Constance to get to the bottom of what she was worried about. At least to reassure her she'd never be so manipulative as to interfere in the relationship between mother and son.

Constance handed her sherry to Archie and unwrapped the parcel.

'Oh, goodness! How wonderful!' She exclaimed as she turned the candlesticks around in her hand. 'What a pity we chose lunch rather than dinner. We could have lit them now.'

'Why don't we?' Nora said.

Constance clapped her hands together. 'Yes! Why ever not.'

Archie beamed at Nora and she felt pleased he thought things had started off on the right footing, even if she was confused about what Constance thought.

'Lunch is served, your Lordship,' Ursula said, popping her head around the door.

Nora almost giggled again. It was funny to hear Archie called that. Since Ursula had referred to him as Archie earlier, she assumed the formality was for Constance's benefit. She probably liked to do things properly.

'Thank you Ursula.' He held out his arm for his mother to take and Nora followed them into the dining room, slightly taken aback by the sudden display of etiquette. But then, she herself had particularly appreciated Archie's manners when they'd been out for dinner.

After Archie had pulled out the chair for his mother and seated her at the table, he pulled out the chair opposite for Nora then took his own seat at the head of the table.

Ursula produced a bottle of wine and proceeded to fill their glasses, checking with Archie first with a simple, 'Sir?' as she offered the bottle, to which he nodded. After Ursula had poured the wine, she went over to a hatch in the corner of the room and lifted it, revealing a dumb waiter from where she carried a tray laden with a silver soup terrine, bowls and a basket of bread rolls over to the table.

'Tomato soup?' she asked Nora.

'Yes, lovely, thank you.'

Ursula served Archie and Constance without asking if they wanted it, but Nora supposed they usually ate everything since the cook probably knew what their likes and dislikes were.

Nora sat with her hands in her lap. She had some distant recollection of the etiquette being that Archie should start first, and Constance seemed to be waiting too. Once he'd started eating, the conversation resumed.

'Have you been to choose your book, Nora? I asked Archie to find out but he never did say.'

'Yes. I've chosen the romance this time. I didn't think I could read another thriller just yet and I wasn't interested in that footballer's biography.'

'I'm surprised at Lois for allowing that,' said Constance.

'It's bound to appeal to some people,' Nora said. There were a fair number of men in the group and Lois had said they tried to appeal to as many readers as possible.

'It's not that long since we had a sports biography. What I'd enjoy is Cher's new autobiography,' Constance said.

Archie's eyes widened, and he looked at Nora, apparently as surprised as she was about that.

'You ought to suggest it, Constance. The romance is We All Live Here by Jojo Moyes, although I don't think it's strictly a romance, more of a book about family and friendship.'

'That sounds lovely,' Constance said, gracefully tipping her soup bowl towards her to scoop the dregs with her spoon. Nora wondered whether it would be bad if she wiped her last bit of bread roll around the bowl to get her own dregs and decided against it. It was her first visit after all, and she didn't want to shock anyone.

After the main meal of ham hock with green vegetables

and delicious herby roasted potatoes, followed by an apple pie with a pastry top that flaked to perfection, Constance excused herself.

'I shall pop to the library with Ursula,' she said. 'It was wonderful to see you Nora.'

'Thank you for having me,' Nora said. She was sorry that she wouldn't have chance to talk to Constance again to reassure her. But she'd see her at book club the following week and it might be better to tackle that conversation in a neutral setting.

'Come on then, show me what happened last night,' she said, intrigued to see more of the house.

Archie led the way back to the hallway and up the staircase to the galleried landing, off which were several doors. He opened the farthest one which led onto a corridor. Another door led into a huge bedroom with a relatively modest double-bed against one wall, a chest of drawers opposite, and not much else. Apart from the pile of wood and plaster in the middle of the floor and the cavernous hole in the ceiling.

'Oh my god!' Nora said. 'Whose room is this?'

'It's a guest room, which is why we hadn't noticed the leak. Last time, with the leak above Mama's bedroom we spotted it straight away. This is a new leak.'

'Oh, Archie.'

'I should have had the repairs done as soon as Simon had come back to me with the quote but I hadn't quite got the cash together. Obviously now, this is going to add quite a bit to that bill.'

They stood together, gazing at the hole in the ceiling. And it wasn't as if it was a plain old ceiling either. It was a grid of decorative plasterwork.

'Come with me,' she said, taking his hand before she realised she didn't know the way back to the room where she'd seen the vase. 'Can we go back to where the china was?'

He smiled, looking puzzled. 'Of course.'

'May I?' Nora said, reaching to slide open the glass door of the cabinet.

Archie nodded.

Nora pulled out a jug and vase which were sitting at the front of the cabinet, laying them carefully on the floor, then gently picked up the Donaldson vase.'

'Archie. This vase is worth thousands. I'm certain. It's in here, doing nothing, not even on show to be appreciated by anyone. Surely, you could sell it to get the roof mended.'

'It's not as simple as that.' He took the vase and placed it back in the cabinet then replaced the jug and vase and slid the glass door across.

'But why?'

'Shall we take a walk in the gardens?'

'Okay,' she said, feeling exasperated.

Once they were outside, Nora having borrowed a pair of Archie's woolly socks and some random wellies, he took her hand and they walked through part of the gardens that she hadn't seen before, tucked away at the side of the house, before the expansive lawns gave way to the farmland.

'None of the things in that house are mine, Nora. I am just the latest custodian of the house and everything in it and I have to do my best to preserve that for the next generation.'

It was all very well having an ethos like that which had been handed down through the generations of his family, but it made no practical sense in the twenty-first century when he was struggling to keep the house from rotting away. She tried to be gentle, knowing this was a topic they were going to struggle to find common ground on.

'All of this used to matter in a way that doesn't make sense these days,' she began. 'Things have moved on and trying to keep everything the way it's always been isn't the way to preserve any of it. If the house falls into disrepair, what kind of legacy is that? Surely it's better to sell a vase no one will miss. Isn't that the bigger picture?'

Archie didn't break his stride, but he dropped Nora's hand and shoved his hands in his pockets. He said nothing, but the set of his jaw was defiant. Nora was shocked. He was behaving like a sulky child and she realised she was seeing a different side to him. Perhaps the more privileged side of him that was used to getting exactly what he wanted with no challenge. Yes, he had the weight of the responsibility on his shoulders and sometimes, Nora could see it almost physically weighing him down. But maybe when he'd told her that all of this was his problem to solve, he meant it. And perhaps supporting him meant giving meaningless platitudes that everything would be alright, rather than him welcoming practical advice.

'I'm sorry,' she said, wanting to breach the divide between them. 'I obviously don't understand but I don't want it to come between us. If you'd rather I stayed out of this kind of stuff, that's fine. I just see how tough it is for you and thought it was a solution.'

Archie stopped walking and faced her. His expression softened. 'It's hard to explain and I'm sorry that I'm not better at it.'

Nora put her hands on his forearms, tempting his hands from his pockets and into hers. 'It's fine. Honestly,' she said. 'It's been lovely coming here, but it's made me realise exactly who you are. When we're down at the lake, you're just Archie. And here, you're his Lordship.'

He shrugged. 'Yes. But that's me. Sometimes, I'd rather be just Archie but that can only ever be a temporary situation and I shouldn't have led you to believe that's who I am. Being Lord Harrington is my life, really, and holes in the roof aside, I'm pretty happy about it most of the time.'

'So this is who I need to get to know, if we're going to be seeing each other,' Nora said, linking her arm in his as they continued their walk.

'I never expected to find what we have now, Nora. If I'd had any idea that we might…end up in a relationship, if that isn't too forward of me to assume, I may have done things differently.'

'Well, I might not have fallen for Lord Harrington in quite the same way as I did for Archie.'

Archie looked surprised and a little hurt.

'No, I don't mean I don't love you being Lord Harrington, it's just that I think when you're down at the lake with me, you're not thinking about all of the difficult stuff. It's like we're in a bubble where you're not his Lordship. The formality and the etiquette and all of that don't matter. And I love that you can be like that with me. The other stuff is still you, but the you that everyone else has.'

'God, Nora.' He took her in his arms and breathed the words into her ear. 'Is it too soon to say that I love you?'

18

Nora was in Stoke glazing the spare stock for a final firing while there was capacity in the kiln and space in her schedule. Once she'd finished, it was lunchtime and she was thrilled to have the afternoon free for a little experiment. Since her visit to Croftwood Court at the weekend, she'd been thinking of designing a new bespoke line. A modern take on early nineteenth century pottery. She'd done some research on the regency era after seeing plenty of pieces on display in Croftwood Court. With the popularity of that era at an all-time high thanks to Bridgerton, she thought it might be something to explore.

She went into the room where they stored the clay and took some ready-wedged balls from a tray that was ready to go to the production line, hoping that Val wouldn't mind. She sat at her favourite wheel and centred the first ball of clay. She worked it for a minute or so, getting used to the feel of it before she began to translate what was in her head, through her fingers and onto the wheel. The first attempt was less than perfect, so it went in the bucket on the floor next to her and she started again. This time was better. She knew where she'd gone wrong the first time and this was all about knowing that and rectifying the next time. Once she was satisfied, she ran a wire between the wheel and the pot and lifted it onto a board. It was elegant, the wide base narrowing to form almost a stem for a pleasingly bulbous pot. The challenge was in keeping the top light but robust at the point where the stem met the pot, so that it didn't collapse into itself with the weight. It would need some delicate handles and maybe even a lid.

'Have you been in here all afternoon?' Val came into the room, taking her apron off and folding it neatly.

'What time is it?'

'Just gone five.'

Nora had completely lost track of time. That's what happened when she was struck by inspiration like this. Just another pot, just another attempt at perfection, and the hours ticked by without her realising.

'Shit. I'm going out for dinner tonight. I'd planned to leave at three.'

'Go. I can clean up for you,' said Val. 'Loving these, by the way,' she said, picking up one of the boards and admiring the pot that sat on it. By this time there were six that had made it onto boards, but more than that were in the bucket.

'It's an idea I had for a new collection,' said Nora, washing her hands at the sink. 'Shit,' she said again. 'I'd better text Archie and tell him I'll meet him there.'

'Where are you off to?'

'Dinner with some friends. It's the first time we've been out with other people and now we're probably not even going to arrive together.'

'Things are progressing,' Val said, her voice reaching a squeal. 'I'm going to need all the details.'

'And you can have most of them next week. I have to go. Would you mind putting the pots in the drying room? I'm not sure the kiln gods will be kind with these. There's a lot of inconsistency with the thickness of the walls.'

'Well, don't worry about that now.' Val began chivvying her out of the door. 'You can't keep the lord waiting.'

'Bugger off, Val.' Nora gave her friend a quick hug. 'See you Monday.'

Hitting the rush hour traffic, which is what she'd been hoping to avoid, made Nora even later. Archie was sitting in his car on the lane outside her house. She turned into the driveway and he pulled up behind her and climbed out.

'I'm so sorry,' she said, opening the door and falling inside. 'I need ten minutes. Come in.'

'I'm sure it's alright. We'll only be half an hour late.'

Archie settled himself on the sofa while Nora raced up the stairs. She had a quick shower, settled for dry-shampooing her hair and then threw on a wrap dress that she always felt good in. She shoved her hair up in what she hoped was a stylish messy bun, and applied some mascara and her favourite tinted lip balm. She grabbed some ankle boots and headed back downstairs.

'Ready! Oh god, let me find a bottle of wine. I meant to get one on my way home.'

'No need. I have one in the car.'

She smiled and sighed with relief. 'Thank you.'

'How was your day? Presumably busy?' Archie asked once they were in the car.

'I was experimenting with something new and I lost track of time.'

'That must be a good sign.'

'It's too soon to say, but I enjoyed it until I realised what the time was. How about you. What have you been up to today?'

'You might be pleased to hear that I spoke to Betsy and Mama about selling the vase.'

'Did you?' Nora had thought that subject was closed. Since the lunch, she'd deliberately put the topic out of her mind.

That and the odd reaction from Constance. At some point she'd have to reconcile the Archie she knew and was starting to love with the Archie that lived at the Croftwood Court, but that didn't need to be now, because it was going to take some getting used to.

'As you pointed out, it's ridiculous to allow the house to crumble around us while we have assets within it.'

'And did they agree?'

'They did. They felt the same way as you. For the sake of putting a single, overlooked vase up for sale, we should be able to repair the roof and have some cash left over to help with the lake project.'

'That's fantastic news.' Nora was so pleased that he'd come to his senses. Not only because it meant that Archie would have the money he desperately needed, but because it meant that the gulf between their ideals had closed a little bit.

Toby was hosting the dinner party at his house because according to Hilary, his kitchen was made for entertaining.

'I'm so sorry we're late,' Nora said as Hilary opened the door.

'Fashionably late,' Hilary said, kissing them both on the cheek as she ushered them in. 'Go through.'

Nora couldn't help lingering in the hallway. The Minton floor was one of the best she'd seen.

'Your hallway tiles are incredible,' she said to Toby.

'I knew I could count on you to notice,' he said as he came over to welcome them.

Seb and Jess were sitting at the kitchen island, sipping wine.

'Good to see you Arch,' said Seb, standing up and clapping Archie on the back.

'Something smells delicious,' Nora said, taking the stool next to Jess.

'We've gone to as little effort as possible,' said Hilary. 'It's lasagne.'

'I'll eat anything,' Jess said. 'It was so busy in the shop today, I only had time to eat a banana.'

'That's not true,' Seb said, lifting his glass towards her. 'I brought you coffee and a pastry for elevenses.'

'You did. And it was much appreciated,' Jess said, blowing him a kiss and then grimacing at the others. 'I hadn't forgotten, honestly.'

'Did you swim this morning, Nora?' Hilary asked.

'No. I set off early for work so that I could leave early.'

Archie chuckled.

'I know. It's my first dinner invitation since I moved here and I was late.'

'Oh, we forgive you, said Hilary.

'Have you been in the lake yet, Hilary?' asked Jess.

'I haven't found the time yet,' Hilary said. Jess and Nora grinned at each other. 'No, really, I do want to.'

'How are the plans for the lake coming on, Archie?' Toby asked.

'We've made a start on tidying it up. The hedge has gone and the chaps are going to start on the paths next week. Then it's just a matter of waiting for confirmation from the council that we can reinstate the entrance on that side of the estate.'

'And get the planning permission for change of use of the lake,' Seb said.

'Yes. Of course,' said Archie.

Nora guessed he'd been dragging his feet because of the lack of money available and wondered if deciding to sell the vase would spur him on.

'It's the perfect time to launch it now that the weather's improving,' said Jess.

'Nora identified a valuable piece of Royal Worcester porcelain that has been in the family for some time, so we're looking into selling that to fund some repairs and the lake project.'

'That's great news!' Seb said, enthusiastically.

Nora was taken aback that Archie would share that with everyone. She'd thought he might feel ashamed that it had come to selling off assets to keep everything afloat, especially after he'd been so against the idea. Yet again, he surprised her with his willingness to admit he was wrong. She loved that. Julian would rather die than admit she'd been right about anything.

'We have some news too,' said Seb, his eyes falling on Jess. 'We've set a date for the wedding. And Archie, would you be my best man?'

'Seb, I'd be… honoured,' Archie said, overcome.

'Congratulations!'

'Where are you having it?' Hilary asked.

'We're having a very small family wedding in Dorset,' said Jess. 'Our engagement party felt as good as a wedding with my sister and her family there, and I can't ask her to come from Australia so we can do that again. So it's just a simple ceremony at the registry office.'

'I can understand that,' said Toby. 'But we will have to have a celebration of some sort in Croftwood afterwards.'

'We'd love that. We're just sorry we can't invite everyone but we're keeping it low key and staying at my parents.'

'No, you mustn't worry about that,' said Hilary. 'Your engagement party will be hard to beat, unless you can talk Archie into a full-blown wedding at the Court.'

'You had your engagement party at Archie's?' Nora asked.

'It was amazing,' said Jess. 'Archie and his staff pulled out all the stops and it was absolutely magical.'

Archie beamed, but looked down at his drink in embarrassment.

'To Seb and Jess,' said Hilary, raising her glass.

'To Seb and Jess!'

'Right. Let's eat,' said Toby.

It was past midnight when Nora and Archie said their goodbyes. After a busy afternoon throwing, and a couple of glasses of wine, Nora was relaxed and happy but keen to get home.

'What a great evening,' she said, sinking into the seat of the Jaguar.

'It was,' Archie agreed. 'It's been a long time since I did anything like that.'

'Me too. I'd forgotten how much fun it can be to talk about everything and nothing.'

Archie reached for her hand and gave it a quick squeeze before he needed it to make the turn onto Worcester Road.

'You told everyone about the vase.'

'Shouldn't I have?' He shot her a worried look before turning his attention back to the road.

'They're our friends, of course you can. I suppose I was surprised how comfortable you are with the idea already.'

'When I was so vehemently opposed before?' he said easily.

'Yes.'

'I'd been wanting to do something like that for a while. I didn't have the courage to talk to Betsy and Mama about it. The way you explained it was so clear, so black and white, it made it easy for me to explain. I couldn't help thinking that selling anything would make me seem like a failure. But as you pointed out, things are different now. Preserving everything doesn't mean keeping everything the same. What's the point of all of these things just sitting there, some of them not even being admired or particularly cherished.'

Nora reached out and put her hand on Archie's thigh, rubbing it reassuringly. 'It's a great decision. For you and for everyone who comes after you.'

He pulled the car into Nora's driveway and switched the

engine off. Making no move to get out, he turned in his seat.

'I can hardly remember life without you.'

Nora took a breath, waiting for Archie to lean in and kiss her. She wanted him. She'd wanted him for a while now but tonight, she wasn't going to let him leave.

'Would you like to come in?' she breathed.

'Mmm.'

His hand was on her thigh now, slowly, easing further upwards. 'Come on,' she said, breaking the spell, because she wasn't sure how much further they could get in this car. Not as far as she'd like.

Archie bolted out of the car, coming around to the passenger side to meet Nora, but she had climbed out herself before he could reach her. Her patience evaporated. All she could think of was getting Archie upstairs and into her bed.

'If you stay, we could have a glass of wine,' she said, suddenly slightly nervous at the prospect of what lay ahead. It was a while since she'd had sex with Julian and even longer since she'd had sex with anyone other than him. At least, she reasoned as she grabbed a bottle of wine and two glasses, Archie had seen a fair bit of her body already at the lake.

He stood awkwardly at the bottom of the stairs, his hands in his pockets and a bulge in his trousers.

'Here,' Nora said handing him the wine bottle. 'This will help.'

Up in her bedroom, she sat on the edge of the bed while Archie poured the wine, handing Nora her glass. He downed his and refilled it before she'd taken a sip.

'Bit of Dutch courage required as it happens,' he said.

'It's been a while for me too,' she said, hoping to put him at ease because however nervous she might be, he looked ten times worse.

She took the glass out of his hand and pulled him onto the bed. Once they'd resumed kissing, she could feel Archie relax

— most of him at least — and he began exploring her body again. This time, he reached bare skin at the waistband of her tights, then pulled away, giving her a look that implored her to be more naked. She pulled her tights down, removing her knickers at the same time. Nora straddled him, loving the feel of his erection against her. She pulled his shirt from the waistband of his jeans and ran her hands underneath, up his torso, and back down his sides. He groaned and lifted from the bed so that she could pull his shirt and sweater over his head. His chest was sparse with hair and lean but lightly muscled. She was surprised how pale his skin was compared to the rest of him, but she couldn't imagine him sunbathing in the garden or working with his top off or anything like that. And she liked she was one of only a very few people to see this part of him. She ran her finger around the waistband of his jeans, letting her finger linger in the dip between his hips and his abdomen, which was enticing her further. He shifted her off so that he could unbutton his jeans, and now it was Nora's turn to groan when she saw him in all his glory.

She pulled his boxers down, and looked at him wide-eyed, never imagining that this had been waiting for her all along. What had they been waiting for? Archie took one end of the tie of her wrap dress, and looked at her with mischief in his eyes.

'This dress…' he said. 'Perfect for tonight.' He pulled the tie and the dress opened, revealing her favourite lacy bra. Thank god she'd had the foresight for that, even though she'd been in a rush. She shrugged off the dress and leant forward so that Archie could reach behind her and undo her bra.

What followed was the most delicious night that Nora could imagine. Archie was a tender, considerate lover, but so masterful. Nora swooned under his touch, knowing she'd been spoilt for anyone else. But if she had needed a sign that this man was someone special, tonight had been it. All the emotions that had been building between them, culminating in a consummation of their building love for each other. And Nora couldn't be happier.

19

It had been a long time since Archie'd had a spring in his step but this morning, after leaving Nora, he drove home and left the Jag in the garage, using the short walk to the house to brace himself for an interrogation from his mother.

'Morning, Ursula,' he said. He'd gone through the back door to give himself half a chance of being undetected in his clothes from the night before, but if he had to come across someone, Ursula was his preference. She was making coffee in the kitchen and gave him a knowing look.

'Good morning, Archie. Coffee?'

'That would be wonderful,' he said. 'Perhaps I should get changed first.'

'Good idea. Her ladyship hasn't noticed that you stayed out last night. In case you were wondering.'

It was exasperating that it bothered him what his mother thought, but it did. And Ursula was proving to be a useful ally.

'Thank you. I take it she's not down for breakfast yet?'

'No, but I have taken her tea up so she won't be long.' Constance always rang down for a cup of tea first thing.

'I'll go up the back stairs then.' He grinned at Ursula, feeling ridiculously happy.

'I'm glad you had a good evening.'

Archie crept up the stairs, feeling like a naughty schoolboy, but thrilled with the whole situation. His room was at the opposite end of the landing to Constance's and even if she headed downstairs now, they wouldn't cross paths but if she did glimpse him in the clothes he went out in, it didn't matter how old he was, she would consider it terribly bad form to have stayed out all night without having planned to.

He looked at himself in the mirror and grinned. No wonder Ursula had been smirking. There was no escaping the fact that somehow, sex with Nora had changed him. Whether it was the way his hair was flopping over his forehead that spoke of her fingers running through it, or whether it was that he couldn't help but smile, thinking of the most incredible night of his life. There was no hiding it.

Jumping in the shower and not caring for once about the lukewarm trickle of water it offered, he then quickly dressed and headed downstairs. Ursula had a steaming cup of coffee waiting for him on the breakfast table. He sat and sipped it gratefully.

'Good morning, Archie,' said Constance, kissing his cheek before taking her seat opposite him.

'Morning, Mama.'

'I take it you had a nice evening with your friends?'

'Very much so.'

'And Nora is well this morning?'

Archie smiled. 'How did you know? I went to great lengths to keep up the pretence that I was simply back rather late last night.'

'I heard the car.'

Archie gave a rueful nod. 'Of course.'

'You're quite old enough to conduct your own affairs without my interference. But it's rather unbecoming for one to wear the same clothes this morning as one wore last night.

Goodness only knows what the staff must think.'

Knowing quite well that this kind of thing mattered to his mother, and Mrs Milton might not share Ursula's relaxed attitude, he said, 'I apologise, Mama. You're quite right.'

'Wonderful. Now, what are your plans for today?'

'I'm delivering the vase to the auction house and making an appointment with the roofing company.'

'Jolly good. Sebastian mentioned there's a planning officer visiting today.'

'For some advice on the stables and perhaps the lake.' It seemed worthwhile to ask as much as possible while the chap was there, especially since the lake project needed to be underway. 'And speaking of Seb, he and Jess are getting married next month.'

'Oh, that's lovely news,' said Constance. 'I shall look forward to that.'

'Ah, no. The wedding is in Dorset with only close family invited.'

'But you're going?'

'Seb asked me to be his best man.' Archie was touched to have been asked. He'd never been best man to anyone before, and it was nice to know that Seb felt they were close friends as Archie did.

'You'll be taking Nora,' Constance said, sounding resigned. As if he'd have taken his mother to Dorset for the wedding even if he didn't have a girlfriend. 'I'm off to the pictures with Penny and Linda. I don't suppose you could take me into town?'

'Of course. What time?'

'In an hour, if that suits?'

Archie finished his breakfast and packaged up the vase by which time Constance was ready to leave.

'Put my knitting bag in the boot, would you darling?' She said, handing him the most hideous, voluminous carpet bag.

'Would you have the vase on your lap, just in case?'

'Good idea. We wouldn't want anything to happen to it. Fancy Nora finding a gem like that in the china room? I never imagined there was anything of any value in there. It's certainly not catalogued with the valuables.'

'I can't help but feel it's somewhat letting the side down.' He'd wondered whether Betsy and his mother thought that selling the vase was the smart thing to do, or were agreeing just to bail him out of the hole he was in.

'Nonsense.' Constance patted his leg. 'We can't live in a museum. The most important thing is to save the house for generations to come. Not every item in it needs to come on that journey.'

'Thank you, Mama.'

It was a relief to hear that from her. Knowing what his sister was like, he had thought that between him being useless and Betsy erring on the materialistic side, that Constance may have felt pushed into agreeing.

'You know if you die before Betsy, she'll sell most of it in one fell swoop.'

Archie let out a roar of laughter. It was absolutely true. Betsy would want the estate and the house but she'd also want the money that went with that, and her husband, despite working in the City, wasn't keeping her in the way she wanted to become accustomed to. But with her baby daughter Florence likely to be the heir to the Croftwood estate, she'd been much keener lately on having a say. 'So cynical, Mama.'

His mother pursed her lips, and he could see she was attempting to suppress a smile. 'I have no illusions where your sister is concerned. Besides, perhaps little Florence won't inherit.'

'I can't imagine why not.'

'You don't think things are progressing with Nora?'

It was far too early for them to have discussed this, but Archie felt sure that neither of them planned to be first-time parents in their forties. 'Not to that degree,' he said. He imagined that if she had wanted children, it is something that would have happened with Julian.

'I know I'm old-fashioned, but I would hope a gentleman would not stay the night with a lady without having honourable intentions.'

Archie wasn't sure what to say to that but stopped himself from saying that yes, it is a rather old-fashioned view and that he was not proposing based on one night spent together. 'It's early days.'

'As long as you understand that integrity and reputation are of the utmost importance. You're not a young man but that does not mean that the same rules don't apply just as they did when you were engaged to Clarissa.'

Archie could hardly believe they were having this conversation. 'Forgive me, Mother, but I will not discuss this with you. As you have pointed out, I am not a young man and am old enough to make decisions about my personal life without any interference.'

Constance harrumphed but said nothing more. Archie's heart was beating ten to the dozen. It wasn't often he stood up to his mother but it felt necessary.

'Just here,' Constance directed, once they reached Croftwood Park and the entrance closest to the cinema.

Archie wordlessly fetched her bag from the boot, and watched until Constance was safely at the door of the cinema.

After dropping off the vase, he grabbed a quick sandwich in the kitchen with Ursula and Mrs Milton then headed to the estate office to meet the planning officer. When he arrived, Seb was chatting to the chap in the courtyard.

'Archie, this is Ben Fletcher from the council. Ben, this is Archie, Lord Harrington.'

'Good to meet you,' Archie said, shaking Ben's hand.

'You too,' said Ben. 'Sebastian's been filling me in on some of your plans. Where would you like to start?'

'Perhaps you could start in the stables here, and then we'll take a look at the lake. I've found the plans of the estate which might be useful as a reference for that. We can take a quick look at them beforehand.'

Ben seemed interested in Seb's various ideas for the stable block. He didn't seem to think there would be any problem securing planning permission for change of use.

'If you're thinking about retail, that's another thing entirely. But workshops or offices are highly likely to be approved. You could even think about holiday accommodation.'

'That's interesting,' said Seb. 'We haven't considered that.'

And with good reason, Archie thought. The last thing Constance would sign off on were holiday lets in the grounds. But he smiled and nodded, making a mental note to let Seb know it was a non-starter.

Rather than take Ben into the untidy estate office, which wouldn't give the impression that they were running a well-organised machine, Archie brought the plans into Seb's storage area on the pretence of their being more space to spread them out.

'Before we head to the lake, one of our queries is whether we're able to reinstate this gate without applying for permission,' Archie said, pointing out where it was on the plans.

'It opens onto the highway,' Ben said uncertainly, 'but it's not a main road. 'As far as I'm concerned, if the gateway is reinstated as it was, it's unlikely to require permission. If you have any photographs of the old gateway that would be useful. We might want confirmation of what materials are going to be used and then I think we could do that on a planning notice under permitted development.'

'That's great news,' said Seb. 'Shall we go and take a look?'

They strolled across the estate to the lake.

'This was a fishing lake, built by my father,' said Archie.

'Did it ever operate commercially?' Ben asked.

'Not officially but I know my father used to run a fishing club. That's why we have these fishing spots, the wooden platforms, dotted around the edge.'

'Ah, I see. The lake itself wouldn't have needed permission but if you're planning to operate it as a business, that would. Are you opening it commercially?'

'Not as a fishing lake,' said Seb. 'We'd like to open it for wild-swimming.'

'Oh, fantastic,' Ben said, surprising them both. 'My wife is in a wild-swimming club, but they're based north of Worcester, so it's not that convenient. She'll be thrilled about this.'

'Does that help our cause?' Archie asked.

Ben laughed, as if that was a joke. 'Ha! Nice one.'

'We're planning on reinstating the gate over there,' Archie said, pointing over to the wall, now visible because the hedge had gone. 'The small brick shed will be the entrance where we'll check people in and out and we plan to build a wooden canopy on the side for a bit of shelter and for people to change under and leave their things in the dry.'

Ben made some notes but didn't comment.

'We're thinking of buying a sauna and a Finnish barbecue shed. It's basically a hexagonal hut with a firepit in the middle,' Seb said.

'Okay. You've given me plenty to go on. It's the perfect setting for it, I will say that,' Ben said. 'I'll be honest, the permission to use the lake for swimming will be determined on whether the site can cope with the expected traffic. When you submit the application, be sure to give us an idea of what you're expecting and how you're going to deal with parking, and think about how much traffic that lane can manage.' He pointed to the boundary wall with his pen. 'The sauna and shed can probably be classed as temporary structures which makes things easier, but it's as well to include everything in the application so that we get a clear picture of what you're aiming for overall.'

'So you don't think there's anything that might cause a problem?'

'I don't think so. You don't have any neighbours. That helps. Get the application in and I'll do what I can to assist.'

'That's great, thank you. Much appreciated,' said Archie shaking Ben's hand.

At that moment, Nora appeared over the wall. She froze as they all turned to look at her.

'Is this your first customer?' said Ben, clocking the fact that Nora was wearing a dry robe.

'This is my girlfriend, Nora. Nora, this is Ben from the council planning office,' said Archie.

'My wife's got the same dry robe as you,' said Ben. 'I think she'd love it here.'

'There's a small group of us that meet here on a Thursday morning at seven-thirty. She's welcome to join us if she'd like to. The others park in the lay-by along the lane and climb over the wall just there,' Nora said.

Now it was Archie's turn to freeze. He had no idea if it was against the rules to allow swimming in the lake before they had planning permission.

'Thanks, I'll mention it,' Ben said, grinning.

'I'll walk you back to the office,' Seb said, leaving Archie and Nora at the lakeside.

'He seemed nice,' Nora said, as she started to strip off.

'What are you doing here? I thought you'd have been already.' It wasn't ideal to have been caught in the act by the planning officer.

She shrugged and smiled. 'I'm not working today so I had a lazy start. For some reason I was feeling a bit tired. Aren't you?'

He couldn't help smiling. She was giving him a look that left him in no doubt that their night together was to blame.

'On the contrary, I'm having rather a productive day.'

'Good for you. Did Constance catch you sneaking in this morning?'

'She did.'

Nora laughed. 'I love that.'

'She's keen for me to make an honest woman of you.'

'Oh god, really?'

Archie laughed. The annoyance he'd felt with his mother earlier dissipating now he was telling Nora.

'Perhaps you could save me the trouble of sneaking around and stay the night with me?'

She was standing in front of him in her swimming costume and he had the urge to slip the straps off her shoulders and see what it would be like to seduce her outdoors. Instead he settled for wrapping his arms around her.

'I don't think I can have sex knowing your mother is in the house.'

'It's hardly a three-bed semi where she'll hear us through the wall. My room is practically in a different wing.'

'You didn't show me your room when I came round.'

'You want to see my room?'

'Yes.'

For some reason, it thrilled him that she did. Forget the fact that his room was nowhere near as comfortable as Nora's bedroom, which was more like a luxury hotel room, he wanted her in his bed.

'Come tonight.'

'Should I drive? Just rock up like a normal visitor? Do you

even have normal visitors?'

'No, we don't. But yes. Drive up to the house and knock on the front door.'

Nora looked at him wide-eyed. 'No way am I knocking on the door. I'll text you and you can come and meet me outside.'

'You want me to sneak you in?' This was an idea he found thrilling. He wasn't sure he'd be able to wait until later to ravage her. It astounded him how much he wanted her. Right now by the lake.

'What are your thoughts on doing... you know... al fresco?'

She laughed softly and buried her head in his chest. 'Are you asking me to have sex with you here?'

He gulped. And nodded.

'Oh my god, Archie. We can't.'

He raised an eyebrow. 'Can't we?'

20

The following week was the next meeting of the date-with-a-book club. By this time, Nora had stayed at Archie's every other night, and he'd stayed at hers on the nights in between. Tonight, because of the club, Nora was staying at his because she'd offered to take Constance with her. It would have been Archie's turn to give his mother and her friends a lift, so it seemed silly for him to turn out when she was going anyway.

Nora and Archie were in his bedroom. It was huge but since Nora had stayed the first night, he'd dragged a sofa in there and made a sort of lounge area around the window. Nora sat there now reading while he was busy making space for her in his chest of drawers and on the bedside table.

'You shouldn't go to the trouble,' she said, watching him over the top of her reading glasses. 'I'm not going to leave any of my stuff here.'

'I want you to feel at home,' he said, shoving a handful of paired socks into a different drawer.

Nora didn't want to point out that it would take more than a drawer for her to feel at home here. She'd only just moved into her own home and she loved it, so however this relationship continued with Archie, she wasn't going to give that up.

'I have a home, Archie,' she said gently. Because it was important for her that they both knew exactly where they stood, and what the expectations were. It was so easy to blindly saunter into a relationship only to find that you had a fundamental incompatibility. Not that she and Julian had been incompatible, but what happened with him made her feel that the next relationship she had; this relationship, needed to be clear of misunderstanding. She was older now. Sure of what she wanted. And that was a great deal more autonomy, and independence from having to run her decisions past anyone.

Archie came to sit next to her on the sofa, lifting her legs up so that he could sit down, and then resting them on his lap. 'Do you think we're at that point where we ought to talk about the future?' he asked.

Nora pulled her glasses off and laid them on her chest along with the book. 'Maybe.'

'Whatever happens, I'd never expect you to give up what you have to become the lady of the manor.'

'Well, that's a relief,' she said, laughing. 'I'm not sure I'd make a very good lady.'

'I think you'd be perfect. But I know that's not what you would want. And the best things about you are the things that make you independent and confident. I wouldn't want to lose those.'

'Neither would I.' Nora wasn't sure she could have explained exactly what her problem was with the idea that Archie might ask her to be his wife, but he had explained it for her. 'I think we're both old and wise enough to know that being together in the more traditional sense would mean too much compromise for either of us to be happy. I don't want to change anything about my life. But when I'm not throwing pots or swimming, I'd like to spend as much of it as I can with you.'

Archie leant over and dropped a kiss onto her lips. 'That's all I want too.'

They went downstairs and ate dinner with Constance.

'Penny told me that Seb is planning on asking some of his and Jess's friends down to Dorset for the wedding,' said Constance.

'I still don't think that means you, Mama,' said Archie.

'It's only us, Oliver and Lois and Patsy and Matt,' said Nora, who had been sworn to secrecy by Seb when he'd told her.

'And Penny and her husband,' Constance pointed out.

'She does run the shop with Jess,' Nora said reasonably.

'Have you looked at where we might stay?' Archie asked, seemingly oblivious to the fact that it might be better to put an end to the subject of Seb and Jess's wedding.

'I've emailed you a couple of options. So did you finish the book, Constance?'

'Dorset can be wonderful in March,' said Constance.

Archie put his knife and fork down. 'Mama. Please.'

'We'd better get going, Constance,' Nora said.

Constance huffed and stood up, her eyes darting to Archie before she headed upstairs to get ready.

'Gosh, she seems quite put out at not being invited.'

Archie sighed. 'I know. I don't think it's about that at all. She has a bee in her bonnet about us, I think.'

'What has she said?' Nora was intrigued. She'd never mentioned to Archie what Constance has started to say when she came for dinner, but presumably it was along the same lines.

'She feels I'm letting the side down by having a relationship with you where there is no commitment. In the traditional sense,' he added quickly.

'And what do you think?'

'I think we've discussed it and we're both happy with how

things are and that's all that matters.'

Nora grinned, pleased that he wasn't about to conform to an outdated stereotype. 'That is all that matters. That and choosing a place to stay in Dorset, because one of them is amazing. It's within a stone's throw of the beach.'

'So you can swim in the sea?'

'Yes, and unless you object, I'd like to book it tomorrow so have a look while we're out and let me know. And might you swim in the sea?' she asked, ever hopeful that one day they'd swim together, even if it wasn't in the lake at Croftwood.

He laughed. 'I'll consider it. But it depends on the size of the waves and how sunny it is.'

'In March, we might be lucky.'

'Are you ready, Nora?' Constance said, appearing in the doorway, her coat already on.

'Yes.' Nora kissed Archie. 'See you later?'

He nodded. Nora had given him a key so that he didn't have to wait until she was in to go round to hers. She was heading to Stoke in the morning so didn't want to stay at the Court overnight.

'I can't keep track of you two,' Constance said, climbing into Nora's car.

'Do you need to?' Nora asked, amused.

'It's nice to know whether one is likely to be eating breakfast alone. Now that Archie has stopped scuttling around, he tends to go straight to the estate office if he's stayed at your house.'

'Perhaps we can come up with a more regular plan,' said Nora. She felt sorry for Constance. It must be strange to have Archie suddenly adopting a different routine to the one he'd had for years and years. He was a creature of habit and it must be unsettling for Constance not knowing.

'I wouldn't dream of allowing you to agree to that,' Constance said. 'Although I'm touched by the suggestion. I'm complaining, but it's a long time since I've seen Archie as happy as this. I only wish you were thinking more conventionally about the future. It's important that Archie, as Lord Harrington, acts in the best interests of not only himself but those of the title itself.

'And what are those interests?'

'To be blunt, my dear, you are having relations out of wedlock and it's not acceptable. I'm not naive enough to think that my son has had no dalliances between Clarissa and you but a dalliance is one thing and can be overlooked. I realise that we are looking at something quite different with you. I must urge you to do the right thing.'

'You want me to marry him?'

'Yes, of course.'

'I think you should talk to Archie about this, Constance. I don't want to come between you two but surely you don't expect us to commit to that degree after only a few weeks?'

Constance sat in silence for a moment, then said, 'I know I'm an old woman who grew up in a different time, but I only want him to do the right thing. I'm not sure that is so very different.'

'Until a few months ago, I had been with the same man for twenty years. I'm not ready, and may never be ready, for the kind of commitment that you're talking about. If you want your son to be with someone who loves him, there's a compromise to be made.' Nora took a deep breath, wondering whether she'd gone too far.

'You love him?'

Nora nodded.

'Then Archie is very lucky to have you.'

Despite having read the same book, the two of them weren't partnered this time, which was probably for the best. Nora's date was with a woman called Steph, who worked for The Hive, the library in Worcester.

'I drive the mobile library van,' she explained to Nora. 'I bring some of my regulars to the book club nights occasionally. 'That's Eunice and over there is her partner, Bill. Isn't he with one of the women you came with?' Nora had picked Penny up on the way.

'Yes, that's Constance.'

'I feel as if I've seen her before,' said Steph.

'She's Lady Harrington.'

'Oh right! She had one too many glasses of Pimms at the festival last year. She was a right laugh. I had to feel sorry for her son, though. He had a hell of a job getting her to leave.'

'So I've heard,' Nora said, making a note to ask Archie about it. 'What did you think of the book?'

'Flipping loved it,' said Steph. 'It wasn't exactly a romance, was it?'

'No, more about family and relationships. I loved it too.'

They chatted for a while, sharing their favourite parts of the book, what they thought of the characters and which resonated with them the best.

'Coffees courtesy of Constance,' Oliver said, setting two lattes down in front of them.

'Thanks,' Steph said, bemused. 'Why is Constance buying us coffee?'

Nora exhaled. After what Steph had said about the festival, she felt she should have admitted her relationship to Constance earlier. 'I'm going out with Archie Harrington.'

'Oh my god,' Steph said, her eyebrows rising in surprise. 'No offence, but I can't believe you're going out with him.'

'He's lovely,' Nora said. She felt defensive, but she knew what Steph was getting at. 'He's ditched some of the tweed.'

Steph roared with laughter. 'You're reading my mind. I really couldn't picture you with the Lord Harrington I remember from the festival. So Constance is like your mother-in-law.'

'Not exactly. But we get on alright. And the house is big enough to have your own space.'

'You can say that again. Oh my god, I can't believe you're going out with Lord Harrington.'

Nora felt much the same as she had on her first visit to Croftwood Court. It was strange thinking of Archie in those terms when, unless she was reminded of it, it wasn't something she thought about. Yes, it was different since she'd started visiting the Court. She'd got used to him being called his Lordship, and the formality displayed in front of Constance was always a reminder of his status. But at her house, or at the lake, or even at Toby's house, until now, she'd never felt that part of Archie's life followed him.

'I didn't know that's who he was when I met him. And he didn't introduce himself as Lord Harrington to me. I don't really think about it most of the time.'

'Sorry, I must sound like a right idiot,' said Steph. 'Going on about him like that when he's your boyfriend.'

'No, it's fine,' Nora said smiling. 'It's going to happen, and I'm not sure my friend Val will ever stop referring to him as the lord.'

Steph laughed. 'There's a friend who will keep you grounded.'

'That's so true.'

'I think it's just because around here, people are slightly in awe of Croftwood Court. When Archie helped out with the festival last year, it was the first time most of us had met him and it's really stupid, but I suppose it's a bit like meeting a royal.'

'It's not stupid at all. From what I gather, Archie's parents' generation kind of encouraged that. I think the circles they moved in were so far removed from Croftwood, it wasn't like they were popping into the local pub for a drink. But it's different now. Archie doesn't do anything like that and

Constance seems to be embracing what the town has to offer.'

'That's true. And that's since the festival. She had the time of her life that weekend,' Steph said, grinning. 'I bet she'll insist on having a yurt this year.'

'Mmm. Once she realises it's basically camping, I doubt it.'

'Perhaps you'll have to hire an Airstream then?'

'I'll let Constance have the Airstream to herself and Archie and I will have a yurt.' The thought of bunking in with Constance was a step too far.

'How about you? Will you go again this year?'

'Definitely. Tom and I did normal camping. It was brilliant. Seb arranged an area so we could all camp together, so there was him and Jess, Oliver and Lois, Toby and Hilary, and Patsy, Matt and the kids. In fact, I think Toby and Hilary might have got together that weekend. Even Bill and Eunice came, but they shared a camper van with a couple from one of my mobile library stops.'

'It sounds amazing, I can't wait.'

'We even had Ned Nokes in our camp. He's friends with Seb's cousin, I think. Something like that anyway.'

'Who's Seb's cousin?'

'You know FL Thorne?'

'I love her books!' said Nora. 'They make me want to visit Iceland.'

'Fliss is Seb's cousin. She did an author Q and A for the festival.'

'I hope it's just as good this year,' said Nora, thinking that she couldn't believe she'd missed out on last summer's, despite not knowing Croftwood existed then.

'Hey, Jess. Tell Nora about the plans for the festival,' Steph said as Jess, Lois, Patsy and Hilary came over to join them now that everyone had finished their book dates.

'It's so hard to keep track,' Jess said. 'Seb's talking non-stop about it but it's hard to keep track of what's happening and what are just ideas.'

'He's booked Melody Farmer,' Hilary said. 'He put it on WhatsApp this afternoon.'

'No way!' Patsy said. 'I love Melody Farmer. We'll have no trouble selling tickets with her as the headliner.'

'I've been talking to Daisy Bailey's agent,' said Lois. 'Fingers crossed she's willing to do a Q and A and a book signing. And she has a new book out a couple of weeks before the festival so I'm hoping we can have that as one of the date-with-a-book choices.'

'You actually do the club at the festival?' Nora asked.

'We try,' Lois said. 'It was a minor miracle that it worked, but it did. As much as Rosemary might drive me mad, she's brilliant at that kind of planning.'

Nora could see Constance and Penny putting their coats on and stood up. 'Thanks for the date, Steph, I really enjoyed it.'

'You're not going already?' Hilary said.

'She's Constance and Penny's taxi tonight,' Steph said.

'Oh, right,' Hilary said, with a knowing smile.

'Shut up,' Nora said good-naturedly. She loved that she was beginning to feel comfortable with these people.

Hilary grinned. 'See you at the lake.'

'Are you actually going in this week?' Nora teased.

'If she doesn't, I'm pushing her in,' said Patsy, making everyone laugh.

21

The wedding in Dorset came around more quickly than Nora had expected. Now that all the women in the friendship group were meeting at the lake on a Thursday, it would be hard to avoid talking about it. And as far as Jess knew, it was only Nora and Archie making the trip to Dorset with them.

After dressing and grabbing her things, Nora headed to the lake. In the past week, the temperatures had started to rise, so she knew that the water would be perhaps as much as a couple of degrees warmer for her friends since the last time they swam.

Jess was already there, and had lit the fire pit and set the chairs out around it.

'Morning!' Nora called as she clambered over the wall.

'Hey, Nora. Beautiful day for a swim.'

'The best kind of day,' Nora agreed. 'Are you all set for the trip?' she asked Jess.

'Pretty much. I've got my dress sorted. That's the main thing. There's not much else to sort. I'll go shopping with Mum tomorrow and get some food for the do back at their house and that's about it.'

Nora knew Jess would be thrilled if she knew everyone was going to be there and that Seb had actually arranged a party at her parent's local pub, but she wasn't about to spoil the surprise. 'We're so looking forward to it. Archie's chuffed to bits to be Seb's best man.'

'At least he doesn't need to bother with a speech,' said Jess, grinning.

'True!' In fact, Archie had been working hard on a speech, having been tipped off by Seb that Jess's dad was making one. He didn't want to let Seb down by being unprepared.

It was a blue-skied spring morning. Although Archie's gardeners had cleared a lot of the growth around the lake, grasses and reeds had come to life on the banks and it was looking much more picturesque.

Now that the hedge had been removed, they could see the others coming over the wall along with a couple of other women Nora didn't recognise.

'Who's that?' Jess asked, frowning, presumably not recognising them either.

'Hey guys, this is Lou and Sam. We found them lurking in the lay-by,' said Patsy.

The women laughed. 'My husband Ben works for the council. He met Nora last week and said we could come along?'

'I'm Nora. I'm so glad you came.'

'I'm Lou,' said Ben's wife. 'We usually swim on the other side of Worcester so this is a real treat. What do we do about paying?'

'Oh, no. We're not charging anything,' said Nora. 'If anything, we're the guinea pigs for whether this will even work.'

'Well, it's beautiful,' said Sam. 'Far prettier than where we swim now.'

They all set about getting ready to swim. Hilary was very quiet, which Nora took to mean she was nervous.

'Are you worried about swimming?' she said to her

quietly.

'I know the thought of it is so much worse than it will actually be,' said Hilary. 'But I really don't want a fish to touch me.'

Nora tried not to laugh. 'I can't count the number of times I've swum in here now, and I've never been touched by a fish. I've seen a couple but only at a distance.'

'That's reassuring, thank you,' Hilary said, looking anything but reassured.

'Come on, let's get in together,' said Nora. Patsy and Lois were already in and happily chatting as they swam side by side. Sam and Lou were easing themselves in off the dock, and Jess was already around the other side of the island.

Hilary started rolling her shoulders and exhaling as if she was about to do a race in the Olympics. 'Let's get it over with.'

Nora lowered herself in from the dock and stood, water lapping at her waist, waiting as Hilary did the same.

'It's not as cold as I expected,' she said, surprised.

'I think you've been smart to hang back for a couple of weeks. It's warmed up a bit since the others started.'

'See? Method in my madness,' Hilary said laughing. She looked a lot more relaxed now.

'Wave your wrists in the water. It'll help you acclimatise before you dip down.'

'Christ, it doesn't feel quite as balmy now.'

'You'll be fine,' said Nora, dipping down into the water so that her shoulders were under the surface.

Hilary seemed to be psyching herself up, then without warning, she dipped straight in and began treading water, even though they were still in the relative shallows. 'I think it's easier if I'm actually swimming. Can we go?'

'Yes.' Nora said, grinning, and pleased that Hilary was breathing normally already. If she was gasping from the cold shock, Nora would have made her stay near the dock until she'd acclimatised a bit more. 'You should be pleased with yourself, Hilary.'

'I am quite pleased,' Hilary said, swimming beside her looking extremely chuffed. 'What was I scared of? It's wonderful.'

'Are you bringing your kit to Dorset?' Nora asked her as they swam together, out of earshot of Jess.

'Absolutely not. I'm planning on a romantic weekend away and this look is not sexy.'

Nora laughed. 'Fair enough. I'm hoping to tempt Archie into the sea. We've booked a place right on the beach.'

'If anyone can persuade him, it's you. If you'd told me I'd be in a lake in the middle of March, I'd never have believed you. And now look at me. Invincible.' It had taken two thermal rash vests, thermal leggings and a full wetsuit before she'd taken the plunge, but she sounded more evangelical about the lake than any of them now.

To prepare for going to Dorset, Nora had spent the past week finishing two overseas orders so that she could take the following week off. The experiments with the new range were still ongoing after a less than successful firing. Neil had given her several notes, as if she didn't know that the thickness of the clay hadn't been uniform enough. Still, she was going to persist, and she was going to win. Because that was part of the fun of pottery. The challenges and frustrations made the triumphs and successes feel amazing. And knowing that was where the joy lay for Nora.

Archie had stayed at the Court the night before they were due to leave for Dorset, so that he could dine and spend the evening with Constance. That suited Nora, who was keen for some time alone ahead of spending a whole five days with Archie.

But it had surprised her how she'd become used to

spending every night together, to the point where she felt the gaping void in her bed that night. She missed him and it was nice to have had the chance to notice that, even if it was unsettling. How had she gone from independent to this in only two months? And was it something she should be worried about?

By the time Archie came to collect her later that morning, Nora was well and truly chilled-out and ready for their break. She'd stayed at the lake, chatting around the fire-pit with everyone, until they drifted off bit by bit to go to work or whatever else they were doing. Nora had come home, finalised her packing, enjoying the fact that she wasn't in a rush. She added in a couple of extra things that had been delivered the day before and were a surprise for Archie for when they were in Dorset.

'Your carriage awaits!' Archie called as he let himself in. 'I'll take your luggage out.'

Nora slurped the last of her tea, rinsed the mug and left it on the drainer, then pulled her boots on and grabbed her bag and coat.

'Ready,' she announced when Archie reappeared at the door. 'You look very dashing,' she said, taking in his smart navy wool jumper and new chinos.

'I thought I ought to dress the part. You've brought quite a bit of luggage for a short trip,' he said, smiling, with an eyebrow raised. 'Do you think we'll fit it all in?'

'I've packed for every eventuality,' she said. In fact, she'd usually pack lighter, but the surprise she had planned for Archie took up quite a bit of room and necessitated an extra holdall.

'I have packed exactly what I plan to wear. Nothing more, nothing less.'

'And what happens if you spill something down yourself?' Nora asked, climbing into the car while Archie held the door open for her.

He shrugged. 'That'll be my hard luck.'

Now that they were underway, Nora was excited. It felt like a real adventure, and being with Archie, away from Croftwood was wonderful. He quickly relaxed, almost visibly. Nora loved watching him drive. The age of the car made her feel like they were in a vintage film and it felt so romantic dashing down to Dorset together for a wedding.

'This is our first holiday together,' she said, feeling as if it was a landmark moment.

He smiled, his eyes crinkling at the corners, making Nora's stomach clench. Her heart was so full. This gentle, kind, beautiful man was making her fall in love with him, and she was ready for it. Falling in love again hadn't seemed like a possibility and certainly wasn't part of her plan. But that was part of what made it so special. The fact that it had happened despite her.

Dorset was playing ball. The sun was shining, even though the wind was still chilly, and as they caught their first glimpse of the sea, it glistened in the most inviting way.

'Oh look! I can't wait to swim in there,' Nora said.

'First things first. Have you got the directions ready? We're almost in Swanage.'

The place Nora had found was off the beaten track and the owner had sent them directions since map apps didn't tend to work very well once you got close.

'Got them.' Nora found the email on her phone. 'Take the turning on the left here. And now slow down because we're turning here.'

She leaned forward and pointed to a road which was little more than a wide path, bordered on either side by hedges. Archie turned in and then stopped the car.

'I don't fancy meeting something coming the other way,' he said. 'Are you sure this is right?'

'Definitely. The directions literally say you need to trust that it's the right way and the road opens out very quickly.'

'Mmm. I hope that's true,' Archie said doubtfully. But he carried on very slowly, and the road did indeed open out. Ahead of them, as they rounded a last corner, a small cove bordered by trees came into view.

'It's exactly like it looked online!' Nora said. 'And look at the little cabin! It's perfect.'

She looked at Archie who was delighting in her excitement. He pulled the car up in the parking spot behind the cabin and came round to let her out.

'It is a rather spectacular spot,' he said. They took the luggage out of the car and went inside the cabin. It was exactly as Nora had hoped. Cosy, with an open fireplace so they could snuggle up and get warm again after a refreshing dip. The host had left a welcome basket for them, which included a bottle of champagne that had been chilling in the fridge.

'Let's take this outside,' said Nora. Archie picked up the glasses that had been thoughtfully left on the side and headed outside to where a tiny patio with a bistro table and two chairs looked out over the beautiful view of the sea.

'This is just about as perfect a spot as I can imagine,' he said, popping the cork on the champagne and pouring it. 'To our first holiday,' he said.

'Our first holiday.'

It wasn't long before the call of the sea could no longer be ignored. Before she would let Archie pour a second glass for each of them, she insisted they take a dip.

Nora opened her holdall and pulled out her dry robe. Then she reached in and pulled out another dry robe. This one was green camouflage with a black fleece lining. A masculine version of her own green one that had pink inside.

'I bought this for you,' she said, handing it to Archie.

He took it from her, but looked unsure. She knew his good manners were ingrained enough that he wouldn't be able to reject the gift. But whether it was enough to entice him into the sea, she wasn't sure.

'You could paddle and see how it goes,' she suggested. 'Going in from the shore is so different to plunging into the lake at home. It gives you chance to take your time and get used to the water. And we can do it together.'

'Alright. I'll come in with you. But not until I've got the fire going.'

Nora threw her arms around his neck. 'Thank you.'

There was a substantial log pile around the side of the cabin. Archie carried an armful inside. There was a basket of kindling next to the chimney breast and a fancy jar of matches. He laid the kindling in the grate and took a match to it. It lit easily, so he piled some of the smaller logs on top, staring into the flames and enjoying the feeling of warmth that seeped into the cabin. Once the kindling was glowing, he placed several of the smaller logs on top and was satisfied that the fire was lit.

'Come on then. Let's go,' he said.

The shingle shore sloped away from the cabin, and it was only about twenty metres to the water's edge. Once they got there, Archie could see how clear the water was. Since it was a still day and there were no real waves, the bottom was visible for as far as he could see. Very different to the lake at home and, he realised, part of the reason he didn't find it appealing. This was much better. At least you could see what you were getting into.

He grabbed her hand and before he talked himself out of it ran into the water.

'Good grief!' The water was colder than he could have imagined and it literally took his breath away.

'Stop!' Nora said. 'You need to go slower to let your body

adjust.'

'My body is never going to adjust to this,' he gasped.

'It will.'

Nora looked entirely at ease in the freezing water, which was up to their thighs. Archie wasn't sure he could even feel his thighs anymore.

'Okay?'

He nodded, noticing that his breathing was back to normal.

'Ready to go a bit further?'

He rolled his eyes and laughed. 'At what point is it supposed to feel as wonderful as you make it out to be?'

'Not yet. This is the hard part.'

'You're telling me.'

Holding hands still, they waded further in, Archie continuing to gasp as the cold water rose up his body, until they were almost chest deep.

'Right, let's dunk our shoulders in,' Nora said.

Thinking it was best to get it over with, to get to the point of it being wonderful as quickly as possible, Archie dunked in.

'Yes! You've done it!'

Swimming helped. It almost felt as if he was swimming away from the cold, and after a minute or so, he actually felt warmer.

'You're enjoying yourself,' Nora said, grinning at him.

'I am.' He felt stupidly pleased with himself. Almost euphoric. And he wondered what had been holding him back from doing it before.

Late that evening after they'd eaten, and after Archie had made love to her, Nora lay in his arms.

'I love you,' he murmured into her ear.

Nora turned to face him.

'It's too soon isn't it,' he said, looking wounded.

'No, it isn't. I love you too.'

'It scares me that I can't imagine my life without you. Already.'

Nora cupped his cheek with her hand. 'I feel like that too. I missed you last night. It took me by surprise.'

Archie laughed softly. 'I wish things were different. I wish I could offer you more.'

'No. Things are perfect. I don't need anything except you. We're both too old to come into a relationship with no baggage. And while I might not be living with my mother, I do have a very needy business and a hangover from my last relationship that means I will probably always want to keep my cottage.'

'And you should. I would never ask you to give anything up.'

'And I wouldn't ask that either.' She paused and idly circled a finger on his breastbone. 'Do you think it's ridiculous to carry on like this? Living in each other's houses?'

'As far as I know, there are no hard and fast rules that say what a relationship looks like. Look at Hilary and Toby, they're making it work. If it makes us happy to arrange our lives like this, who is anyone to tell us that's wrong?'

'And you think Constance will go along with that?'

'I may live with my mother, but I'm my own man.'

Nora stifled a laugh. 'I love that you think that.'

Archie pretended to be affronted but couldn't help grinning. 'I suppose sneaking into my own house after spending the night with you doesn't make me seem particularly masterful.'

'I think you're very masterful. Just scared of your mother and Mrs Milton.'

'That's a fair assessment. But I have told Mother that where our relationship is heading is no one's business but ours.'

'Thank you. I like your mother, Archie, you know that. But I do worry that she's putting pressure on you to…I don't know, make some kind of commitment that I don't think either of us want.'

'Well, you mustn't worry,' he said, tightening his arms around her. 'Things are perfect just as they are.'

22

The day of Jess and Seb's wedding dawned bright and sunny. Nora had been out for a swim as the sun rose while Archie had coaxed the fire back to life and made some breakfast. She didn't mind that he wanted to sit this one out; she'd been more than happy that he'd at least tried it the day before and didn't want to push her luck.

The ceremony was at eleven o'clock, and they'd booked a taxi, which picked them up at the end of the lane that led to the cabin and took them to Swanage where they'd arranged to meet the others outside the registry office. Nora was wearing one of her favourite summer dresses, which was long, so a little warmer, and had paired it with white trainers and a cardigan with elbow length frilled sleeves. She'd left her hair down, and it fell in waves around her shoulders. Archie had been intent on wearing a suit, but she'd persuaded him it was better to be less formal, so he was wearing some new chinos and the jacket that Constance had bought him along with the shirt Jess had made, which felt right.

The Town Hall was a pale stone building with an ornate doorway. It was right on the street, so the taxi pulled up at the door. Patsy and Matt were already there, and Lois and

Oliver were walking up the road as Archie and Nora arrived.

'Morning! What a fine day for a wedding,' said Oliver as the men shook hands with each other.

'No sign of Hilary and Toby yet?' Nora asked Lois.

'No. I think they're staying at the pub where the reception is. Penny and her husband are there too, so I guess they'll come together.'

Another taxi pulled up and deposited the final four guests outside the Town Hall.

'I thought we were going to be late,' Penny said, looking flustered. 'I had to pick up the buttonholes from the florist on the way. Here you are.' She handed out yellow roses with pretty pink edges to the petals to the men. Nora helped Archie with his.

'This is my husband, Paul,' said Penny, introducing him to everyone. 'We'd better get inside or we'll be stood out here when they arrive.'

Archie and Nora stayed behind, since Jess and Seb were expecting to find them there, while everyone else went in.

'I feel nervous,' said Archie, rolling his shoulders. 'I wonder how Seb's feeling?'

'I'm sure he's taking it in his stride. I bet he's looking forward to Jess realising everyone's here.'

'This is the kind of wedding I'd have wanted,' said Archie. 'There's something so elegant about it being a simple ceremony with only the people who really matter.'

'I always thought I'd have eloped,' said Nora. 'Julian and I talked about it a couple of times, and it seemed romantic until I realised the romance is in the spontaneity of it and talking about it in advance ruins it.'

Archie laughed. 'My mother would have had a fit if I'd eloped. Before Clarissa broke things off we were on course for the wedding of the century. Would have cost a fortune.'

'Just as well we're past all that sort of thing then.' She

wrapped his arm in hers and rested her head on his shoulder.

'Things are perfect as they are,' he agreed, dropping a kiss on the top of her head. 'Oh, look, the groom's here.'

Seb and an older man, presumably his father, were striding down the road together. They were both wearing sunglasses. Seb had a big grin on his face and looked anything but nervous.

'Arch! You remember my father, Charles.'

'Good to see you again, Archie,' said Charles, shaking hands with Archie.

'You too, sir. This is Nora Hartford.'

'Lovely to meet you, Nora.'

'You two look very dashing,' she said. 'I love the sunglasses. It makes you look like the Blues Brothers.'

Seb guffawed and took his sunglasses off, putting them in his inside pocket. 'We had a couple of whiskies last night. The sun's not our friend this morning.'

'Come on, son. We ought to get inside before your bride arrives.'

The four of them went inside where everyone else was waiting, already seated. Seb and Archie walked to the front where they had a word with the woman officiating before they took their seats in the front row. Nora sat behind them with Charles.

It wasn't long before the music started and Jess walked down the aisle with her mum and dad on either side of her. Her dress was simple yet beautifully elegant. It was made of the most delicate cream tulle that was embroidered with tiny flowers. The bodice was a fitted princess line with a neckline that skimmed Jess's collarbones, and a skirt that flared from the waist to a ballerina length. Her hair was gathered into a chignon and a simple rose that matched the ones the men wore was nestled in it. She took Nora's breath away.

Jess was beyond thrilled to see everyone, the surprise clear on her face, her eyes watering as she walked down the centre of the room, seeing all of their friends there to share their happiest day.

The ceremony was short and sweet and very traditional. When Seb was making his vows, Archie looked for Nora and winked at her. Her stomach flipped and she wondered whether there was something in the idea of getting married after all. Saying these vows to each other in front of everyone, well perhaps that was the ultimate way to show that you loved someone? Perhaps when you were so in love with someone, you simply had to let it out, and this was the best way?

They gathered in the foyer of the Town Hall afterwards, everyone chatting and laughing.

'Come on, you lot,' Jess's dad, Joe, called out. 'The carriages await outside!'

'What? I thought we were getting a taxi back to your house?' Jess said.

They all went outside and found two vintage VW campers waiting for them. One was orange and the other was blue and they were decked out with bunting in the windows. Everyone piled in, finding plastic champagne flutes and ice buckets of bubbly waiting inside.

'Charge your glasses for the journey!' Joe instructed. 'See you on the other side!'

The VW campers took them back to Corfe Bay, the village where Jess had grown up and where her parents still lived. Having thought that the reception was a bite to eat at her parents' house with Archie, Nora and Charles, it was a wonderful surprise to find that her new husband had organised a proper party in the function room in the village pub.

Nora was feeling tipsy and in the mood to be romantic with Archie but the perils of being the partner of the best man, even at a relatively informal wedding, were that he had a lot of things to do. And Archie, well-practiced in etiquette and with his excellent manners, was being the consummate host on behalf of the happy couple. The numbers swelled as friends of Jess's and her parents from the village arrived for the evening do.

'Speech!' People began to heckle Joe. 'Come on! Father of the Bride, let's hear it!'

Joe raised his pint and grinned while Jess's mum, Clare, smiled and rolled her eyes. His speech was lovely and brought a tear to everyone's eye when he mentioned Jess's first love, Jon, and how proud they were that Jess had got through her grief and found Seb.

'Clare and I, we love Seb like he's our own kid. He looks after Jess, lets her flourish, loves and supports her. And as we know,' he said, hugging his wife to his side, 'That's the most important thing. To Seb and Jess, Mr and Mrs Thorne!'

'Mr and Mrs Thorne!'

'Right, I'm up,' said Archie, taking his speech from his breast pocket and making his way over to Joe and Clare.

'Sebastian and I haven't been friends for very long, so I'm unable to regale you with tales of his teenage misdemeanours.'

'Thank god!' Shouted Charles, making everyone laugh.

'But what I can do is vouch for him as an excellent friend.' Archie went on to tell everyone about the summer before when they'd worked on the Croftwood Festival together and how much fun it had been, but how hard Seb had worked to use it as a way to turn his life around. 'He gives his all to everything he does, and I'm sure his marriage will be no exception. Seb and I met at about the same time he met Jess and it's been wonderful to see their relationship grow and strengthen. They deserve every happiness. Please raise your glass with me to toast their enduring love.'

As everyone chorused the toast, Nora found her eyes watering. Her heart was filled with so much love, it was almost overwhelming. Because of the wedding — the love in the room was incredible; because Archie was being an amazing best man but perhaps just because she was letting herself be open to the idea that love was wonderful and to let it pass her by would be the worst mistake she could ever make.

After Julian, she'd never thought she'd find love again but now, the way she felt about Archie made her realise that it had barely been love with Julian at all. She'd never had this feeling of being overwhelmed by the way she felt about someone. She'd thought it was a bit like the Emperor's New Clothes when people banged on about how in love they were as if it were some kind of magical state that was different and special compared to what she thought love was. But this was different and very special and okay, she might not be about to suggest that they needed to get married, but she was certain now that her future lay with Archie.

The party was like an old school disco. There were some floor fillers and crowd pleasers before it finished off with a few slow dances. It was the first chance Nora'd had to grab Archie since the speeches and she cherished every second of having him pressed up against her. He had his hand on the small of her back and his other hand held hers to his chest as they swayed together to Tony Bennett singing The Way You Look Tonight. Archie began softly singing the words into Nora's ear and she thought her knees might give way with the romance of it all. She felt as if he was sweeping her off her feet, right here in a Dorset pub.

Before she could suggest that it might be a good time to leave, the song ended and Joe announced that Jess and Seb would be leaving. Everyone flooded out to the front of the pub to wave them off as they were chauffeured away to a hotel back in Swanage by the orange VW camper.

'What a wonderful day,' Nora said.

'Fantastic,' Archie agreed. 'Come on, let's grab one of those taxis before everyone else decides to.'

He saw Nora into the back of a taxi and then dived back into the pub to collect his jacket, then got waylaid saying goodbye to Jess's parents.

'I've promised we'll be at their house for a fry-up at eleven in the morning,' he said as he climbed into the back seat next to her.

'That's okay. We've got plenty of time until then,' Nora said, leaning against him and closing her eyes for a moment.

The next thing she knew, Archie was trying to make her get out of the taxi when she was so comfortable and they couldn't possibly be back at the cabin already.

'Come on, sleepyhead,' he said, sweeping her into his arms as soon as she'd stood up.

That was enough to wake her up. 'Don't carry me! You'll hurt yourself!'

She was awake now, but he seemed compelled to see the chivalry through. 'I'm trying to be romantic,' he said, although he sounded out of breath. 'Can you reach the key? It's in my right trouser pocket.'

'Archie, put me down.'

'Not on your life.'

She felt for his pocket and he held her closer to him. She could feel his breath against her neck.

'Got them,' she said, managing to open the door as Archie burst through, then kicked it closed behind him before he headed for the bed.

'I've waited all day for this,' she said as he laid her down, slightly less elegantly than he'd picked her up. 'And you carried me in here. So masterful…' She pulled him towards her by his lapels. He gave a low laugh, straddled her and took his jacket off followed by his tie.

When she'd first seen Archie from across the lake, it had never seemed possible that she might ever think he was sexy but now, he exuded it.

'I feel like you've been teasing me all day,' she said. 'Keeping me just at arm's length enough to make me wild with desire.'

He chuckled. 'Really? Wild? Show me how much you wanted me.'

Nora grinned wide-eyed, loving that he was playing along. It was so out of character, it only turned her on more. She slowly unbuttoned his shirt to his navel.

'Roll up your sleeves like you mean business.'

'Oh, I do mean business,' he said, sitting back on his haunches while he stared her right in the eye and rolled his sleeves up to mid-forearm.

Nora thought she might melt right there on the bed. Then Archie took charge and did things to her that she never would have imagined he'd even know how to. And she knew then, what she'd suspected for the whole day; Archie was it for her. No matter how the differences between them might need to be overcome, she would do whatever it took and she knew he would too. They had a connection that went beyond everything else and Nora wasn't about to let that go.

23

Spending five days together had left Nora wanting more. It had been heaven. She felt as if they'd transcended how things had been before they went to Dorset, coming back to Croftwood with their relationship in a completely different place.

That morning, when she'd arrived at the lake for a swim, she found Archie waiting for her. He was sitting on the dock wearing his dry robe as if he was a regular. It touched Nora's heart that he'd really meant it when he said he was a convert to wild-swimming.

'I missed you last night,' she said, sitting down next to him and leaning in for a kiss.

'I'll come to you tonight,' he said.

'You sound like someone from a Regency romance. I like it.'

'Good,' he said, kissing her and running his hand underneath her robe.

'Hey. Someone might see.' Nora pushed his hand away.

'Spoilsport.'

She kissed him, then stood up and undressed. Archie sighed as he followed suit.

'Are you worried about going in?'

'It's not the same as the sea. I liked the gentle shore. This feels like all or nothing in comparison.'

'It'll be better when the steps are in.' They'd commissioned a joiner to make steps into the water and a Monet-style bridge to link the island to the shore.

'Perhaps, but it doesn't help me today.'

'You don't have to come in,' Nora reasoned, although she knew that would be exactly the thing to say to make him think he had to.

'No. I want to. I ought to have first-hand experience of my own lake if I'm asking other people to swim in it.'

Nora lowered herself off the dock first and waited for Archie. 'It's not as cold as the sea, if that helps?'

He grimaced as he lowered himself in. 'Liar.' But once they started swimming, he relaxed and seemed as happy as he'd been in Dorset.

'It's rather wonderful, actually, swimming in one's own lake.'

'How much land do you have?'

'Not as much as we used to. Around fifty thousand acres all told.'

Nora had no idea how much that was, but it sounded a lot.

'My father sold off some of the farmland in the nineteen-eighties, so there are pockets of our land all around Croftwood. It's not all surrounding the house. And obviously we have the arrangement with the trust for the majority of it.'

It struck Nora how odd it was that a family could be so rich in assets and yet be struggling to make ends meet. It wasn't as if they led a flamboyant lifestyle. Archie and Constance lived nothing like the way most people might assume, given the scale of the estate.

'Are you feeling cold?' Nora asked once they had done one loop of the island.

'No, but I'm going to get out while the going's good,' he

said. 'I've enjoyed it.'

They climbed out together and raced to dry and put their robes on. Now that they were entirely comfortable with each other, they both stripped off without worrying about modesty, which made getting warm and dry much easier and quicker.

'I should have lit the fire-pit,' Archie said. He pulled the hood up on his robe and shoved his hands in the deep pockets. 'It's really not the same when there's no log fire waiting for you.'

'That's why Seb suggested the Finnish hut. It's much better than the fire-pit, especially when the weather's bad. It's one thing swimming in the rain, but it's much harder to get warm afterwards.'

'What are you doing today, my love?' Archie asked, taking her in his arms as soon as she'd zipped her robe.

'I'm going to Stoke. I've been desperate to see how my new pots have fired. I could just text Neil, but I'd like to catch up on things with Val. How about you?'

'I've got nothing pressing on. Could I come with you? I'd love to see where you work.'

'I'd love that!' Val would love it more, Nora thought. 'I'll come and pick you up as soon as I've showered.'

She was so excited. It hadn't occurred to her that Archie might be interested in visiting the pottery, but she was thrilled that he was. And she also knew that while she faffed around with her pots and caught up with Val, he'd be quite happy. In fact, she might even get him on the wheel.

'Are you sure you're ready for this?' They were just about to go into the pottery. 'Everyone's eyes are going to be out on stalks.'

Archie took her hand. 'I'm ready for anything,' he said, grinning.

'Tell me that again in a couple of hours.'

Nora's first stop was the room next door to the kiln, where Neil would have put her pots. If they'd survived the firing.

'Oh, yes!' Nora said, picking one up and feeling the weight of it. 'They're okay.' There were one or two missing, probably amongst the first ones she'd tried, but considering she'd been concentrating more on the form than the construction, she was pleased.

'How are you going to decorate them?' Archie asked.

'I'm not sure yet. I don't know whether to paint a design on them or let a clever glaze do the work. I was channelling the regency period and if I'm true to that, they would have had a fairly intricate design on them. But that's not really me. If it's going to be my new collection, it needs to look like it's mine. You know?'

'I do,' he said, nodding. 'May I?'

'Of course.'

Archie picked up one of the more robust looking pots. 'I can't help but be reminded of some of the pieces we have at home.'

'I did make these the day after I'd been to yours for the first time. It was inspiring, and actually, the vase that you're auctioning, that kind of thing isn't my vibe. But I loved some of the less showy crockery. Beautiful things you can use every day.'

'Nora! Back from the wilds of Dorset.' Val came into the room, not noticing Archie at first since the door hid him. 'Oh. Hello.' Her eyes darted from Archie to Nora.

'Val, this is Archie. Archie, Val is the production manager.'

'Very pleased to meet you, sir,' said Val.

'No, don't call him sir, Val. It's fine,' said Nora.

'Please. Call me Archie. It's lovely to meet you.'

Val was uncharacteristically silent. Nora knew it's because she'd been set on getting the low down about the wedding and their mini-break and couldn't think what to say instead.

'I wanted to chat to Mel about glaze for these new pots,' said Nora. 'Have you got time to give Archie a quick tour of the pottery while I do that? Then we're going to do some throwing.'

'Oh, are you a potter, Archie?' Val asked.

'Not at all. This is the first I've heard about it, but I've always wanted a go.'

'As long as it doesn't turn into the scene from Ghost,' Val said, laughing. 'Right, come on then.'

Mel was the person who knew the most about glazing and finishing out of everyone who worked at the pottery, and although Nora did all the finishing and glazing on her bespoke collections herself, it was brilliant to have an expert like Mel on hand for advice. By the time Nora had settled on a couple of different treatments she might try, Val had delivered Archie back to her.

'It's an incredible operation,' he said to Nora. 'Impressive to say the least.'

'Thank you. I've got an incredible team,' she said, grinning at Val.

'Come and find me before you go,' Val said. 'Good luck with the throwing,' she said to Archie. 'You'll need it.'

Archie laughed. 'Oh. You're not joking,' he said, when he realised Nora and Val weren't joining in.

'I mean, you might be a natural,' said Nora. 'But it's unlikely.'

'People watch the pottery show on television and think it's easy,' said Val.

Archie looked at Nora, his eyes wide.

Once Nora had been through the basics with him, helping him throw a couple of simple pots, she left him to practise while she sat at the wheel next to him and began her own.

'It's fascinating watching you,' said Archie. His wheel was still, the lump of clay he was working on centred, but nothing else. 'I feel as if I'm using all my strength to keep the clay doing what I want, whereas you make it look effortless. As if it's bending to your slightest touch.'

Nora looked at him. She could see the admiration and love in his eyes, and it made her feel quite emotional. She stopped the wheel and wiped her eyes with the back of her hand.

'What's wrong?' Archie got up from his wheel and came over, hugging her awkwardly to avoid getting his clay-covered hands all over her.

'I'm going to sound sappy,' she sniffed.

'I've got no problem with sappy,' he said gently. 'Tell me.'

'It just means so much to me that you admire what I do. That you understand what all of this means to me and recognise what I've achieved. It hasn't been like that before.'

'You mean with Julian?' Archie exhaled. 'I may be speaking out of turn, but it astounds me that someone, especially in the same profession as you, can fail so spectacularly in supporting the person he loved.'

'Being with you has given me a new appreciation for what love really looks like.'

'Nora…'

'Really, Archie. My relationship with Julian was born of friendship and mutual interest. I know that now. And thank god I realised before I ended up spending the rest of my life with someone who didn't make me feel anything like as wonderful as you do.'

'I'm sorry. I am going to cover you with clay now,' said Archie, taking her cheeks in his hands and kissing her so thoroughly that she almost started crying again. 'I love you so much.'

'I love you too.'

He clasped his hands around hers and kissed them, getting clay on his own face too.

By the end of the afternoon, Nora had fed her urge to

perfect the pots for her new collection, and Archie had thrown six wonky but functional pots of his own.

'Come on, help me get all this in the drying room,' she said.

'You think these are worth drying?' he said, pointing to his board of pots.

'Of course. They're not perfect, but you enjoyed making them, right?'

He grinned. 'Loved it.'

'In which case, they are perfect.'

They washed their hands and Archie took a paper towel to Nora's face to get the clay off, then she did the same for him and they went to find Val before they headed home.

'I knew you two would get up to no good!' she said, picking a bit of dried clay out of Nora's hair.

'Shut up,' Nora said. 'That happens all the time.' She looked at Archie and grinned.

'I've got some more Christmas samples to run by you,' said Val.

'Oh fantastic! Let's see.'

Nora signed off on two new bauble designs and a couple of mugs.

'These are great,' said Archie. 'Could we buy some from you to sell at the Christmas market?'

'Of course,' said Nora. 'We can do mate's rates, can't we Val?'

Val raised an eyebrow and nodded. 'Would you be interested in a special design? A collaboration between Croftwood Court and Hart Pottery?'

'That's a brilliant idea!' said Nora. 'We could do some candlesticks based on the chimneys. I wonder if we could produce enough mugs to use them for the mulled wine and hot chocolate and give people the option to keep the mug?'

'Hold your horses,' said Val. 'That might be difficult. The

production schedule is almost full. We can manage some baubles, but a load of mugs might be tricky to fit in.'

'We can bear it in mind for next year,' Nora said. 'The baubles would be a good start. We'll send over some design ideas and we can get some mock-ups done.'

'Wow. Easy as that,' said Archie.

'It's all about who you know,' said Val. 'And Nora has never been afraid to say yes. That's what makes Hart Pottery so successful. She champions ideas from everyone in the company and it keeps us innovative and morale is through the roof.'

'We're a team,' Nora said firmly. 'And you can't be a team unless everyone feels part of it.'

'I like the idea of collaborating,' said Archie on the drive back to Croftwood. 'It makes me wonder what else we could do.'

'You could do all sorts of things. We could try for a collab with a dry robe company. See if they'd do a limited run of robes in Croftwood lake colours that we could sell. We could talk to Jess about having some bespoke hats knitted.'

'We need a brand,' said Archie. 'For all of this, Croftwood Court needs a brand.'

'Don't you have a coat of arms or a family crest or something like that?'

'Of course, but it's rather dull. Who wants a stuffy old crest on a mug?'

Nora laughed. 'Exactly. But we can take elements of it to come up with a contemporary brand that you can use for anything. The lake, the Christmas market and anything else you end up doing.'

'I can't wait to get started,' said Archie. 'That's how you felt today, isn't it? Desperate to put your ideas for your new pots into action. It's like an itch that needs scratching.'

'Exactly. I can't keep my mind on anything else once that

feeling comes. It was all I could do to make myself go to the lake this morning instead of setting off for Stoke before dawn.'

Archie laughed. 'Well, I'm very pleased that you waited so I could go with you. It's been a wonderful day.' He reached over and patted her thigh.

'Are you going home for dinner first?'

'Not on your life. I'm taking you straight to bed.'

Nora giggled. She loved this side of Archie. The playful side he'd only recently revealed to her now that he had gained more confidence in their relationship. It was intoxicating knowing how he felt about her and feeling exactly the same way about him.

24

The following week, the Court was a hive of activity. After the excitement of the vase selling at auction for far more than even the auction house had predicted, the work to repair the roof was underway. It was still a patch-up job, but a thorough one that would last long enough to enable Archie to have a breather from worrying about leaks every time it rained for a few years. And hopefully by then, a couple of years of income from the lake and the Christmas market would be enough to fund a proper renovation of the roof. Unless a more urgent maintenance issue cropped up in the meantime, but that was old houses for you.

Seb had submitted the plans for the lake shortly after their meeting with Ben from the planning office. Ben had recommended the plans be approved, so they hoped it would be only a formality. Work had already started to reinstate the gateway and to clear an area for car parking between there and the little brick shed.

The removal of all the greenery that had been allowed to run riot made the area around that side of the lake feel bare and exposed, so the gardeners had suggested planting a living willow hedge that gave almost instant privacy and separated the lake from the car park quite nicely.

The Finnish hut had been delivered in pieces and was waiting until the planning permission was in place before being erected, as was the canopy that would extend out from the brick shed and act as a changing area.

'You know we were thinking about what to do with the island now that we're having the bridge made,' Seb said, when they strolled down to the lake to see how the hedging was coming along.

'To save Tatty having to swim across every day?' Archie joked. The dog still jumped in, swam, rested on the island and then swam back when Archie headed home.

'Yes, purely for the convenience of your dog,' Seb said, drily. 'Actually, I was thinking we could have the sauna over there.'

They'd applied for planning permission for everything they wanted to do now, but they'd do the work in phases, as funds allowed. The sauna was less important than the Finnish hut to begin with and at the moment, it had to be either or.

'That sounds pretty idyllic, a sauna on a little island.'

'It might help us police who's paid for the sauna on top of a swim. I don't know how, exactly but we can work it out.'

'Nora thinks we ought to have a lifeguard on the island because it'll give them a clear view of the entire lake. So I suppose they could check people across the bridge.'

'Sounds good to me.' Seb sat on the edge of the dock. It was the only one remaining now that the others had been taken out. They were trying to cut down on entry points into the water to make it easier to monitor who was in the water and how long they'd been in.

Archie sat down next to him, idly picking a piece of grass and tying it in knots.

'So you and Nora had a good time in Dorset?'

Archie grinned. 'We both loved it. Jess's family are wonderful. How was the honeymoon?'

'Bloody fantastic. I'm very lucky.' He and Jess had enjoyed a week in the Italian Lakes, a last-minute wedding gift from his father.

'Great that your father came.'

'That was completely unexpected. I think Clare and Joe had a hand in that. I had no idea until he rocked up at theirs the night before. Do you think you'll be next?'

'No. We've talked about it but neither of us want to change how things are,' said Archie. 'It's working for us.'

'Is Constance going to be happy with that? Because of your title?' Even though Seb's family life had imploded when his mother had died, before that he'd grown up in a privileged family, so he knew better than most the kinds of pressures Archie sometimes faced.

'I've explained it to her. I'm not sure she is happy, but what's the alternative? I'm not going to compromise to suit an outdated view of what might be expected of a lord. Even so, there's a lot of baggage that comes with me, not least the house, and it doesn't seem fair to ask Nora to take that on. It means a lot to her to have her independence and her own place. I can't see her ever wanting to live at Croftwood Court with me and Mama.'

'So what's the plan? You carry on like you are now? Living between places?'

'That's it exactly,' Archie said, grinning at his friend. 'And I feel very lucky to have it.'

'After that contract I did in Germany last year, I knew I couldn't bear to be away from Jess like that again. It was torture.'

'Slightly different for us. We see each other every day and spend most nights together. I think it's working.'

'Good for you, Arch. And I know it's not what you want, but I can't recommend being married highly enough.'

'Glad to hear it.'

'And you should talk to Nora properly. I'm not sure this is going to work as a long-term plan for you.'

Archie wasn't sure whether to be amused or affronted that Seb thought he might not have thought of any of this. 'What would I do without you?'

'I think you'd still be working up to asking Nora out for dinner for the first time,' Seb laughed.

Archie gave Seb a friendly shove. 'Careful. Although I admit, I couldn't have pulled it off without Andy the barber.'

'Lending you all my secrets, you see? But seriously, Archie. If what you have with Nora is anything like I feel about Jess, do whatever you can to keep it. I've never seen you happier.'

'You sound like my mother.'

'Constance knows what she's talking about,' said Seb. 'And she likes Nora from what I hear. That's not an easy battle to have won.'

'Nora seemed to have the measure of her from the start. It helped that they'd met at the book club before anything started between us.'

'At least they'd get on if Nora did move into the Court.'

'I'm not sure *I* would get on with that,' said Archie. The thought of living with his mother and Nora filled him with dread. Yes, the house was big enough that everyone could have their own space, but it would never feel like home to Nora in the way that her cosy little cottage did. She'd never be able to put her own stamp on it.

'You've got to go with what's right for you both,' Seb said. 'It'd be nice to have someone to share all of this with, though.'

'I'm not sure I'd have pursued the lake project were it not for Nora. But I can see what the attraction is now. I know it's not the same swimming in the sea as it is in the lake, but I have to say, I quite enjoyed it while we were in Dorset.'

'Jess had me in there on New Year's Day last year,' Seb said shivering. 'You won't get me in there, unless we're in the middle of a heatwave.'

'I need to get back and see how the roofers are getting on. They're going to try one of Nora's chimney pots up there today.'

'I still can't believe she can actually make stuff like that,' Seb said. 'There's got to be a way to make that into a money-spinner.'

'Yes, it's called Hart Pottery.' Archie said. 'I went to work with her last week. Honestly, Seb, it's incredible. It's a proper factory with a production line. Way beyond what I was expecting. Her factory manager suggested a collaboration. They're going to help us design a bespoke Croftwood Court Christmas bauble that we can sell at the market.'

'Now that's what I'm talking about!' Seb said, clapping Archie on the back as they began strolling back to the Court across the fields. 'I knew you'd find your entrepreneurial spirit eventually.'

Archie grinned and shook his head. 'Sometimes I wonder if you think you came up with the idea for the Croftwood Christmas market.'

Seb frowned. 'I thought that *was* my idea.'

Simon, the roofer, and the other two men in his team were working hard when Archie went up through the attics to check on the progress.

'How are you getting on?'

Simon stood up and put his hands on his hips. 'Not too bad. You've got some rotten roof timbers, so we'll get started on replacing the worst of them. We haven't found anything we weren't expecting, which is good news for you.'

'That is good news,' Archie said, finally feeling as if he was beginning to regain control over the parts of his life that had felt so overwhelming. Why, he wondered for the millionth time, hadn't he thought to try and sell something like the vase before? He could have saved himself so many sleepless nights.

'And we offered up your new chimney pots. They fit a treat. What we've done is swap a couple of the more ornate ones over so that the plain new ones are less visible.'

Because Nora had made the chimney pots, it seemed ungrateful to relegate them to somewhere they wouldn't be seen. But then, she had made them as an experiment and if she decided she wanted to embark on making more elaborate ones, they could give those pride of place. At least this way, there was no great rush if she decided not to.

'That's fantastic, thank you.'

'Bloody good pots, those are. The frost isn't likely to touch those in a hurry.'

'I must remember to pass on your praise to my potter. She'll be thrilled.'

'Seb let on that you're seeing Nora Hartford who runs Hart Pottery. I suppose that explains it,' Simon said with a smirk.

'It does,' Archie agreed, full of pride for Nora. He'd had very little experience of being proud of someone that he loved. Of course he was proud of his parents in the way that anyone would be; particularly of how his mother dealt with losing his father, picking herself up again and making a different life for herself. But the pride he felt for Nora was making his heart swell, and he was constantly surprised at how much he loved her. Surprised that it was possible to love anyone this much. And it felt quite marvellous, especially when he allowed himself to contemplate that she might just love him that much too.

'Archie!' Constance called him from across the landing as he was heading back outside. 'I've just had word that Betsy et al are arriving on Friday evening and will be spending the weekend.'

'Ah, right.' It was always with mixed feelings that Archie

welcomed his sister to the Court. Betsy was high maintenance and expected to be waited on hand and foot. He could already imagine Ursula's face when she found out. 'What's the occasion?'

'She wants to meet Nora and she's mentioned that she'd like to talk about the proceeds from the sale of the vase.'

Archie wanted to ask his mother how Betsy knew what the vase had fetched, but he suspected that she already knew she'd made a grave error in confiding about that to her youngest child.

'I am sorry, darling.' Constance looked devastated.

'No bother, Mama. There's very little to talk about since we've spent the money already.'

'I think she may be expecting something by way of a cut.'

'No. I shall explain to her that every penny has been spent on investing in the future of the estate, in one way or another. It's her family who will benefit from it, and I am very happy to remind her of that.'

'Oh, darling. I do enjoy this new commanding side of you. Being with Nora has given you a new confidence.'

He hoped that's what his sister would see rather than the weak, hopeless excuse of an older brother and head of the family that he'd been until a few months ago. Things were different now and he would make sure his sister understood that.

'It has,' he said, because he didn't mind crediting his relationship with Nora for the change in him. Even at the age of forty-one, he felt as if his life was just getting started again. 'I'd better make sure Nora's forewarned.'

'And you will be here over the weekend, won't you?'

'Of course. Don't worry about anything. I'll talk to Ursula and Mrs Milton and we'll arrange everything.' He walked over to Constance and kissed her cheek.

'Thank you.'

He called into the kitchen on his way back to the office and let Mrs Milton know that Betsy, Caspar and Florence would be staying for the weekend. Mrs Milton loved Betsy and doted on Florence so she was thrilled.

'I'll make some butterfly cakes for the little one,' she said. 'And I'd better ask Ursula to put the blackout blind over the nursery window.'

The last time they'd visited there had been terrible trouble getting Florence to sleep because the curtains didn't block out every tiny sliver of light and poor Ursula had been sent out to source a blackout blind, which fortunately had been available in Worcester. But Betsy had made Ursula feel personally responsible for the full moon daring to shine right outside the nursery window.

So it was no surprise that when Ursula found out Betsy was coming, she gave Archie the most sullen look she could summon.

'Oh lovely. Your sister is a delight. I'm so looking forward to it,' she said in a monotone voice, leaving Archie in no doubt about her feelings. He didn't blame her at all.

'I'm so sorry, Ursula. I will make it up to you somehow.' He'd love to promise her the spruce up her rooms so desperately needed, but even though selling the vase had taken the pressure off, they were a long way from any other revenue coming in, so he bit his tongue.

'You don't owe me anything, Archie. It's an absolute pleasure working here. And don't worry, I won't let on how much I detest your sister. Sorry,' she added, not looking it in the least.

'Perhaps Nora being around will encourage Betsy to be on her best behaviour.'

'We can but dream.'

When he was finally on his way to the estate office, Archie's phone buzzed with a text from Nora. She was in

Stoke today for the final firing of the test pieces of her new collection and she was throwing for a new bespoke order.

I'm feeling under the weather so going to stay here tonight. Back tomorrow xx

Rather than text back, to find out what was wrong, he called her.

'What's wrong? How are you feeling?'

'Disgusting. Sicky and tired. It's just a bug but I can't face driving back today.'

'You poor thing. Is there anything I can do?'

'No. Val's booked me a hotel so I'm going there now and I'll sleep it off. I'll call you tomorrow.'

She sounded tired and he didn't want to keep her. 'I love you. Take care of yourself.'

'Will do. Love you too.'

He'd hoped to talk to her about Betsy's visit. He wasn't sure whether it was too much to ask that she stay one of the nights at the weekend at the Court with him. He certainly couldn't disappear to Nora's house now that he'd promised his mother he'd be around but he hated the thought of being apart from Nora just when he needed her supporting influence to help him navigate the weekend with his difficult sister.

Still, she'd be back tomorrow and then they could spend the evening together before he would have to be back at the Court the following day to greet Betsy. It would all fall into place.

25

Waking up after a very sound night's sleep, Nora felt better. She was hungry but reluctant to eat, in case it made her feel sick again. She rang down to the hotel reception, organised a late check-out and then made herself a cup of tea and went back to bed, sipping the tea and nibbling on a biscuit while she watched some morning television.

After half an hour or so, she decided perhaps it would be best to drive back to Croftwood while she felt better. She called Val to let her know.

'If you've got a bug, it's always nicer to be in your own bed. Are you sure you're alright to drive?'

'Yes, I feel okay and I haven't been sick today.'

'That's a relief. I was half wondering whether you might be pregnant!' Val laughed.

Nora laughed too. 'Not much chance of that.'

'That's what you say, but you and the lord have been busy.'

It was true, but Nora had been on the pill for years and had never even had a scare. 'Thank god for reliable contraception, is what I say.'

'Look after yourself. Better still, get the lord to look after you. See you when you're better. Want me to get Neil to send pictures of your pots?'

'No, that's okay. It's more exciting seeing them in person.'

'I know. You're bonkers. I'd be desperate to know if they'd survived the kiln or not.'

'It's all part of the fun. Got to go.'

A wave of nausea hit and Nora ran to the bathroom, but then it passed. She shouldn't have eaten the biscuit. She went back to bed and, when she felt better, she made another cup of very sweet tea. It was a long time since she'd felt as rough as this, but then there had been lots of norovirus outbreaks reported on the news. Perhaps it was a mild version of that.

Playing it safe, she headed back to Croftwood on the A and B roads rather than the motorway, so that she could pull over if she felt ill. As it was, she made it back without any further episodes of nausea. But she felt exhausted and fell into bed as soon as she got back.

It was dark when she woke. She heard the front door open and then Archie called up the stairs.

'Come up!' she called, snuggling under the covers to wait for him.

'Oh, my love,' he said, sitting on the bed next to her, his hand automatically feeling her forehead for a fever. 'Are you still feeling poorly?'

'I feel okay, actually. I'm just a bit tired.'

'Have you eaten yet?'

'No, and I'm starving. Have you?'

He shook his head. 'I had a sandwich earlier. Mama's gone to her knitting circle tonight and they were having pizza delivered.'

'I can't imagine Constance tucking into pizza,' Nora giggled.

'Neither can I. Let me conjure up some food for us while you get up,' he said, patting the duvet in the general area of her arm. 'Unless you'd like a tray?'

'No. I'm getting up.' She pulled Archie down for a hug.

'I've missed you.'

'I've missed you too.'

'I miss being in Dorset together. I loved that so much.'

'I know.' He kissed her nose. Nora didn't blame him. She'd avoid a proper kiss too if she were him.

When Archie had disappeared back downstairs, she got up and pulled on some jogging bottoms, a voluminous hoody and her favourite pair of fluffy socks and ventured down after him.

'Have I got any food?' She sat at the kitchen table while Archie busied himself at the stove.

'Will beans and cheese on toast do?' he asked over his shoulder.

'Ooh, yes. Lovely.'

A few minutes later, Archie presented two plates of steaming hot beans on toast with grated cheese that was melting into the beans.

'I always forget how much I enjoy beans on toast,' said Nora. 'It's delicious.'

'Any plans for the weekend?'

'No, apart from hanging out with you. Maybe we could go out for brunch with Hilary and Toby.'

'Actually, I need to talk to you about the weekend. My sister and her family are coming to stay.'

'Oh, brilliant,' Nora said, smiling enthusiastically. 'Well, why don't we all go?' She'd been looking forward to meeting the elusive Betsy.

Archie shook his head. 'I don't think that's a good idea.'

'Why?'

'Because she's not like you. She won't fit in with what we've arranged. She'd want to change the plans to suit her and the whole thing would turn into a nightmare for all of us.'

Nora was surprised to hear Archie talk like this. As an only child, she'd always longed for a brother or sister and so found it odd when siblings didn't get on. He'd mentioned that his sister was high maintenance, but she'd thought he was joking.

'What do you usually do when she visits?'

'Survive.'

'Archie. It can't be that bad.'

He looked at her with a resigned expression. 'You'll see. She wants to meet you and Mama says she's keen to talk about the vase.'

'What about the vase?'

'I think she wants some of the money.'

'It's as good as spent, isn't it?'

'Yes, but I don't think Betsy will take that very well.'

Nora put her knife and fork down. 'I'm looking forward to meeting your sister. But I'm going to find it very difficult not to stick up for you if she starts demanding things like that. It's none of my business, I know that, but selling that vase hasn't added to the personal wealth of you or Constance and so Betsy shouldn't be expecting that for herself. You're using the money to enhance the assets that she may one day inherit.'

'I suppose she will feel that the vase belongs to the family,' Archie said weakly.

'It belongs to you. It's kind of you to consider the wishes of Constance and your sister, but at the end of the day, you're the one who inherited. And you are the one carrying the burden of the estate on your shoulders, not Betsy. So don't let her waltz in for the weekend and call the shots.' She'd gone too far. She was sure of it. It wasn't her place to tell Archie how to manage his family. She would never truly understand the position he was in, and she acknowledged that. But at the same time, it filled her with rage that his sister was so intent on material gain that she'd put that ahead of Archie's priorities, which in the main were preserving her family's legacy. 'I'm sorry,' she said. 'It's not my place to tell you how to deal with your sister, or anything else for that matter.'

Nora slipped onto Archie's lap for a cuddle.

'You're right, though. Everything you've said is absolutely right. And I want to tell her that, but it's so hard. I regress into being a pushover, unable to stand up for myself whenever I'm around her.'

'It's important to make her understand,' Nora said, trying to take the aggression out of her tone. 'It's too much for her to expect any more than she already has. You could threaten to start charging her a nominal rent for the London flat.'

Archie buried his head in Nora's shoulder and laughed. 'God. Are you trying to start a war?'

'No. As I said, nothing to do with me.' What was wrong with her? She couldn't let it go. 'I don't want to see you being railroaded into things by someone who's supposed to love you.'

'If you're there, perhaps she won't.'

'Are you planning to use me as a human shield against your sister?'

'Yes. Is that alright?'

'I'll do whatever I can to help. But it's probably best if I leave the talking to you.'

'Perhaps.' He kissed her nose again.

'Or maybe we'll get on like a house on fire and be best friends forever.'

The following day, Nora was still too under the weather to feel like swimming. Archie had stayed over and unusually, they had actually slept rather than talk late into the night or make love.

'Morning, my love. How are you today?' Archie said, setting a cup of tea down on the bedside table. 'I popped a teaspoon of sugar in there to give you a bit of a boost.'

'Thank you. It's ridiculous, but I still feel quite tired,' she said, yawning.

'Why don't you have your tea and then go back to sleep? I must go and see how the roofers are getting on. Oh, I forgot to tell you. The chimney pots fitted a treat. Simon the roofer was incredibly impressed. Look.'

He pulled his phone out and showed her a photo of the chimney pots in situ.

'Your chimneys are so beautiful. I'd love to go up and have a closer look sometime.'

'I can arrange that. Let's wait until the roofers have finished, though. You'll be feeling better by then.'

'I hope so.' She was desperate to get back to the pottery so she could concentrate on fulfilling her latest order.

'Look, there's no need for you to meet Betsy this time. I can make your apologies. Perhaps we'll go to London for a weekend instead.'

'No, I'll be fine later,' Nora said. She had been yesterday, and at least she wasn't feeling so sick anymore. 'I think I must have had a bug, and it's wiped me out. I want to come and hang out with you this weekend. And your sister.'

'Liar. But thank you from the bottom of my heart.'

Thankfully, by the time Nora and Archie got to the Court later on, Betsy and her family had not arrived. Constance was sitting in the drawing room perched on the edge of a sofa but craning her neck so that she could see the driveway.

'Archie, Nora. I'm so relieved you've arrived ahead of Betsy,' she said.

'I think we're all a little on edge,' said Archie, bending down to kiss her on the cheek.

'Is there anything I can do?' Nora asked.

'Ursula has it all in hand, but thank you for offering. How are you feeling? Archie said you've been under the weather.'

'Much better today, thanks,' Nora said, not sure it was true now that she'd had to go to the effort to get ready and leave the house. 'It was only a twenty-four-hour thing.'

'They're here, your Lordship,' Ursula said, popping her head around the door.

'Best foot forward, Mama,' Archie said, offering Constance his arm.

Nora followed them, finding it intriguing that they were both dreading the visit.

A huge black Range Rover had pulled up outside the front door. The passenger door opened and Betsy climbed out. Nora's first impression was that she was glossy. She looked expensive in the way that only certain people who had been privileged their whole lives could.

'Mama!' She headed for Constance, who did a good job of looking pleased to see her daughter. They kissed on both cheeks, and then Betsy turned to Nora, ignoring Archie entirely.

'You must be Nora. It's wonderful to meet you,' she gushed, enveloping Nora in a cloud of expensive perfume as she leant in and air-kissed her.

'It's lovely to meet you, Betsy,' said Nora. Archie had started helping Caspar to unload the boot. There was already an enormous pile of luggage and baby paraphernalia stacked beside them.

'Have you over-packed, darling?' Constance said.

'It's mostly Florence's. Caspar! Can you get Florence out of the car?' she snapped at her husband. Then, when he didn't put down the bag he was unloading in the two seconds since she'd asked, she sighed and flounced back to the car. 'Florence, we're at Granny's house,' she said, taking the child out of her car seat and carrying her over to Constance. 'Say hello to Granny.'

Florence hid her face in her mother's shoulder, then

peeked out shyly.

'I can see you,' Nora said in a sing-song voice, remembering Val doing something similar when one of the women at the pottery had bought their grandchild in to visit. That child had thought it was a brilliant game, and Florence thought the same. She hid her face, then looked at Nora again, smiling, waiting for the game to start again.

'I can see you,' said Nora, then ducked behind Betsy to trick Florence into thinking she'd disappeared. Florence looked for her and then Nora said 'Boo!' from behind her and she started chuckling in the marvellous way that babies do.

'Oh, Nora, she loves that game, don't you Florence?' said Constance.

'Please don't get her overexcited. She needs to go down for a nap,' said Betsy, striding into the house. 'Caspar! Bring the cot in first!'

Constance rolled her eyes at Nora. 'And so it begins,' she said.

Nora followed them back into the house, trying not to cringe when Betsy started interrogating Ursula about what sheets had been put on the bed they'd be sleeping in.

'Can you help bring the luggage in, Ursula?' Betsy said.

'No need, Ursula,' said Constance, out of earshot of Betsy. 'If you could make a pot of tea, though I'd be grateful.'

Ursula, equally grateful, escaped downstairs while Constance headed back into the drawing room. Nora went outside to help ferry everything in.

'Caspar, this is my partner, Nora,' said Archie.

'Lovely to meet you, Nora,' said Caspar, beaming at her despite the weariness emanating from him. 'Sorry for descending on you.'

'Not at all,' said Archie, clapping him on the back. 'It's always nice to see you.'

26

'If you want to make your excuses for dinner, I'd quite understand,' said Archie when they were both lying on his bed before they had to get ready for the evening meal.

'Given that Betsy has barely even said hello to you yet, I wonder what she might unleash over dinner. Do you think she'll bring up the vase with me there?'

'Probably. If she's already told Mama that she wants to talk about it, she won't be able to keep it in. That's probably why she's been avoiding me. It'll be the first thing she says.'

Nora snuggled into his side, her cheek resting on his shoulder. She loved being with him. She'd never felt so safe with anyone. And she needed Archie to know that he could rely on her in the same way. And that was why, even though she was already exhausted by the whirlwind of an afternoon, she was going to show up for everything all weekend.

'We'll get through it. Your sister intimidates people to get what she wants. Don't let her do that to you. Remember how you've turned things around in the last few months by having the Christmas market and then starting the lake project. You're lord of the manor, Archie, and you're doing a great job. And it's not your job to support your sister when she has a capable partner in Caspar.'

'You like him?'

'I do. I think he's henpecked to death and needs to stand up for himself a bit more, but perhaps he does when he's not here with us,' said Nora. She knew Betsy had told Archie and Constance that Caspar wasn't able to provide the standard of living she required, but having met both of them now, and with an outsider's perspective, she thought it was more to do with Betsy's unrealistic expectations than anything Caspar was lacking.

'I've never had the chance to get to know him,' said Archie. 'It's always like today has been. A bloody circus, even before they had Florence.'

'Why don't you take him out for a drink tonight?'

'I can't leave you with Betsy and Mama,' he said. 'It's not fair.'

'Yes, you can. And it might be good for you to hear Caspar's side of things. Get a feel for whether they really are struggling financially. Because if they're not, you can stop feeling guilty about not being able to help her out.'

'You're so wise,' Archie sighed. 'It's so obvious when you say things like that, yet I never think of it myself.'

'It's only because I'm not as close to it as you. And my view isn't coloured by knowing anything about what's gone on before.'

'Do you think everyone has things like this going on in their families?'

'Yes. Look at Seb, he's had all kinds of issues with his dad, hasn't he?'

'But you don't.'

'I think it helps that I'm an only child from a very ordinary family. My mum and dad went straight from steady jobs they'd had all their lives to living a very full life between their retirement village and several holidays a year. They're no trouble, just hard to keep track of.'

'We should invite them up to stay,' Archie said.

'One family at a time,' Nora said, closing her eyes for five minutes.

Dinner started out as a relatively civilised affair. Florence was in bed and the baby monitor sat on the dining table next to Caspar. Betsy had still barely said a word to Archie and was now sitting on his left opposite Constance.

'I thought we might venture out for a drink later,' Archie said to Caspar.

'He doesn't want to do that,' Betsy said at the same time that Caspar said 'That sounds great.'

'Oh, come on, darling,' Constance said, 'let the men have some fun. Us girls can open a bottle of bubbly or something. It'll give you and Nora the chance to get to know each other. How does that sound?'

Betsy harrumphed but said nothing else.

'Where's your local?' Caspar asked.

'If you don't mind walking, we can take a shortcut through the woods to the Cricketers Arms. It'll take about twenty minutes.'

'Looks like a lovely evening for a stroll,' Caspar said. 'It's nice to get some country air, isn't it, Bets?'

'Perhaps tomorrow we could take Florence for a romp around the garden,' said Constance. 'You two loved running on the lawns when you were toddling. It's nice and soft if she falls over.'

'Lovely idea, Constance,' said Caspar.

'Is anyone going to address the elephant in the room?' Betsy said.

'Not tonight,' said Caspar, in a warning tone, that made Nora think he had balls after all.

Betsy gave Caspar a mutinous look, but said nothing else. Nora braced herself for an evening which wasn't shaping up to be much fun. But she wanted to help, and she was pleased

Archie had gone with her suggestion of taking Caspar out.

'We could play poker,' Constance blurted out, surprising them all.

'Is that what you've been doing when you're out at your knitting circle?' Nora teased her. 'Playing poker with Penny and Mary?'

Constance laughed and when everyone else did too, even Betsy, despite herself, it diffused the tension and by the time Caspar and Archie left for the pub, she seemed to be in a much more amenable mood.

'I'll just pop up and check on Florence,' she said.

Nora and Constance went into the drawing room.

'Shall I light a fire?' Nora asked, thinking that it was too chilly in the room to sit comfortably.

'I can ask Ursula,' said Constance.

'I don't mind,' said Nora. Ursula had more than enough to do already.

'Thank you for staying tonight. I'm so pleased Archie and Caspar have gone out together. I'm sure that was your idea, and it's wonderful.'

Nora didn't want to take the credit because, although she'd suggested it, she knew it had been a big step for Archie to actually ask Caspar. 'Hopefully it'll help Archie understand where Betsy's coming from.'

'Because Betsy was still so young when her father died, I overcompensated and spoiled her. She used to be such a loving child, and now she seems so cross with me and Archie all the time. It can be very difficult.'

'Hopefully, now Archie has got things on track with the estate, she will see how hard he's working to secure it for Florence's future. That must be important to her.'

'I do wonder whether she's thinking of that, or the short-term gains to be had from selling everything we own now. Still, at least we've managed to avoid the topic for tonight.

Long may it continue.'

Ursula delivered a chilled bottle of Prosecco on a tray with three beautifully delicate champagne coupes and some nibbles.

'Oh, lovely Ursula, thank you,' said Constance.

By the time Betsy came down, Nora had a roaring fire going and Constance had poured them each a glass of bubbly and was curled in the corner of the sofa.

'I thought you said champagne, Mama,' said Betsy, sitting on the sofa opposite Constance and making a face as she sipped her drink.

'I said bubbles, darling. We don't run to champagne anymore.'

'If I'd known, I'd have bought a case with me.'

'It's lovely, Constance,' said Nora, seeing Constance's face fall. It was no wonder Betsy felt she needed her funds topping up if she was buying champagne by the case.

'So, you spotted the vase that we sold the other week,' said Betsy to Nora.

Nora looked at Constance, who looked horrified.

'Yes. Just a lucky find. I think it's one of those things that goes in and out of fashion and perhaps wasn't considered valuable until recently.' This wasn't true, but Nora was wary about seeming too knowledgeable about anything in case Betsy wanted to check every nook and cranny of the Court for other things to sell. And anyway, that wasn't the point. The Court was full of beautiful things that were worth some money. But those were the things that had been handed down through the generations and it seemed very different to sell anything like that rather than a vase that had been languishing in a cupboard for who knew how long.

'Mmm, makes one wonder what else might be here,' Betsy said.

'I think it was very much a one-off. We won't be doing it

again,' said Constance, hoping to put an end to the conversation.

Nora was desperate to chip in and say that it wasn't any of Betsy's business, but that was difficult since it wasn't her business either. So she kept quiet.

After another sip of Prosecco, Nora was overwhelmed with nausea. 'Sorry, could you excuse me a moment,' she said, trying not to run out of the room as dramatically as she felt she needed to, while also trying not to throw up on anything expensive.

She ran for the nearest toilet, which was thankfully just down the corridor and was sick. She sat on the floor trying to compose herself, but was clammy and not at all sure that being sick had helped her to feel better. Perhaps the Prosecco had been a bad idea after having had an upset stomach. She felt awful, leaving Constance to deal with Betsy alone, but all she wanted to do was go to bed.

Once she was sure that she could leave the safety of the toilet, Nora headed back into the drawing room.

'I'm so sorry, but I'm not feeling too well. I'm going to head to bed.'

'Oh, Nora, is there anything you need? Perhaps the food was too rich,' Constance said, looking concerned.

'Thank you. I'll be fine. It's nothing a good sleep won't fix.' She was certain it wasn't the food since she'd barely eaten anything at dinner.

As she left the room, she heard Betsy say, 'Do you think she's pregnant?'

'I don't think so, darling. Archie says she's had a bug. It's not exactly morning sickness at this time of night, is it?'

Nora lingered outside the door. She remembered Val had said the same thing. Was she being stupid not to consider that? However reliable it had been until now, the pill wasn't a hundred percent effective.

'I had a friend who was sick at all times of the day and night when she was pregnant. But you're right, she's probably too old, anyway.'

Nora was aghast at this comment and had to stifle a giggle as she crept away from the door and went upstairs. Perhaps to Betsy, who was probably almost ten years younger than her, she seemed old, but certainly not too old.

She lay in bed, one hand on Tatty, who was dozing on top of the covers and snuggled into her side, mulling over what Betsy had said. She'd dismissed the idea that she might be pregnant because she was on the pill. All the time she'd been with Julian, she'd had no cause to worry, but then it felt as if they'd had less sex in the past twenty years than she and Archie had had since they'd met. Surely it didn't become less effective the more work it had to do?

She was spiralling. But tomorrow she'd buy a pregnancy test to put her mind at rest. Being stressed about it wouldn't help her shake off the virus or whatever it was.

27

Nora had been asleep when Archie got back from the pub last night. They hadn't stayed out late but his mother said that Nora hadn't been feeling well so had gone to bed early, He hoped that's what had happened and it wasn't that his sister had been too much to deal with.

He woke the following morning to find Nora gone. He checked his phone and found a message from her saying she felt better and had gone to the lake and she'd be back after lunch. It was after nine now, so even if he went down to the lake she probably would have left by now. She'd pop home for a shower and some peace and quiet and that was completely understandable.

Archie and Caspar had a surprisingly good time at the pub. Away from the rest of the family, Archie found Caspar good company. He loved Betsy but was under no illusions as to how difficult she could be at times.

'She's got a bee in her bonnet about this vase,' he told Archie. 'I think she forgets that although she's part of the family, she's not in that sense anymore. She sees the estate as belonging to the family rather than to you.'

'I can understand that. She was young when Papa died, so technically I was looking after her financially, and there was never a time when she was told she had to stand on her own two feet.'

'To be frank, it doesn't sit well with me that we live in your flat rent-free. I've tried to put my foot down about it but the fact is we'd have to move out of central London to find somewhere affordable and she won't leave Chelsea. The idea of living in the suburbs horrifies her.'

Archie laughed. 'I can imagine. I'm glad we're having this conversation, Caspar. I only hear through Mama what Betsy says about your circumstances. I didn't want to assume anything. And if things were difficult for you, of course I'd want to try and help.'

Caspar shook his head. 'I can only imagine how tough it is keeping Croftwood Court going. I've said to Betsy, it's wrong to expect anything from you when all you're doing is trying to preserve the place for your family. For Florence.'

'It's a constant headache. The bloody roof has cost a fortune to repair and even then, it's thousands for a relatively temporary fix. That's where the money from the vase went. And towards the set-up costs of the wild-swimming at the lake.'

'Look, Archie. I think we both know your sister well enough to know that she's not going to change. And for me, I wouldn't want her to change. High-maintenance as she is, she's the woman I fell in love with,' he said. 'But let's do each other a favour and agree that Betsy and I don't need any help. So even if she asks, know that it isn't coming from me.'

'In that case, we must also agree that if anything changes, you come to me. I can't guarantee that I can do an awful lot to help financially, but I'd want to try. Florence is the sole heir to the estate, so it's only right.'

'Deal,' said Caspar. 'Same again?'

Archie felt much more positive about the rest of the weekend now that he and Caspar were working as one.

Betsy's comments about the vase continued but he found it easy to stand his ground, explaining what the money had been spent on, and even going so far as taking her into the bedroom upstairs where the ceiling had collapsed. It was still in a state of disrepair since he had been concentrating on fixing the cause; the interior side of the repairs could wait without causing any further trouble.

'I had no idea it was this bad, Archie,' she said. 'When Mama said the roof was leaking I didn't think it was on this scale at all.'

'It's not for you to worry about,' Archie said, kindly. 'But also, I need every penny I can get my hands on to stop the place from crumbling around us. None of the investment in the lake or the Christmas market is giving me or Mama any income. Everything is going into the estate.'

'It doesn't seem right that you're not benefiting when you're working so hard,' said Betsy, doing an about-turn.

'I have enough from the wage I pay myself from the money we receive from the trust. I don't need much.'

'You need to buy some trendier jeans,' she said. 'And I don't mean from the place in Croftwood where Dad used to get all of his clothes.'

Archie didn't mention that his latest wardrobe additions had all been from there.

'I'll send you a couple of pairs from the place Caspar gets his from. Now you've finally got a girlfriend, you don't want to frighten her off with your terrible fashion sense.'

'Thank you. I wouldn't want that either. So are we all happy?'

'Archie I'm sorry. Caspar told me not to ask you for any money. He says we don't need it, but I want things to be nice for Florence, like they were for me.'

Archie knew she was looking back with rose-tinted glasses, as he did himself. Their childhood memories, particularly from the time before their father died, were idyllic. But Archie knew that his father had been fighting the same battles back then around how to make ends meet. If anything it had been worse, because of the pressure of keeping the family name and reputation intact. Any sniff of money struggles would have been scandalous in a way it wouldn't be now. And that must have added a whole lot of extra anxiety to their parents that they'd never been aware of.

'You know Florence will have a wonderful childhood with you and Caspar whether it's the same as ours or not. The privilege we grew up with wasn't about where we lived. All of that is superficial. We had loving parents who did the best for us, always. And that is all Florence needs.'

Betsy threw her arms around Archie and hugged him. He couldn't remember the last time that had happened and it brought a lump to his throat.

'You're the best big brother in the world,' she said, squeezing him tightly. 'Nora is a lucky woman.'

'You like her?' Archie asked, slightly afraid of the answer.

'I do,' Betsy said. 'She's strong and you need that. If I'd come here six months ago asking for some of that vase money, you'd have given in. You've got a confidence I haven't seen before and I can only assume that's come from your relationship with her.'

Archie nodded. 'She's the most wonderful thing that's ever happened to me.'

'It's a shame you didn't meet earlier in life. Things could have been so different.'

It was strange that she assumed it was too late now for things to be different. Things were going to be different. It felt like the start of everything.

'I think things have turned out for the best. Neither Nora nor I might have been ready for each other if we'd met earlier. It seems now is the right time for both of us.'

'I'm thrilled you're happy. Come on, let's take Florence out for a walk, wear her out before dinner then we can eat in peace. Is Nora feeling better today?'

'I think so. She's heading back over.'

Archie was in the bedroom when Nora arrived back at the Court.

'Gosh, you still don't look very well, my love,' he said when she came into the bedroom. If anything she looked worse than she had on Thursday. 'You should have stayed at home. I've had a chat with Betsy and we've cleared the air.'

'Oh, that's great,' she said, fussing Tatty and then sitting down on the sofa by the window. 'I need to tell you something, Archie. This bug I have, it's a baby.'

'A baby?' It slowly dawned on him what she was telling him. 'You're pregnant?'

28

A baby. As soon as she'd seen the positive result on the test, Nora realised that she really hadn't been expecting that result. Whether or not she wanted a baby seemed beside the point. She was a grown woman with years of experience of not getting pregnant and now – at what felt like the last minute – she'd failed.

So as she sat there, waiting for Archie's reaction, she still hadn't equated the test result with any of the consequences of what it was going to mean to have an actual baby.

'Oh my god, that's incredible,' he said, pacing in front of her, running his hands through his hair. He had a stupid grin on his face. At least that was something. He was thrilled, and that made Nora feel better about it.

'I'm so sorry. I don't know what happened. I'm so careful about taking my pill.'

'It's a surprise, an unexpected marvellous surprise, but nothing to be sorry for at all. Christ, Nora. We're having a baby.'

'At our age.'

'That doesn't matter, does it?'

'I don't know. I feel too old to have a baby. It's like the last-chance saloon.'

'That makes it all the more special. It's a gift. I never thought I'd be a father. I let the idea that I might be go a long time ago. There is so much pressure to produce an heir and for a long time I felt like I'd failed my family.'

'Well, not any more,' said Nora. 'Although Betsy probably won't be very pleased about Florence being usurped.'

'We must get married.'

'No, this doesn't change anything. The way things are between us are perfect. It's not necessary,' said Nora.

'It is now,' said Archie his eyes shining. 'We need the baby to be the legitimate heir.'

Nora put her head between her knees, fighting another wave of nausea. This was too much. How had she gone from having the perfect life? A life of independence, having the best of all things with Archie to now having to get married because the baby she'd known about for only a couple of hours was the heir to the Croftwood estate.

'I don't think we should get married, Archie. It'll change everything.'

'But everything *is* going to change now.'

'Why?'

'Because it's not just us anymore. There's a child to consider.'

'That's not the only consideration. What's wrong with keeping things as they are? We both agreed on how we see our future together and I don't think a baby needs to change anything.'

Archie chuckled and Nora sat bolt upright, incredulous that he could find anything about this amusing.

'Nora, my love, this baby is heir to the Croftwood estate and the title. They can't be brought up between us. They need a proper home.'

'They'll have a proper home,' she said. 'Having a baby doesn't mean we're going to get married and live at

Croftwood Court happily ever after.'

'What other option is there,' he asked, frowning.

'The fact that you even think that means you don't understand how this is for me at all.'

'You're not pleased?'

'It's not about being pleased,' Nora said in frustration. If only it was that easy. She'd love to ignore the way it was going to drastically change her life, even without these hereditary considerations that were seemingly so ingrained in Archie. This was what she'd wanted to avoid; a relationship that would mean she had to give herself up to it, and yet that was where she was. And it was all her own doing. Why had she insisted that they could rely on her contraception when there was so much at stake? 'It's about how we're going to navigate this. And that doesn't necessarily include getting married or me moving in here.'

Archie slumped down on the sofa next to her. 'I'm thrilled, Nora. And yes, there is plenty to discuss but surely nothing that can't be overcome. Can't we enjoy this moment?'

Nora managed a small smile and allowed Archie to take her in his arms. Her own worries weren't shared by him at all, and to an extent she could understand that. But suddenly she felt alone.

There was a knock at the door.

'Come in,' Archie called, standing up.

'Your mother asked me to come and fetch you. It's dinner time,' said Ursula, popping her head around the door. She looked them up and down, realising that neither of them were dressed for dinner. 'Is everything alright?'

'Yes, fine. We'll be down in a few minutes.'

'We're just going down to dinner like nothing's happened?' Nora said when Ursula had left.

'Yes,' Archie said, as if there was no other option.

'I can't sit through dinner with your family. I think I'd

better go home.'

'Nora, please. They'll be as thrilled as I am. There's nothing to worry about.'

'We're not telling anyone yet. It's too soon. And as soon as we tell anyone, they're going to ask all sorts of questions. I'm not ready for that yet.'

'No, of course it's too soon. I'm sorry.' He sat down again and rubbed Nora's leg. 'Why don't you stay? You don't need to come down for dinner, you could stay up here and Ursula could bring you a tray.'

'I need some time to think. This is a lot for me to get my head around.' It seemed Archie was taking it in his stride to the point where skipping dinner wasn't even a consideration for him. Their world — *her* world — had been rocked and he was carrying on as normal.

'But you are happy about the baby?' His eyes scanned her face in desperation, and her heart ached for him. Because she couldn't give him what he wanted, what he thought a baby ought to mean for their relationship.

'Of course I am.' She tried to smile, wanting to reassure him, but it was all still too raw. 'I can't celebrate yet, it's been such a shock.' Saying she was happy was a step too far. It wasn't that she didn't want the baby; not having it wasn't an option for her. She knew she could love a baby and that Archie would make the most loving father she could wish for, but at the same time, this news was the start of grieving for the life that wasn't going to be hers anymore. It was selfish to worry about how it was going to affect her, but an unplanned pregnancy at her age was going to upset the course of her life. Just as she had established the business, she was going to have to take time away from it, maybe even stop with the bespoke side of things and settle for overseeing the production line. And she needed to think all of this through.

'You go down to dinner. I'll see myself out.'

He kissed her and then went over to the doorway. 'I'll call you later,' he said.

Nora couldn't help herself. She started crying. Did he understand where she was coming from at all? They'd had such a connection but now she felt as if she was in this on her own, battling to understand what the future might look like when to Archie it was all so clear; get married, move into the Court, live happily ever after.

Once she'd had a cry, she felt a little bit better and headed downstairs while she knew the family would still be eating dinner and she wouldn't be intercepted. As she headed through the kitchens, aiming for the back door, Ursula caught her.

'Nora, I don't want to pry, but if there's anything I can do,' she said, with a sympathetic look on her face.

In the face of Ursula being so kind, the tears threatened again. Nora rubbed the back of her hand across her eyes. 'Thank you, that's so kind but I'm okay. I'm heading home.' She paused. 'Keep an eye on Archie for me?'

Ursula nodded and laid a hand briefly on Nora's arm. 'Of course. He'll be fine, you mustn't worry.'

He would be fine, she knew that. His excitement about the prospect of becoming a father outweighed anything else that might be concerning about becoming a first-time parent at the age of forty-one.

Nora thanked Ursula and, managing a tearful smile, headed outside to where she'd left her car at the side of the house.

Going home suddenly didn't seem like a very inviting prospect. What she really needed was to talk things through with someone who could listen to her woes without judging her.

'Are you at home?' she asked when Hilary picked up.

'Yes. Toby's away for the weekend on some work-related

golfing thing. Do you fancy coming round?'

'I'd love to.'

'Brilliant! I'll put the kettle on.'

Nora smiled. If Hilary had suggested opening a bottle of wine, that might have been the last straw.

'I thought you were staying at Archie's this weekend, what with the dreaded sister visiting,' she said as soon as she opened the door.

'I was feeling under the weather. Nothing catching,' she added. Telling someone other than Archie that she was pregnant felt weird.

'Bit too full on was it?' Hilary led the way into the lounge and turned the television off. She sank into the corner of the sofa and Nora did the same.

'Betsy's okay. I mean, she's exactly what I expected but I didn't see much of them.'

'What's up?' Hilary frowned. 'Has something happened with you and Archie? You're not just under the weather.'

'I'm pregnant.'

'Oh my god! Are you? God, Nora.'

Hilary's reaction was exactly what Nora had hoped. She hadn't jumped from shocked to congratulating her, hadn't glossed over the brutal fact that this was the most shocking thing that could have happened at the beginning of a new relationship. At the beginning of a new start.

'I know. I can't get my head round it. I've been on the pill forever. I really thought it was just a bug, then I overheard Betsy telling Constance that she thought I could be pregnant, which thankfully Constance dismissed, and it made me wonder. Even so, I didn't think for a minute I would be.'

'And you've told Archie?'

'Just told him. He's thrilled. Totally oblivious as to why I might not be. And then merrily went down to dinner when he was called.'

'God.'

'I know.'

'If you weren't pregnant, I'd pour us both a brandy.'

'It's such a relief to talk to someone who understands,' Nora said, the tears falling again. 'Archie's first thought was that we need to get married so the baby's not illegitimate. He thinks that solves everything.'

'What do you want?'

'I want to not be pregnant.'

'Have you thought…'

'I don't want to do that.'

'No, you just wish it hadn't happened in the first place.'

Nora nodded. 'If it had happened with anyone else, we could keep things how they are. Manage things between us without needing to get married or move into the sodding Court. But because Archie's who he is, this stuff matters to him. And it didn't matter to either of us particularly before now. We could have carried on forever dipping in and out of each other's houses, like you and Toby do. That's how I pictured things.'

'I'm sure Archie thought that too. He's not so set in his ways that he was insisting on making an honest woman of you before. Perhaps there's a compromise to be made. I'm sure you can do something these days to make sure the baby's seen as the heir, assuming that's the driving factor, without having to go all in lady of the manor.'

'Well, if there is I haven't thought of it yet.'

'It's such early days. You have plenty of time to think about what you want to do and plenty of time to talk things through with Archie.'

'It's so ridiculous getting pregnant by accident at my age.'

'Not at all. Can I ask, did you and Julian ever think about having kids?'

'I used to think about it, but it never seemed like the right time. And on some level, I knew he was too selfish to be a father.'

'Whereas Archie…'

'I know,' Nora said, managing a smile as she thought of him. 'He'll be amazing. That's not what I'm worried about.'

'Look, I know I had my boys when I was much younger than you, but it still had a massive impact on my life. Mike was far from ready to be a father and right from the start, it wasn't a partnership. I had to bring those boys up by myself and most of the time it was a slog, especially once Mike left me. But they were worth putting my life on hold for. No one can tell you what it's like to be a mother, Nora. It will change your life, and at the moment, you only know how it's going to change what you have now for the poorer. You probably feel you've only just begun your new life, on your own, without Julian, and now it's being ripped away from you.'

'That's it exactly,' said Nora, sniffing. 'I feel like I've hit my stride for the first time in years. And before Archie came along, I thought that's all I needed. I never imagined he could change my life for the better, but he has.'

'Whatever happens, you have to do what's best for you. Think about what's going to make you happy. Don't think about Archie and all that baggage he comes with. Think about how you see the future that you want working. With the baby, if that's what you want.'

'I do want the baby. But I want my work too.'

'Nora, plenty of women are working mothers. And you're in the unique position of being your own boss. I know you've got the factory, but from what I can gather that pretty much runs itself.'

'That's true. And I can take the baby to the factory when I need to go. It's the other stuff. That I can lose myself in throwing whenever I want to. I can bugger off to Stoke and experiment when the urge hits me to start a new collection.'

'You're not going to lose your freedom.' Hilary said. 'You just have to organise yourself a bit differently. But you'll have help. I'm sure Archie will help with childcare.'

'I don't know. He's so traditional. I expect he had a nanny when he was little.'

'A nanny would have been amazing. I'd have happily gone along with that tradition when mine were little. Right. More tea?'

29

Archie went downstairs for dinner reeling from the news that he was going to be a father. He was desperate to share the news, but wanted to respect the fact that Nora wasn't ready. Whether it was because she was feeling poorly, or whether the news had overwhelmed her and hadn't quite sunk in yet, he was a little sad that she hadn't been more excited.

'Darling, is Nora joining us?' Constance asked as Archie escorted her to the dining table.

'She sends her apologies, she's not feeling well, Mama.'

'Oh dear. This bug does seem to be lingering.'

'Are you sure she's not pregnant?' Betsy said.

Archie felt like a rabbit in the headlights. 'Why would you think that?'

'I was telling Mama, I have a friend who had morning sickness at all times of the day and night. It took her ages to cotton on that she was pregnant. Nora seems to be similarly unwell.'

He couldn't bring himself to lie to his sister, but his loyalty to Nora, having promised not to tell anyone, made him. 'It's probably some nasty gastric flu. I'll suggest she see a GP next week.'

After Ursula had served the food, the conversation turned

to the festival. Constance had been part of an impromptu planning session at the Croftwood Haberdashery and had already volunteered to help man the craft tent.

'I feel I simply must stay on site this year,' she said to Archie.

'You do know there won't be a flushing toilet in your tent, don't you, Mama?' Betsy said, winking at Archie.

'I think a motorhome like Eunice and Bill had would suit me better,' said Constance.

Archie almost choked on his wine. 'That'll cost a fortune!'

'I shall have a word with Sebastian,' she said, confidently.

Before Archie could point out that he doubted Seb had an in with anyone willing to hire out a camper van in prime festival season for next to nothing, Betsy had chimed in.

'We ought to come to the festival, Caspar, don't you think? We could hire something like an old VW camper. Wouldn't that be amazing?'

'They most definitely don't have a toilet,' Caspar said, grinning at his wife.

'If we park next to Mama, we can use hers.'

'No one needs to stay on site. It's the other side of the estate, not the other side of the country,' said Archie. 'Of course, you're very welcome to stay here if you decide to come,' he said to Betsy.

'Perhaps Ursula could babysit Florence?'

'No,' said Archie firmly. 'Ursula and Mrs Milton will have the festival weekend off, as will the rest of the estate staff.'

'Really? Well, I'm sure I can find someone to look after her.'

'There were lots of children there last year,' said Constance. 'Florence might enjoy it.'

'Yes, but I won't,' Betsy pouted. 'What's the point of going to a festival if you can't have a drink and let yourself go?'

Aware that he was going to sound like the party police, Archie said, 'It's not really that kind of festival. It's a book festival with a few other things thrown in for good measure.'

'But you had Ned Nokes there last year.'

'Not officially,' Archie pointed out.

'Having an unofficial person like Ned Nokes means it was *the* festival,' Betsy continued.

'I didn't realise you're a Ned Nokes fan, Bets,' said Caspar, raising an eyebrow.

'Of course not. I'm just saying having a secret appearance by someone of his calibre is something. Come on, Archie, you must have some idea of who they're getting this year,' said Betsy.

'No idea. I'm not sure anyone knew Ned was turning up. It was entirely unplanned as I understand it,' said Archie.

'He's very charismatic,' said Constance. 'The girls at knit and natter are quite taken with him.'

Betsy stifled a giggle.

'I hear you're developing a swimming lake, Archie,' said Caspar, trying to divert the conversation away from Ned Nokes and festivals that he might get dragged along to.

'The lake was always there, we're just giving it a bit of a makeover,' said Archie.

'Eww. You haven't been in there have you? Remember when we were children and Papa tried to get us to swim in there?'

'I have been in,' said Archie, thrilled to be able to get one up on his sister. She briefly widened her eyes which told him she was impressed, although he knew she'd never admit it. 'It's rather wonderful. There's a group of local women who have been swimming regularly on a Thursday morning for the past few weeks and they've given us invaluable feedback.'

'I must have a walk down there sometime. I'd be interested to see what you and Nora have been up to,' said Constance.

'Nora's involved?' Betsy asked.

'Very much so,' said Archie. Mindful of what he'd promised Nora with regards to the baby news, nevertheless, he needed his sister to understand the nature of his relationship with her. Perhaps then, when they did announce the pregnancy, it wouldn't be such a shock. 'Nora and I are serious about each other,' he began.

'You're getting married?' Betsy said, putting her hand on her chest in shock.

'Not necessarily. Nora left a long-term relationship and is a very independent woman. Actually that's one of the things I love best about her. But I think it's important that you know she's going to be part of my life whether we marry or not.'

'God, Archie. You can't be lord of the manor and be...' Betsy stalled, but she'd said enough.

'Be what? Shagging around out of wedlock?'

'Archibald!' Constance said.

'Forgive me, Mama. But we're not youngsters, and we're not living in the last century. The expectation on me to follow a traditional path fell away a long time ago. I want to be happy with the woman I love, that's all. I doubt anyone, aside from my family, it appears, would bat an eyelid these days.'

'Hear, hear,' said Caspar, raising his glass, then lowering it again when he realised no one was joining in.

Archie took a large gulp of wine. It would be so satisfying to tell them about the baby. But Nora's voice rang in his ears. *I don't think we should get married, Archie.* He really wished now that there had been the time for them to talk all of this through properly before he'd had to rush off for dinner. Who knew what she must be thinking now?

'Please excuse me,' he said, pushing his chair back from the table.

'Archie! Wherever are you going?' Constance said.

'I must check on Nora. I'll see you all tomorrow.'

Having had a drink, Archie set off on foot to Nora's

cottage. Her car wasn't there and there was no sign of her being at home. Perhaps she'd popped out for something. He felt in his pocket for the key to her front door.

'Damn.' In his haste, he'd left it in his other jacket.

He dialled Nora. It rang a couple of times then went to voicemail. Had she rejected the call?

I'm at your house. Can we talk? A x

It was a few minutes before he received a reply.

I need some time. I'll call you tomorrow.

He tried not to read anything into the fact that she hadn't finished the message with a kiss as she usually would. That sort of thing wouldn't have crossed his mind a few weeks ago and if he wanted to keep his sanity, it shouldn't now.

But he knew he'd messed things up. He had no idea what Nora thought about the pregnancy and hadn't taken the time to ask. Instead, he'd blundered into saying they needed to get married, as if he was living in the bloody nineteen-fifties. It had seemed like the obvious thing to suggest, but seemed to have been the catalyst that made Nora leave.

There was nothing to be gained by waiting at her house. He had to give her time as she'd asked. And that would give him time to think things through properly. To consider what her concerns might be, and perhaps even come up with some solutions.

The walk back to the Court was a sombre one. He felt so alone. He'd imagined finding Nora in her cottage, apologising, and then spending the night together making plans. He lingered outside, reluctant to go back in and face the Spanish Inquisition from his mother and sister about where he'd been and what had happened. That could easily lead to him blurting out the news, and that wouldn't improve the situation at all. It just showed that all those years of being single could still trip one up. He wasn't used to putting himself in someone else's shoes.

He pulled his phone out and called Seb.

'I don't suppose you're in the pub are you?' he asked hopefully when Seb answered.

'The next best thing. I'm at the Backstage Bar at the cinema. There's a relaxed showing of Jaws but Jess is sat with her knitting friends so I'm hanging out with Jack.'

'Would you mind if I join you?'

'Course not. Jack will be relieved he hasn't got to entertain me for the rest of the evening. I'll have a pint waiting for you.'

Since he'd already been drinking, Archie put his best foot forward and set off for Croftwood Cinema. It wasn't as far as the pub the night before, and once he got out of the estate, it was only a fifteen-minute walk and it wasn't dark yet.

The cinema backed onto a secluded area of the park, and they had festival lights strung through the trees. The back door had been slid open slightly to allow the warm spring evening air inside and to allow people to wander outside if they wanted a break from watching the film. Archie slid inside and found Seb on a barstool, as Jack served another customer.

'I haven't been here since the festival,' said Archie, looking around. The bar was designed with an Art Deco theme to match the original features of the rest of the building. There were mirrors behind the bar and Archie caught sight of himself, shocked that he looked so dishevelled.

'It's a nice quiet spot to have a drink. What's up, then?'

Now that he was here, he realised he'd have to break his promise to Nora. Did it count if it was to get advice?

'Come on, spit it out. You look bloody awful.'

'Thank you. I've had some unexpected news today and it's rather thrown me.'

Seb took a sip of his pint and waited for Archie to continue.

'Can I ask that what I share with you goes no further.'

'Course, mate.'

'Nora's pregnant.'

Seb gulped his pint and started coughing. 'Christ, Archie!' he said when he'd recovered. 'Congratulations, that's amazing news!'

Archie glanced behind him, worried at who might have heard Seb, but aside from Jack, there was no one else in the room with them at the moment.

'It is,' he said, grinning and feeling on top of the world again for a moment, just as he had when he'd first heard. 'But I think I've buggered things up with Nora.'

'Go on,' Seb said, pushing Archie's pint towards him.

Archie paused for a sip, then carried on. 'I'm not sure she's that pleased yet. I suppose it's the shock. I hope that's what it is.'

'You haven't talked about this yet?'

'No. It was just as dinner was served so there wasn't time.'

Seb raised his eyebrows. 'And you went down for dinner mid-conversation?'

'Bugger.' Suddenly it seemed so obvious. What the hell had he been thinking? 'I should have said sod it to going down for dinner. It's just… I always go for dinner, Seb. It's so habitual, it didn't occur to me not to.'

'And Nora?'

'Nora left.'

'Ah.'

'I went after her as soon as I realised we needed to talk it all through, but she's not at home. She texted and has asked for some time to think.'

'That's tough. But knowing Nora, that's what she's doing. She's not the type of woman to punish you by cutting you off, Arch. Yes, you're an absolute Charlie for going down to dinner after an announcement like that, for crying out loud, but that won't be what's riling her.'

'No, I think that's probably down to me suggesting we get married.'

'So you managed to propose between her telling you she's pregnant and you going down for dinner?' Seb chuckled and shook his head. 'Oh Arch. You need so much more help from me than the name of my barber.'

'I know,' Archie said mournfully. 'It's very easy to see all of this with hindsight.'

'Look. She's probably freaking out. She's how old? Forty odd? This wasn't in her plan. It's different for you. You're gaining everything in this. A child, an heir, someone to share your life with. You have nothing to lose here.'

It dawned on Archie like a cold hand on his heart. He nodded. 'She will be feeling like she's losing everything. And when she's only just started again after Julian.'

'I'm sure that'll be it. God knows, I'm not an expert by any means, but for me, building up my business and then losing it when Covid hit was devastating. I know it's not the same thing, but I bet Nora's thinking along those lines.'

'And then I wade in suggesting we get married as if I want her to leave everything behind and be a wife and mother,' said Archie, his elbows on the bar and his head in his hands as he thought it all through. 'You're absolutely right, Seb. I need to think about how we do this together, so it's not the end of her life as she knows it, but not the end for us either.'

'There you go,' said Seb, patting him on the back. 'And I've got a smashing idea to start you off.'

30

After a restless night, desperate to speak to Nora but wanting to give her the space she'd asked for, Archie could bear it no more. Dawn was not yet breaking, and he took a punt on the fact that if Nora needed time to think, that probably involved her going to the lake for a swim. He pulled out his swimming kit and dressed, putting the ridiculously big dry robe on instead of a jacket, and headed with Tatty at his side, across the fields to the lake.

There was no sign of Nora, so he pulled out one of the chairs from under the dock and sat down to wait while Tatty did her customary swim over to the island for a nap. Having had no sleep, and with the beginning of the dawn chorus to lull him, he ended up taking a nap himself. When he woke, his neck was painful from his head lolling against his chest and he was stiff from being sat in one position for too long. How long had he been asleep? Judging by the sun, only an hour or so. He stood up, groaning as his body complained equally loudly at being stretched as it had about being asleep in an uncomfortable chair.

Knowing that there was still hope, that it wasn't too late for Nora to come, he moved from the chair onto the dock. He took his shoes off and dangled his feet into the water in an effort to keep himself awake while he mulled over the whole issue of marriage and whether he'd been an idiot to suggest it at all, or whether Nora's reaction had been more to do with his timing being off.

If the baby was a boy, he could only inherit the title if he was legitimate and that meant marriage. The estate itself could still pass to him if he and Nora didn't marry, but he would never be Lord Harrington. And despite Archie's own misgivings about what that had brought to his own life, he still felt duty-bound to protect it in tribute to his forebears, if nothing else. If the baby was a girl, the title would die out with him anyway, unless Betsy produced a boy, so there would be no need to marry. And thinking about this made him sympathetic to Nora's point; that the baby shouldn't be a reason to get married. The only reason he was giving her to marry him, he realised, was to preserve the title. And leaving his own feelings aside, how important was that? Important enough to drive a wedge between him and Nora?

He started to feel fidgety and having his feet in the water made him keen to have a swim, something he had never expected to want to do other than to keep Nora company. He took off his dry robe and the rest of his clothes and, feeling brave, launched himself gingerly in from the edge of the dock, even though he had the option of the brand new wide wooden steps that went into the water allowing for a gentler way of getting in. Taking a moment to make sure he had his breathing under control, he set off. The water was warmer than he'd expected, and it was interesting to note the changes that had taken place at the lake in the couple of weeks since he'd last swum there. Reeds had pushed themselves up from below the surface of the water, and the branches of the weeping willow trees on the island were almost kissing the water as they grew after their winter slumber.

As he headed around the island, he turned onto his back

and sculled his hands at his sides, looking back at where he'd come from, so that he would see if Nora had arrived before that side of the lake disappeared for him. When he emerged again, he could see Nora's dry robe and other things piled on the dock next to his. She must be around the other side of the island, probably not that far behind him, but not visible yet. He climbed out using the new steps and wrapped in a towel, his dry robe around his shoulders and sat at the end of the dock again, waiting for her to appear.

It felt very similar to the first couple of times he'd come to the lake to find Nora here. His stomach was in knots, this time from the pain of knowing he'd hurt her with his lack of understanding, rather than the painful awkwardness he'd felt just being around her to begin with. It seemed like such a long time ago.

He raised a hand as he watched her glide through the water, faltering briefly when she spotted him. She smiled, at least. Perhaps finding her at the lake, in her happy place, was a blessing.

'Good morning,' he said, as she pushed herself out of the water onto the dock.

'Thank you,' she said, taking the towel he handed her.

'You must be feeling better?'

'I am now. The water's perfect.'

'I'm so sorry about yesterday, Nora. I would love to blame the shock for me being such an absolute idiot, but I'm not sure that would be true.'

'It's okay. It was a shock. It was also a shock that you thought going down for dinner was more important.'

Her words were like a punch to his gut. They were true, but it hurt that they had come to this. That they could be this brutally honest with each other.

'I'm mortified about that. I was on autopilot. Terrible excuse, I know.' What else could he say? 'I'm so sorry.'

'It's okay,' she said again, but Archie worried it wasn't.

'I came to find you last night.' He wanted to tell her he had felt a pull to her like never before. That he'd realised he'd upset her and wanted to make things right. But if he said that, and she rejected him, he wasn't sure he could bear it.

'I know, you texted me. I stayed the night at Hilary's.'

'Right. And how is Hilary?' Why he was enquiring, he had no idea. It was habit more than anything.

Nora smirked despite herself. 'Hilary's fine. Look, I know this is difficult, Archie. Neither of us saw this coming, and it's going to take some talking through.'

'I've had a great idea about how we can change the stables —'

'Archie, I'm not ready to think about anything other than the fact I'm having a baby. I'm sorry. But please, I need time.'

'I love you.' He felt as if he was baring his soul. Even though he'd said the same thing to her before, many times, the meaning behind it now was greater than ever. But how to convey that with those three words? He wasn't sure he could.

'I love you too, Archie,' she said with a sigh. 'This has happened because we love each other. It's not a problem to be solved in that sense. I need to get my head around how my life is going to change and I need to do that before I can think about anything else. Even about us.'

Tears sprang to Archie's eyes, and he turned his head away so Nora wouldn't see. 'I understand,' he managed to say. 'I'm sorry. I should have respected that you'd asked for time to think.' He stood up and gathered his things. 'I'll wait for you to let me know when you're ready to talk.' He risked looking at Nora, smiling at her too brightly. 'Take care of yourself.'

Without a backward glance, he walked around the edge of the lake and headed back to the Court, not even wanting to turn back to call for Tatty. But the dog sensed it was time to leave and soon caught him up.

He'd brought this on himself. She'd asked for time and he'd selfishly overlooked that when the very reason she'd left last night was because he'd not paid enough attention to how she was feeling. He'd made things worse by coming to the lake to see her. He should have waited. And now she would think he wasn't listening to her. His conversation with Seb had buoyed him into thinking he could solve everything, but it was still too soon for her. He could see that now.

'Oh my god, you're a dry robe wanker!' Betsy said helpfully. She waited at the top of the stairs as he came up, with Florence in her arms.

'Lovely language in front of Florence,' he said, smiling at his niece and pretending to take her nose. He'd started doing it yesterday, and it had gone down very well. She seemed utterly convinced.

'You look a sight, that's all.'

'I don't think it counts as being a w-word if one's using it for its intended purpose.' The brutal sibling banter lifted his spirits.

'I have nothing against other people wearing them. I'm talking specifically about you,' she said. 'I suppose Nora bought it for you.'

'Yes.'

'And where is Nora today? Not still poorly, I hope?'

'She's swimming and then I imagine she has work to catch up on since she missed a couple of days this week.'

'On a Sunday?'

Good point. 'She works whenever she feels like it.'

'It's a shame we didn't see more of her. Perhaps you could both come and stay for a weekend sometime? Although, we'll be back for the festival in the summer.'

'Lovely. We'll make one or other of those happen.' Which was the lesser of two evils, he wasn't sure.

'We're leaving after lunch. We're walking to the chapel

with Mama to visit Papa. Are you coming?'

It might be just what he needed to take his mind off things. 'Give me ten minutes to have a shower.'

He was dressed and rubbing his hair dry with a towel when someone knocked at his door.

'Come in,' he called. 'Mama,' he said in surprise when he saw Constance. 'I'm coming.'

She came in and closed the door behind her. 'Archie. Is everything alright? I saw you walking over the lawn looking so forlorn, and Betsy says she thought you might have been crying.'

He almost laughed at the fact his sister had given him a hard time about the dry robe when she thought he'd been crying. It was a perfect example of how hard they both found it to express themselves with anything related to emotions.

'I'm fine, Mama. Nora and I have had a minor… interruption to business as usual. Nothing to worry about. We're giving each other some space, that's all.'

'Am I right to think that it's Nora who needs the space rather than you?' Constance said gently.

He nodded, not trusting himself to speak.

'Oh, darling.'

It was all Archie could do to not fall into his mother's arms and weep. Constance took a step towards him and he crumbled.

'I've ruined it.'

'Nonsense,' said Constance, leading him over to the sofa. 'I'm sure it's nothing that can't be fixed.'

'Nora's pregnant.'

'I wondered if that might be it.'

'Did you?' Archie said, surprised.

'It's the first thing one thinks of when a woman has a mysterious bout of sickness. And that coupled with what you've told me, about her needing space. I put two and two together.'

'I asked her to marry me.'

'Of course you did, darling Archie. And she declined your proposal, which is where you find yourself now.'

It was odd that his mother somehow knew the whole story with no one having told her.

'Unfortunately, it was an expectation rather than a proposal.'

'Ah.'

'And she asked for time to think about everything, and I went to the lake knowing she would be there. I talked things through with Seb and I have a brilliant plan, but she's not ready to hear it.'

'I know you must be thrilled at the thought of becoming a father, as I am about being a grandmother again but it must be an awful shock for Nora. And you must know that the way she is feeling now is probably nothing to do with how she feels about the baby. But you must allow her the time she needs, otherwise you risk driving her away.'

He nodded. 'I know that now. I've left it to her to get in touch with me.'

'That's for the best,' Constance said, patting his leg. 'My darling. All will not be lost. I'm certain Nora loves you as much as you love her. She'll come around and these few days while you're apart will make you stronger in the long run.'

'Thank you, Mama,' Archie said, kissing her cheek as they stood up.

'Archie. You understand the importance now of making things official between the two of you. It's unacceptable to continue living as you are with a child on the way.'

For a moment, he'd thought Constance was entirely on his side, worried only about how he was feeling and how he and Nora might navigate the future. But apparently not.

'You think I should insist on marriage?'

'You would be happy for your child to be illegitimate? To not bear your name? Come. Let's visit your Papa and then we can send your sister on her way and enjoy a peaceful evening together.'

Archie followed his mother out of his room wondering whether there was any solution at all that was going to suit Nora as well as satisfy everything else he had to worry about. If there was, he had no idea what it was.

31

The next couple of days were busy for Nora, and a welcome distraction while she mulled over what the future might look like. Her heart had ached when she saw Archie put a brave face on her asking him for more time to think, but it was what she knew she needed. She couldn't talk to him about the future without having some idea of how that might look.

As soon as she'd got back from the lake after seeing him, she headed to Stoke and threw herself into work. Although it was Sunday and the production line was closed, Neil was in to supervise the production kiln, which fired every day of the week. The test firings of her new pots had been successful and the glazes she had chosen worked perfectly, matching the idea she had in her head as closely as was possible to achieve. It was a relief to know that, because she'd begun working on this collection before she'd really needed to. Now it was going to help plug the gap there would be while she was on maternity leave. Aside from telling Hilary she was pregnant, she'd also told Val first thing on Monday morning. It was only fair to give her as much notice as possible.

'Oh my god! I knew it! Didn't I say the other week when you were sick?'

'You did,' Nora said, grinning at her friend's reaction.

'See? The pill is obviously not up to working against the quality of his sperm.'

'Val!'

'Well! How else do you explain it?'

Nora wasn't about to go any further with this topic of conversation. 'How are the Christmas lines coming along?'

'Spoilsport,' said Val, giving her a side-eye. 'We're all confirmed. Everything's scheduled. We're starting with your special Croftwood range just so we can get it out of the way.'

'I love the design we settled on,' said Nora, filling the kettle and then rummaging in the cupboard for two mugs. The midnight blue bauble had a simplistic gold outline of the Court dusted with snow — glitter would be added as a final step — its twisty chimneys radiating to the top of the bauble and meeting at the hanging point where a gold ribbon would be the final flourish. 'And the mugs came out okay?'

'Yep. They look so good, I wonder whether you'll need a second run of them? Anyway, I've pencilled in a second batch at the end of November. If you don't need them we'll fill that with some extra runs of the normal Christmas mugs ready for the website rush the week or two before Christmas.'

'Perfect.'

'So you're happy about the baby?' Val asked. She tipped a few custard cream biscuits onto a plate and set it on the table.

'Yes, so happy, although it was the biggest shock I've ever had seeing that positive test.'

'And Archie's pleased?'

'Yes. But the moment I told him he launched straight into suggesting we should get married.'

'I suppose he's trying to do the right thing,' said Val.

'Yes, and on one hand that's lovely, but on the other hand, do I want to leap from a twenty-year relationship that ended only a few months ago, to marrying someone just because I'm pregnant?'

'I'm guessing not.'

'Correct. But even though I know what I don't want, I don't know what I do want either. Except for everything to be like it's been these past couple of months. I love Archie but I don't need to be married to him or live with him just because we're having a baby. Is that mean?'

'I can imagine there's quite a lot to consider for the lord,' Val said tactfully.

Nora sighed. 'It's so complicated. I know he'd like to get married but it's so far removed from how I saw our future a couple of weeks ago, I can't bring myself to think it's the best plan.'

'I get that. And it's still so soon after Julian. You probably feel like you've jumped from one thing into another without a minute to yourself.'

'That's it exactly. And I don't want to lose what I've worked for all these years. I know you'll hold the fort here for me. And I know I can get childcare and still work afterwards, but it isn't going to be the same.'

'It won't be,' said Val. 'When I had my girls, it cost more to put them in nursery than I could earn. That's why this was my first job for a few years. At least you won't have to worry about that.'

'No, I'm very lucky. And I think Archie will be a hands-on dad.' She hoped he would be. She couldn't imagine being at the beck and call of a baby twenty-four hours a day. 'The thing I'll miss the most is my little cottage. It's not as if Archie can move in with me. There would hardly be room for the three of us anyway. But I've never lived anywhere before that's just mine.'

'Get used to it. Nothing is ever just yours again. Especially if you have a girl, nothing is off limits. If they're not rooting around in your handbag for a loose fiver, they're "borrowing" your hair straighteners and you have to fetch them out of their bedroom every time you want to use them.'

Nora laughed. 'You love it.'

'I do, and there will come a point where you won't even remember worrying about all of this now because you'll love it.'

It was almost exactly what Hilary had said, and Nora began to realise that although it felt like she was giving up everything for this baby, there were things to look forward to that she would love, she just didn't know exactly what the good stuff was yet.

'I think I'll have to sell my house,' she said.

'I wouldn't rush into any big decisions. That's a knee-jerk reaction,' Val said through a mouthful of custard cream. 'You don't want to move in with the mother-in-law yet, do you?'

'I can't imagine that at all,' said Nora. 'I get on all right with Constance but Archie is different when he's at home. He's more buttoned-up and formal when he's there, which I totally understand, I'm not sure I can live with that Archie all the time, though.'

'I thought when the Lord got married, the mother moves out to a cottage. That's what happened in Downton Abbey.'

'He can't ask Constance to move out. Anyway, the place is huge enough that you're not on top of each other, but he might not be my Archie anymore.'

'Keep the cottage as a love nest,' Val suggested.

'Tempting. We haven't talked about any of this yet. I told him I needed time to think.'

'So you told him you're pregnant and then what?'

'He suggested we get married and then got called down for dinner and I left.'

'Oh god, Nora. And you've left it like that?'

'I can't think about what he wants, Val,' Nora said, pleading her case. 'I need to think of some options that seem workable because otherwise my head will explode. He doesn't understand how huge this is for me. Everything's going to change.'

'One thing at a time. Have you made an appointment with the midwife yet?'

'God, no! Do you think I should?'

'Yes,' Val said firmly. 'I hate to break it to you but you're what they call a geriatric mother so they'll keep an extra special eye on you. It's best to get everything checked out just in case.'

'Geriatric?' Could things get any worse?

Nora lost herself in throwing for the rest of the day. It gave her time to think and helped her relax. The more she thought about it, the more she wondered whether she'd been unfair to Archie. Yes, perhaps his marriage suggestion had been unwelcome and he shouldn't have robotically gone down to dinner at the worst possible moment, but he had said sorry, so he'd obviously had time to think about things while she'd been at Hilary's. What had he said about the stables? Was he suggesting they turn them into somewhere for them to live? She couldn't imagine he would feel happy about leaving Constance in the big house alone, even with Mrs Milton and Ursula there. And that wasn't what she objected to anyway. Constance was great, but starting a new relationship, fast-tracked by having a baby so soon after meeting and then moving into somewhere that was more museum than home, with his mother. It was a lot.

That evening, while she was relaxing in her hotel room, indulging in some mindless television, she suddenly felt lonely. She missed Archie. Maybe she didn't feel ready to make decisions, but they weren't decisions she should make alone. That wasn't fair. Of course it felt as if all of this was going to have a bigger impact on her than it was on Archie, but shutting him out while she worked out how she felt wasn't helping. She realised she needed to talk things through. And that could only be with him.

I'm sorry about this morning. I'll be home tomorrow. Come to mine for dinner? x

I'd love to. I'll bring dinner with me. A x

Nora immediately felt better. The next day, she already felt as if a weight had been lifted and found she was looking forward to seeing Archie and talking things through now that the immediate shock had worn off. She had thrown like a whirling dervish for two days and the drying room was full of pieces for her current collection so that she could build up a stockpile, and to a lesser extent her new experimental collection which still needed some refining before it was ready to be unveiled to anyone aside from Neil and Val.

'You're off then?' Val said when Nora sought her out to say goodbye.

'Yes. Archie's coming over for dinner so we can talk.'

Val grinned. 'That's good. You look happy about that.'

'I am. I've missed him.'

'That's a good sign. I'm sure you two will work out a fine plan,' Val said, giving her a hug. 'Take care of yourself.'

'Will do. See you next week.'

Nora had time to shower when she got home, blasted her hair with the hairdryer and then put on her most comfortable clothes; leggings and a long oversized hoodie that had "I'm kiln it" emblazoned on the front. Archie rang the doorbell just as she was coming back downstairs.

'You could have used your key,' said Nora, sad that he thought things had changed that much.

'It didn't seem right,' he said, coming in and kissing her on the cheek. 'You look wonderful. How are you feeling?'

'I'm fine, thanks. Less nauseous today.'

'Good. I've brought dinner courtesy of Mrs Milton. It's a shepherd's pie.'

'Lovely.' Nora led the way to the kitchen, feeling that there was a level of awkwardness she probably should have expected, but hadn't. She took the dish from Archie and put it in the oven to warm through.

'Cup of tea?'

'Thank you,' said Archie, sitting down at the kitchen table.

'I'm sorry about yesterday at the lake. It wasn't fair of me to make you wait before we could talk about things.' She wanted to tell him that she'd missed him but he seemed a little distant and she could see in his eyes that he was uneasy.

'No, it's perfectly understandable. I should have respected you when you asked for time to think.'

Nora sat down and reached her hand across the table. It felt like a test. Because if he didn't reach out, that said everything about how he was feeling. She would have pushed him away too far. Hurt him too much.

But he reached for her hand and leant towards her. 'I know this is harder for you than it is for me and that you've had so much change in your life recently. Our relationship is so new, having a baby is a frightening prospect.'

Nora could only nod and squeeze his hand. She was overwhelmed with relief that he understood after all. He was her Archie, the man who was tender, loving and committed to her. Not the Archie who'd left her in his bedroom to go down for dinner. Whatever he'd told her, she knew it had been shock that had driven that. He'd been clinging on to the closest, easiest thing to do next that could reassure him that everything was still the same; dinner.

'I don't want to do this alone. I want to find a way to do it together but I don't know what that means. There's so much to think about.'

'We don't have to get married if that isn't what you want,' Archie said. 'The baby should be something wonderful for us, not something that comes between us.'

'But it brings all the differences between our lives into

focus. All of the things we didn't need to consider or think about before. A lot of that matters now. But I'm sorry for saying I don't want to marry you. I love you and I wanted that to be enough.'

'It is enough. I don't want to get married because of bloody traditions, either.'

'But it's important to you that the baby is your legitimate heir.'

Archie sighed. 'I wish it wasn't but it's ingrained in me. Look, I'm not an expert in the legal side of any of this. It's always been straightforward in my family, until now, so that's all I know. Why don't I take some advice on what the options are?'

'Okay. Thank you. Are you upset that I won't just get married and live happily ever after?'

'Not at all, my love,' he said, pulling her hand so that she got up and went to sit on his lap. 'Your independence is what I love about you. I hadn't thought through what I was actually asking of you.'

'We were both in shock. It was a five-minute conversation in the heat of the moment that we ought to forget,' said Nora, stroking his cheek. 'We're having a baby. Let's give ourselves time to get used to the idea before we start thinking about all the practicalities.'

'That sounds like a very sensible first step. I want to decide all of these things together, but I know I'm from a background where normal is not terribly normal so you must shoot me down if I make any idiotic suggestions. This is going to be a learning curve for both of us.'

Nora finally felt as if they were in it together. Perhaps this is where they could have got to sooner on Saturday night, not wasted the past two days, but that didn't matter now. She sank her head into Archie's shoulder and nuzzled his neck.

'I think we have half an hour or so before that's ready,' she said. 'Come on.'

32

Archie had taken Constance into his father's study to let her know that he and Nora had worked things out.

'It was wrong of me to assume she would be willing to marry just because of the baby,' he said. 'I think it's likely we'll come to some other arrangement.'

'You will allow the child to be illegitimate? It's out of the question,' Constance said in a tone that said there was nothing else to be said on on the matter.

'But, Mama. I told you that I'd proposed and that Nora had turned me down,' Archie said in confusion. 'You were very understanding.'

'Yes, but I assumed she would come around to the idea. After all, what other option is there? She must understand that a child cannot be born into this family out of wedlock. It simply isn't an option.'

Archie had kept his word to Nora and taken advice on what the legal position of the child would be whether or not he and Nora were married. It seemed that the matter of inheritance was straightforward enough; Archie could bequeath the estate to the child whether or not they were legitimate. However, the only way to pass the title down was through a legitimate heir.

He sighed. 'Things have moved on. It's not necessary for Nora and I to be married. A civil partnership will give us the same legal status.'

'But you won't have a wife, Archie. Lady Harrington will not exist.'

'That's the only part of it that wouldn't be the same.' He braced himself. 'And that doesn't matter to Nora and me.'

'Archibald. If your father was here —'

'Papa is not here,' he said as forcefully as he could muster. 'If he were here, I perhaps wouldn't find myself in the position of being a single man in his forties who's been stuck on an estate in the middle of Worcestershire for twenty years.'

Constance's eyes filled with tears.

'I'm sorry, Mama. That was uncalled for.'

She dabbed her eyes with a handkerchief and sat down in the window seat. 'Your father would be proud of you. You've kept the estate running and looked after your sister and me exactly as he would have done. I know it has curtailed your life. Meant you had to make sacrifices and carry burdens that aren't yours to bear. But if you allow this chance to build a family pass you by, to fail to continue the line when the opportunity has come to you right at the very last moment, you are a fool.'

His mother's words were like a knife to his heart. He was shocked at how black and white her view was. What did she expect him to do? Issue Nora with an ultimatum when they had only just come together again? He was fairly sure he knew which way that would go, and he wasn't about to risk upsetting the delicate balance between them again.

'I'm sorry you see me as a fool. But I will not issue an ultimatum to Nora which could very well result in me losing her and the child altogether. I realise that there is a way things are done, a way things have been done in the past, but that doesn't mean that is the right way now.'

'So you would see your child lose their right to inherit the title? See the Harrington name die with you?'

'If that is the price I have to pay to have a family, yes.'

Constance shook her head and dabbed her eyes again. 'I know you love Nora and I have never seen you happier, but she is asking too much of you.'

'She hasn't asked anything of me. I haven't told her any of this yet.'

'Perhaps when you do, she will understand.'

'Perhaps. But I don't want her to feel pressured into anything. Fate brought this child to us. It wasn't something we planned and I don't expect Nora to sacrifice her independence when that means so much to her. It has to be her decision.'

'So what do you propose? You want me to move out into the cottage?'

The cottage had long been rented out on the assumption that it would never be needed as it grew increasingly unlikely that Archie would get married. He had no intention of asking Constance to leave Croftwood Court. But otherwise, he had no plan until he and Nora could settle things more definitely.

'Your home is here. There is no question about that. I don't know yet what our arrangements will be, but you must realise that it's a possibility that we may live here. Married or not.'

Constance looked at him as if she may say something about that but thought better of it. He certainly hoped she was in no doubt that her feelings on the situation were not to be aired in front of Nora.

'It's your house to do with as you wish,' she said. 'I will respect your decision, whatever that may be.'

'Thank you. Right, I must go. I have a meeting with the planning officer.'

He took a deep breath as he left the room and headed

straight out of the front door, striding towards the estate office, trying not to worry about how much he might have upset his mother. He was in no doubt that he'd done the right thing. He had to put the needs of his family first. And his family was Nora and the baby now.

Seb and Ben were waiting in the courtyard outside the estate office.

'Morning,' he said to both of them.

'Morning,' said Ben. 'I was just explaining to Seb that because your planning application is still in progress, we can change the classification of this building without delaying the outcome. Having said that, I know you have an opening date at the beginning of June pencilled in for the lake. I'm afraid I think that may need reviewing.'

'Why's that?' Seb asked.

'It was always at the quick end of the timescale,' Ben said. 'The concerns around the parking held things up. That's ironed out now, since you submitted the additional information on how you'll provide parking in the grounds, but it's added a couple of weeks to the process.'

'It can't be helped,' said Archie. 'But this change of use for the stables is extremely important. Even if it delays the application, I want to do it.'

'No problem. Talk me through what you're thinking.'

Archie had a very clear plan in his mind. He would renovate the old stables into a house for him and Nora. It was a stone's throw from the main house so he was still on hand for Constance. It would give them the flexibility to keep her company but to have their own space. A space he hoped Nora would feel as hers as much as his. Somewhere she could put her own stamp on and turn into a home.

'And the estate office, I'd like to turn that into a workshop,' he said to Seb's surprise. 'I don't need an office. I can use one of the rooms in the house.'

'There's plenty of room in the roof space over the other side. You can have an office next to me,' said Seb.

'What kind of workshop?' Ben asked.

'A pottery. I'd want to glaze both ends of the walkway and knock that through to where the office is now. I think the drying room and the kiln could go in there. Nora would have to finalise what she wants, if she even agrees, but from what I've seen of where she works now, I think it would work.'

'I can't see any problem with that. A renovation like this is more to do with the materials you're going to have to use to comply with the building regulations for a building of this age, but I expect you're used to that.'

'I am.'

'It sounds like an expensive business, this renovation. How are you going to pay for this?' Seb asked after Ben had gone and they were having a cup of tea in the office.

Archie didn't mind in the least that Seb had asked. He was the only person aside from Nora who knew the full extent of the Court's finances. Or lack of them.

'I'm going to sell the fish from the lake and I've asked the auctioneer who sold the vase to come round and value what we have. We ought to be doing it regularly for the insurance, so as far as my mother knows, that's all it is. I'll have the discussion with her once I know what I might sell.'

'Blimey, Arch. I've never seen you so driven.'

Archie shrugged. 'I have no choice. I have to provide for my family and that means solving the biggest problem, which is where we're going to live. I only hope Nora thinks this is an appropriate compromise.'

That evening was the highly anticipated anniversary showing of The Breakfast Club at Croftwood Cinema. Nora's enthusiasm for it had waned in the face of the pregnancy, which she was finding exhausting. But Archie knew she'd been looking forward to it, and all they had to do was turn up and watch the film. She could sleep through it if she wanted to.

He'd found an old coat of his father's which was too big for him but which when paired with an old check flannel shirt gave him the Judd Nelson vibes he was after. He drove round to Nora's in the Jag and let himself in.

'Only me,' he called.

She appeared at the top of the stairs, looking every inch like she'd stepped out of the nineteen-eighties. Her hair was huge, with an enormous floppy bow tied in it. She had a pink sweatshirt hanging off one shoulder and was wearing leggings, leg-warmers and lots of neon bead necklaces and bracelets.

'Wow!' he said, grinning. 'You look like…' He floundered, but Nora grinned.

'I was going for early Madonna,' she said, coming down the stairs and kissing him before she snuggled into his chest. He wrapped his arms around her, glad that they were back to where they'd been before the baby news.

'You look amazing. You feeling okay?'

'Mmm,' she murmured. 'I'm looking forward to it. I came home early and had a nap so I'm raring to go.'

She seemed anything but raring to go, though Archie was pleased they were. They hadn't had much fun in the past few weeks.

He'd booked two tickets for seats in the circle, since it was quieter up there and the seats were more comfortable. They parked the car on the road nearby and walked the long way through the park to the cinema, joining the short queue to get in. Everyone in the queue was dressed in similarly nineteen-eighties clothes with a scattering of other Judd Nelsons and Madonnas amongst them.

'You two look great!' Patsy said, checking their tickets. She was wearing a ra-ra skirt with three tiers each in a different neon colour and a vest top with a mesh t-shirt over it and a pair of mesh fingerless gloves. 'We're doing Long Island Ice Tea cocktails and mocktails. Grab one before you head upstairs.'

With their drinks in hand, they climbed the stairs to the circle and settled themselves into the comfy seats.

'The planning officer came round today,' he began.

'Oh, was it Ben?'

'It was. We discussed renovating the stable block into a house for us.'

Nora turned to look at him. She was biting her lip, looking unsure.

'And we could set up a pottery studio for you so you can work from home.'

'We'd move in together?'

'I hope so,' he said, still not sure if she thought it was a good idea. 'And there's no pressure for you to sell your cottage. You ought to keep that if you want to. But we need somewhere that's ours. Somewhere that's never been mine or yours, where we can start our family together.'

A tear escaped down Nora's cheek. Archie leant over and wiped it away, his heart sinking into his stomach.

'It's okay. We can think of something else. It's not the only option.' It was the best he could come up with though, and he'd thought it was as close to perfect as they were likely to get.

'It's a wonderful option,' she said, taking his hand and squeezing it just as the lights went down.

After the film, they headed through the stalls to the backstage bar where there was an after party that was spilling out of the doors and into the park.

Nora pulled Archie by the hand outside into the park before anyone could intercept them.

'I want to pay for the pottery workshop,' she said. 'It's the only way it can work. I can't explain it very well, but it's important that it's mine. I need it for my business and it's only right that I pay for it.'

'And you think the house is a good idea?' he asked, his heart filled with hope again.

She nodded, her eyes sparking. 'I do. How will we pay for it though without selling the cottage?'

Archie explained his plan. 'I know my mother and Betsy won't be pleased but it's the best option for us and that's the most important thing. I hope they'll understand that holding onto paintings and vases that no one ever sees but us, things that don't even have any sentimental value to any of us, is ridiculous when compared to building a future for our family.'

'I think it's the perfect solution. Thank you.'

Nora looped her arms around his neck and pressed her cheek to his. 'I love you so much,' she whispered into his ear.

'My love. I feel so lucky to have this chance of a new life with you. I love you.' Archie thought his heart might burst. It had all come together and they had found a way to be together. Nothing else mattered now.

33

Epilogue

Two Months Later

The planning permission for the lake had taken longer than they'd hoped, and opening at the beginning of June was looking unlikely. It was frustrating, but Archie and Nora were living in a bubble of bliss now that they'd embarked on planning to renovate the stable block, so to them it hardly mattered. Seb, however, who was hoping to have squared away the lake project before he had to start working full time on this summer's Croftwood Festival, was a ball of anxiety.

'We're going to end up opening on the same weekend as the bloody festival at this rate,' he said to Archie in the middle of May.

'If it comes to that, we'll have to manage without you,' Archie said, pragmatically.

'No. You won't. No offence, Arch, but your mind's not on the job anymore.'

It was a fair point. Archie and Nora, who was past the twelve-week point of her pregnancy and starting to feel better, had understandably been concentrating on getting the plans for renovating the stables finalised so that when the planning permission finally came through, they could start right away. Although they had continued to live between Nora's cottage and the Court, Constance was increasingly vocal about the fact they were having a baby out of wedlock, and it was becoming difficult for them both. Archie felt guilty about spending more time at Nora's and leaving his mother alone, but he'd had enough of hearing about how he was wiping away his family's legacy. Abandoning the title.

'Why don't we open for an evening, have practice run?' Archie suggested. 'Everything's ready to go, isn't it? We can mock-up the opening using friends and family as guinea pigs.'

'I suppose so,' Seb said. 'It makes sense to have a dry run. Iron out any kinks.'

Later that afternoon, Archie and Nora were sitting in the sunshine on the patio at the back of the cottage.

'I think we should get married,' Nora said.

'Where has that come from?' Archie asked. 'I thought we'd decided on the civil partnership.'

'I've been thinking about it and it's not right for me to be the one deciding that our baby doesn't inherit the title.'

Archie was surprised at how much it meant to him to hear Nora say that, but he needed to be certain it was what she wanted. 'We could wait to find out whether the baby is a girl or a boy. If it's a girl, there's no need to get married. It won't change anything.'

'Archie. You keep telling me that it doesn't matter to you. But it does. And you're willing to sacrifice all of that for me. But it's not right to take that away from our child. Whether they're a boy or a girl, they should be part of your family. Properly. And if it is a boy, inheriting the title isn't going to mean the same thing for him as it did for you. It doesn't have to be something that defines him or limits the kind of life he wants to have. Either way, they belong to your legacy. I want to get married.'

'That's wonderful,' he said, with tears of happiness in his eyes. He slipped out of his chair and knelt at her feet. 'I've always wanted to do this,' he said, as she laughed at him in delight.

'I don't mind at all.' Her eyes were full of tears as well.

'Nora Hartford. I want to marry you more than anything in the world. Would you do me the honour of becoming my wife, my partner in life and love?'

'Yes, Archie Harrington! Yes!'

They chose the summer solstice as the date for the dry run of the lake opening. Everyone was invited. In all, they were expecting around fifty people, which made Archie and Seb nervous, but it was important to know that they could deal with that many cars, that many people changing, swimming and warming-up afterwards.

'Seb, the planners want a meeting with us in town this afternoon at one,' Archie said, finding Seb in the Finnish barbecue hut putting the finishing touches to the grill.

'Today? Christ.' Seb ran his hands through his hair. 'Fine. I'll meet you at the estate office at half twelve.'

'Can I meet you there? I'll be in town already. I promised Mama a lift to Jess's at noon.'

Archie was waiting outside the council offices ready to intercept Seb. He spotted him striding across the car park looking harried, and felt a little guilty.

'Come on then. Let's hope it's good news,' Seb said.

'Actually, we're not here for a meeting with the planning office. I'm getting married.'

'What? Now?'

'Yes, now. I was hoping you'd return the favour and be my best man.'

Seb was very rarely lost for words, and Archie couldn't help but grin. 'But… I'm wearing dirty jeans.'

'It doesn't matter.'

'And you're wearing jeans. You can't get married in jeans.'

'It's fine,' said Archie, putting an arm around his friend. 'Come on.'

Nora and Hilary were waiting in the foyer, similarly underdressed for a wedding.

'I imagine this was as much a surprise for you as it was for me,' Hilary said to Seb.

'You can say that again. I didn't think you two were into the whole marriage thing.'

'It's just a formality,' Nora said. We didn't want a fuss. 'We thought the solstice swim tonight would be a lovely way to celebrate it, though.'

Seb grinned. 'The solstice swim is your bloody wedding reception? What is Constance going to say about that?'

'Constance will find out as soon as we've finished here and hopefully she'll be so relieved we're married, she won't care that the reception is in a barbecue hut,' said Nora.

'I wish you'd warned us,' Hilary said. 'Look at the state of Seb, and I'm wearing my shop flip-flops.'

'It doesn't matter,' said Nora, beaming. 'It really is just a formality for us. The bare minimum, purely to give the baby everything it deserves.'

'And because we love each other,' Archie reminded her.

'That too,' she said, kissing him.

'Harrington and Hartford?'

'That's us,' said Archie to the woman dressed more smartly than any of the wedding party.

Seb and Jack were stationed at the new entrance, directing cars where to park. The small dedicated parking area was full, but there was plenty of room on the grass either side of the estate road, which was fine since the ground was dry and meant a short walk back to the ticket office.

One of Val's teenage daughters was in the office signing people in, because although it was free to swim tonight, they needed to keep strict records of who was there for safety reasons. The only person to have flouted this was Constance, who had arrived on foot from the Court, accompanied by her new daughter-in-law, bypassing the official entrance.

'We ought to have a proper party at the Court,' Constance said as Nora led her to the area they'd set up with benches and chairs on the far side of the dock, away from the route between the changing canopy and the steps into the lake.

'This is all we want, Constance. A celebration with our friends at the place we met.'

'There is a certain romance to that,' Constance admitted. 'I would have liked a big wedding. I would have liked to have been there,' she said, pointedly, 'but I'm grateful you've done the right thing.'

As much as Nora wanted to point out that her reasons for agreeing to the marriage weren't to do with preserving the hereditary title for its own sake, but simply because she wanted to give Archie everything he deserved. Whatever he said, it mattered to him and so, she came to realise, it mattered to her. Being married didn't have to mean that she was losing anything because it all came down to what the marriage meant to the two of them. And what it meant for both of them was security for their child. So she said nothing. Constance would never understand how important her independence was, and that was okay. But Nora knew now that being independent didn't mean being alone.

'Thank you.'

'And you'll be Lady Harrington as well, now.'

'Oh, no. I'll be sticking with Nora Hartford.'

Constance looked aghast, but perhaps realised that she'd

already won the biggest battle. 'If that's what you want.'

Before they'd even known it was a celebration, Jess and Seb had gone all out to make the lakeside look spectacular. They'd tied bunting from the trees to the corner of the roof of the Finnish hut and to the roof of the changing canopy. Fire pits were dotted along the lakeside surrounded by logs for people to sit on, and Oliver was setting up a trestle table where people could pick up food to toast on the fire, or cook on the grill in the Finnish hut. Everything from a simple slice of bread to crumpets, teacakes and sausages and burgers. There was something for everyone. Big plastic tubs filled with ice and cans of soft drinks were also dotted around since swimming and alcohol weren't a mix they wanted to encourage, but nobody minded that at all.

'Are you coming in?' Nora asked Constance.

'Not on your nelly! I've brought my knitting,' she said, patting the bag on her shoulder. 'I'll join Penny and Mary over there. We much prefer to watch.'

Nora slipped her dry robe off and headed over to the steps, looking out for Archie but not seeing him anywhere. The water was so warm now that she had abandoned her gloves and socks, and it was possible to dip straight in and start swimming. There were quite a few people in the water. The day had been sunny and hot, so it was the perfect evening to enjoy a swim. Nora swam around to the far side of the island.

'Hey!' She turned towards where the voice had come from, the island, which was a sea of greenery as yet untouched since they were still waiting for the bridge to be completed.

Archie was leaning against the trunk of a weeping willow in his swimming trunks, almost hidden from sight by its branches that swept down towards the water. He moved towards the edge and reached out a hand to her. Nora had swum around the island many times, but never gone onto it. She placed her feet down onto the silky mud at the bottom of the lake and found that the water was only thigh deep at the edge. She took Archie's hand, placed a foot on the island and he helped her out of the water, handing her a towel.

'What are you doing over here?'

'Waiting for my wife,' he said, smiling as he took her face in his hands and kissed her.

Nora didn't think she'd ever seen him look so happy. And she felt the same way. It was ridiculous that a piece of paper they'd spent ten minutes obtaining that afternoon could shift the way you felt.

After a moment more of kissing, Archie led her further onto the island.

'When did you do this?' Nora said in delight as they came to an old-fashioned canvas A-frame tent with the flaps tied open, revealing an inviting-looking bed, covered in blankets and cushions. It looked as if Archie had raided the airing cupboards in the Court.

'A couple of days ago while you were in Stoke. I was hoping the weather would be kind to us and that we might spend our wedding night out here. What do you think?'

'I love it,' said Nora, crawling inside and lying on the bed. It smelled of freshly washed linen and was gloriously squashy. 'How did you get all of this stuff over here?'

'I bought a blow-up boat. One of those you find at the seaside.'

'And how many trips did it take?'

He grinned and rubbed the back of his neck. 'Quite a few.'

'It's perfect. I can't wait.'

Archie lay down on the bed next to her. 'How does it feel to be Lady Harrington?'

'It feels wonderful, actually,' Nora said, surprised to find herself saying that. 'I can't believe how amazing it feels to be married. I thought it was a formality, but it feels more significant than that.'

'I can't tell you how much it means to me,' Archie said, squeezing her hand.

'Have you told Betsy yet?' They'd invited Betsy and Caspar for the evening but hadn't let on that it was more than just a dry run for the lake.

'No. I decided to wait until they arrive.'

'Come on,' Nora said, sitting up and making her way out into the sunshine. 'I'm starving. I need my husband to cook me a sausage.'

They lowered themselves back into the lake, which felt a little fresher since they'd warmed themselves in the sun and swam back around to the steps. Nora grabbed her towel and dried herself off before putting her dry robe on.

'Where did you two disappear to?' Seb said, handing them both a can of lemonade. 'It's time for my best man's speech.'

Before either of them could say anything, Seb had climbed onto the dock and shouted for everyone's attention.

'Ladies and gentlemen,' he began. 'You may not know, but tonight we are celebrating more than Croftwood lake being ready to open as soon as the planners give us the thumbs up.' Seb raised his can to Ben, who was there with Lou.

'Any day!' Ben shouted, and everyone cheered.

'Today, I was best man for my friend and colleague, Archie.'

There were gasps of surprise, and everyone started talking. Nora and Archie grinned at each other, quite enjoying Seb revealing their secret.

'So tonight we're celebrating the marriage of Archie and Nora in the place where it all started, a few months ago. I know they were hoping to keep this on the down-low, but if you're anything like me, I'm sure you all feel like this is something worth celebrating. Archie's been there for me since I moved to Croftwood and seeing him and Nora find each other when neither of them was looking, well, it warms my heart.'

Everyone cheered and clapped. The people nearest Archie and Nora patted them, and Val came over to give Nora a kiss. 'I can't believe you didn't tell me!' she said. 'You dark horse!' she said, kissing Archie on the cheek.

'To Lord and Lady Harrington!' Seb shouted.

'To Lord and Lady Harrington!'

The End

Sign up to my exclusive mailing list to find out about new releases, special offers and exclusive content. Go to www.victoriaauthor.co.uk

Also by Victoria Walker

Croftwood Series
Summer at Croftwood Cinema
Twilight at Croftwood Library
Festival in Croftwood Park

Icelandic Romance Series
Snug in Iceland
Hideaway in Iceland
Stranded in Iceland
Ignited in Iceland

The Island in Bramble Bay

Author's Note

Thank you for choosing to join me at Croftwood Lake! If you enjoyed Nora and Archie's story and you have a couple of minutes to leave a review, I'd be so grateful. Reviews are the best way to help other readers find out about books they might enjoy.

The idea for this story came to me when I started cold-water swimming for the first time last summer. I'd always wanted to try it, mainly because I love swimming in the sea on holiday, but also, I wanted an excuse to buy a Dryrobe. So when a lake opened close to where I live, I decided I was going to swim once a week, come rain or shine, and I've loved every moment of it. I was determined to swim throughout the winter and I did that, although I'll admit it was a struggle through January and February when the water was hovering around two or three degrees, but now it's on the up again, it feels good to have ditched the wetsuit.

I should mention that although Nora's experiences are based on mine as far as the swimming side of things goes, the practicalities of changing the lake from a fishing lake into a swimming lake, particularly regarding the planning permissions required, are entirely fictional. I've based it on research, but in the end, that doesn't always fit with the story!

Thank you to Berni Stevens for another wonderful cover and to Catrin for editing and proofreading, and for being my new writing retreat buddy. Thanks to James for proofreading and story advice and for coming to the lake with me right at the start. Thanks to Jake and Claudia for website and marketing support. Love you guys.

You can find me in these places:

* * *

Facebook - Victoria Walker Author
Instagram - @victoriawalker_author
www.victoriaauthor.co.uk

Printed in Great Britain
by Amazon